STOLEN
SOUL

THE YLIASTER CRYSTAL

BOOK 1

ALEX RIVERS

To Iftach, whose excitement knows no bounds

ONE

The cold October night air blew against my cheeks as I cycled down the street, my backpack full of dreams, potions, and magic-infused crystals. The sky was cloudy and dark, the occasional shimmering star peeking from behind the gray curtain. The moon was a sliver of white, shining down the narrow street. I smiled in exhilaration, the sound of the wind increasing to a tormented shriek. I could hardly hear it: My earphones were playing Taylor Swift's "Look What You Made Me Do," the volume set to the max. My nose and ear tips were frozen stiff but the rest of my body was getting warmer, my heart pumping, my lungs burning.

God, it was awesome to be outside, to move, to breathe fresh air. As much as I adored my lab, it tended to smell of alchemy. And alchemy, when done right, never smelled good.

The breeze carried the distinct scent of the sea. North End has a large wharf in the Boston Main Channel and, cycling through the neighborhood, I could appreciate the salty tinge in the air. I would have to visit the beach soon. Saltwater was an important ingredient in some antidotes, and was also used for making Verna's glowing crystal. Though for Verna's recipe, the seawater had to be collected using a copper ladle with seven holes, which was an utter pain in the ass.

I shook my head, dislodging the train of thought as I cycled even faster. It was getting late, really late, and I didn't want my client going to sleep before my delivery. I needed the cash tonight. Tomorrow morning, Breadknife would be knocking on my door for his monthly payment, and I was still a bit short.

I nearly missed the apartment building, a typical three-story red-brick structure. This one was a bit dirtier and shabbier than the rest, the graffiti on it sprayed in layers, tags and signatures painted over each other, intermingling into an unpleasant dark mess. I hit the brakes, jumping off the bicycle before it stopped completely.

A man in a trench coat leaned against the wall, smoking. The orange tip of his cigarette burned brightly in the shadowy street, casting an eerie light over his face. He gazed at nothing, not even sparing me a glance.

I walked it over to a nearby streetlamp and took out a thin chain from my backpack. Looping it around the lamppost, I attached it to my bike and brought the chain ends together. A silvery light flickered in the darkness and the chain was sealed. I peered back at the smoking man suspiciously. He didn't seem like a bike thief, but you never could tell. Just to make sure, I leaned closer to the chain and whispered, "Angustus." The chain tightened, its links shrinking, locking the bicycle even tighter to the metal pole

I texted my client, informing him that I was here. As I waited for his response, I hopped from foot to foot, the adrenaline that pumped through my blood nudging me to move. As I waited, I took a cursory look in a nearby window's reflection. My wavy dark hair was a mess, set in windblown-to-the-right style. I brushed my fingers through it, fixing it as best as I could. I smiled at the girl in the reflection. Small mouth, eyes I liked to think of as chocolatey. A bit short, angled nose, loose purple shirt, dark blue jeans. And freaking awesome black boots, a gift from my friend, Sinead, for my twenty-third birthday five weeks ago. The backpack with my products was slung on one shoulder, worn from use.

The 21st century had seen a boom in quaint mystical shops. Every aged hippie or goth chick could start selling energy-cleansing crystals and so-called magical herbs. But my shop had a large volume of repeat clients, and I constantly found new ones. Word of mouth was all the advertising I needed, because my potions actually *worked*. And I let everyone know I delivered my products to their door.

Lou Vitalis—your friendly neighborly alchemist, here to help you out. For a reasonable price.

Still no response from the client. I called him. It took twelve rings before he finally answered, his voice slow and sleepy. At first I thought I had woken him up, but then I remembered that was just the way he talked. He buzzed me in and I headed up, ignoring the subtle aroma of piss in the building's lobby.

His door was brown, dirty, no nameplate. I knocked several times until I finally heard him say, "Coming, man, I'm coming, hang on."

A lock clicked, followed by the sound of a bolt sliding. He opened the door—a pale man in his twenties, unshaven, with red-rimmed eyes and stained, drab clothing. Behind him, in a living room decorated in the universally grimy style of stoned bachelors, two men sat on lumpy pillows, sharing a hookah.

"Hi Ronald," I said, stepping into the living room, circumventing an empty discarded Coke bottle and an ashtray.

"Hey, man. Did you bring the stuff?"

I nodded, breathing shallowly, and only through my mouth. The room's smell of sweat, smoke, and old cheese mixed together unpleasantly. Opening my backpack, I took out a small nylon packet containing a thin purple powder, which seemed to glimmer as I held it to the light. Ronald held out his hand, his body tensing with urgency. I looked at it, and then at him. I didn't like the needy desperation in his eyes.

"Ronald, have you been injecting this stuff?" I asked, my voice cold.

"No, man, no way! Only snorting it, like you said!"

I raised an eyebrow doubtfully. Children's sweet dreams were potent stuff, but they weren't addictive when inhaled. They just assured a good night's sleep, accompanied by a measure of nearly unattainable innocence. There was something wonderful in going to sleep without thinking about anything beyond your toys, or the friend you met in the park, or the fire truck you saw that afternoon.

But boiled and injected, those dreams became much more potent. And highly addictive. Innocence and purity-of-heart on steroids.

I wasn't happy about this. I liked repeat customers, but I didn't want addicts. For one, addicts were unpredictable and dangerous. And besides, my moral compass, though not the cleanest, felt uncomfortable with it.

Still, I needed the money.

"Cash first." I folded my arms.

Ronald rummaged in his pocket and retrieved two crumpled bills, handing them to me nervously. I glanced at them, not touching.

"We agreed on five hundred," I said, my voice becoming even more frosty.

"Bitch, take the money and give us the dope," one of the hookah-smoking guys barked.

I glanced at him, my expression bored. He was bald, his eyes sunken, his shirt torn, his stomach bulging underneath. But under the flabbiness of his belly there was strength. He was large, and I pegged him at about two hundred pounds. Which was about ninety more than me.

A sudden air of menace filled the room. My hands began pulsing, getting warmer, reacting to the tension.

I met the man's stare dead-on, then rummaged in my pocket, retrieving a crumpled pack of cigarettes. Almost bored, I fished one out and placed it in my mouth.

I don't usually smoke, but this cigarette contained more than just tobacco. I inhaled the contents, not bothering to light it. I felt the powder in my mouth. Rancid, dry, *evil*. I leaned against the peeling wall, and said, "Why don't I just leave, taking the stuff with me, asshole?"

The large man stood up. He was much taller than me, which was no great feat, but he towered over Ronald as well. This was a guy who didn't simply stand. He *loomed*. His face twisted in a mixture of anger and superiority—a man used to scaring people into compliance. "The bitch has a mouth on her."

Tendrils of smoke started rising from my palms. In a room filled with hookah smoke, they went unnoticed.

"Dan, there's really no need for violence," Ronald told him, voice quavering. "Lou and I agreed on the price beforehand. I have the rest in my room, I'll go get it, I—"

"Shut up," Dan grunted. "Two hundred is more than enough for this shit."

I sighed, mentally nicknaming him Big Dumb Dan. "Really? Are you an expert on dream value?"

He took a step toward me. It was like looking at a bulky, very sweaty glacier approaching. "You know what? Why don't I just take it?"

"Go on, give it a try," I said. I could almost feel the powder I'd swallowed intermingling with my blood, dissipating, spreading in my body.

Children's dreams were potent stuff, but not all were sweet. Some were nightmares.

A child's nightmare could be infinitely worse than an adult's, their rampant imagination unhampered by years of experience. And a talented alchemist knew how to distill those nightmares as well.

I was a *very* talented alchemist. And the nightmares were coursing through my veins.

My usually delicate hands morphed into rough, deformed claws, the nails long and broken. My skin became gray, dry, lifeless, sections of it peeling to reveal rotting flesh underneath. My hair twisted on my scalp, like a writhing pack of angry snakes.

Big Dumb Dan's eyes widened, his mouth going slack. Behind him, the other guy said, "Her eyes—oh god. Look at her *eyes.*"

I smiled and licked my lips with a tongue that felt long and serpentine. "Well?" I asked, and my voice echoed strangely in the room, the words reverberating with an otherworldly, high-pitched, tortured scream. "I thought you wanted to take it. What are you waiting for… bitch?"

"I'm… sorry." Big Dumb Dan took a step back, his voice shaking. "You're right, of course. Your price is fair."

I turned to Ronald. "The price just went up," I said, my voice still echoed by the tormented wail. "It's six hundred now."

Ronald went for the money quickly while I stared flatly at the two other men, occasionally licking my lips with that strange tongue. If Big Dumb Dan had decided to risk rushing at me, he would have found out I could easily be overpowered. My appearance was nothing more than smoke and mirrors— parlor tricks to impress the crowd. A punch in the face would have knocked this nightmare out easily.

But you don't punch nightmares. You cower from them, trembling, hiding under the blanket, crying for your mother.

Neither man acted, their eyes clear windows to the terror that paralyzed them.

Ronald returned, shoving a bundle of bills into my outstretched claw. I handed him the powder, and he shuddered as my dry, peeling skin touched his. With a final smile full of bared teeth, I left the apartment.

TWO

My hands were pulsing with infernal heat as I closed the door behind me. The skin of my palms burned, itching for relief. I unfurled my fingers, still long, gray, and misshapen, and let the flames erupt.

The fire covered my claws in the blink of an eye, orange and red flames licking my skin, enveloping my hands up to the wrist. If anything, I was even scarier now, a nightmare with her hands ablaze. But unlike the nightmarish illusion that cloaked me, the flames were real, my body's reaction to the mixed anger and fear inside me. They would burn for a few moments until I calmed down. I considered waiting out there in the hall until the flames—and the nightmares' effect—subsided.

But it stank, and I didn't want Big Dumb Dan to have a change of heart and find me standing just outside the door.

I left the apartment building, my flaming hand leaving the front doorknob pulsing with heat. To my chagrin, the man in the trench coat was still outside. He had moved slightly, and now stood directly by my bicycle. To retrieve it, I would have to approach him, looking literally like a nightmare.

What I had done just now was bad enough. These men would tell their friends about this, and it would start a rumor about a witch, or a monster, or the bogeyman. A local tabloid might hear about it, publish an article. It would get some undesired attention. And *that* was bad. It was the one thing we all agreed upon. Magicians, witches, alchemists, demons, monsters—all the creatures beyond the veil tried to avoid being discovered. Because if there was one thing more deadly than us, it was the mass hysteria of regular people.

No, I wouldn't risk another man seeing me like this. In a few minutes, the effects of the nightmare powder would wear off, the flames on my hands would dissipate, and I would look like a regular human being again. I turned my face quickly away, trying to hide my burning claws with my body. I walked a few feet into the gloom, away from the dim streetlights.

In the dark, I glanced at my blurry reflection in a rain puddle, and nearly recoiled in horror. The eyes staring back at me were the eyes of a demon—orange and dark, something flickering inside them. My tongue was forked and black, and my hair was styled in a manner popular among Medusa and her friends. No wonder those guys were terrified.

I gazed at the puddle, wondering what would happen if I took a selfie and posted it on Instagram. *Woke up a bit cranky this morning. #NeedMoreCoffee.*

Someone cleared his throat behind me. It was that man. "Are you okay?"

I nodded brusquely, not turning around. I clenched my fists, trying to hide the flames.

"Isn't that your bicycle over there? I hope I didn't scare you away."

"I'm fine," I said sharply. My voice was echoed by the sound of a tormented, agonized shriek.

There was a moment of silence. "You don't sound fine. Cigarette?"

Damn it. I turned around, eyes full of fury, giving him an eyeful of a creature from hell. "Leave me alone!" I snarled, and bared my teeth, unfurling my claws to let the flames rise.

His eyes widened. Now he would pee in his pants and run into the night, screaming about a demon.

Instead, something almost like amusement touched his eyes. He rummaged in his pocket, taking out a cigarette. He put it in his mouth and then, to my utter shock, leaned forward and lit the tip with the flickering flame on my palm.

I gazed at him in confusion as he straightened, meeting my stare with intense, grass-green eyes.

Now, up close, I saw him clearly. His hair was jet black, and had a richness to it that made me want to run my fingers through it. He was unshaven, with sharp cheekbones, his lips quirked in a seemingly perpetual half-smile. An aura of smugness emanated from him, as if he was in on a million secrets I didn't know.

He exhaled the smoke sideways, then took the cigarette from his mouth and offered it to me. "You look like you need it."

"I don't smoke."

"Worried it'll blacken your tongue?"

"What do you want?" I contemplated walking to my bicycle, but curiosity got the better of me.

"Just wanted to talk." Despite his casual behavior, his tone had an iron edge. "You're selling dreams to those people up there. You really need to stop."

"I don't know what you're talking about."

His smile widened. "I thought we'd be beyond the stage of denial by now, what with your whole horror-movie getup. What's someone like you doing with guys like these, anyway? You seem like a..." He paused, hesitant.

"Nice girl?"

He let out an amused laugh. "Well, maybe not right now. But when you're not wearing your nightmare costume."

My claws were slowly morphing back into regular hands. My skin looked healthier. The effects of the powder were wearing off, though the flames still danced around my fingers. "You don't know me. And what I'm doing is none of your business." The tormented shriek was gone.

"You're wrong." His smile disappeared. "What you're doing *is* my business. You'll stop selling those dreams, girl. And trust me when I say those people are nothing but trouble. Stay away."

His eyes flickered for a moment as he spoke, the green color shimmering, changing to jet black. Then he blinked, and the color shifted, becoming green again.

I wanted to come up with a retort. Lou Vitalis didn't let strange men tell her what to do. I opened my mouth, but then shut it, the words momentarily gone.

He flashed me a final smile as he dropped the cigarette on the ground, stubbing it out with his shoe. "I personally prefer *this* look on you. It's a mild improvement."

Turning away, he went over to the door of the apartment building. He pushed the door, which opened easily. I clearly remembered shutting it behind me. It should have been locked.

Instinctively I knew he was going to Ronald's apartment.

I decided not to stay around to see what happened when he got there. My anger gone, the flames on my hands had shimmered away to nothing. I whipped the chain off my bike, leaped onto it, and furiously pedaled away.

THREE

My second client, and a childhood friend, billed herself as "Madame Isabella King, Psychic and Tarot Reader," but I called her Isabel.

"You want some sugar in your tea, hon?" she called from the back room.

"No thanks," I called back, glancing at the eerie human skull in the corner of the table. I wanted to believe it was a plastic model, meant to instill an atmosphere of mystery and of the occult.

It seemed kinda real, though. Creepy bugger.

Isabel's shop was definitely selling the cryptic and mysterious fortune-teller vibe. The general decor was crimson velvet everywhere, accompanied by beads, bones, and candlelight.

There were several runes etched into the thick wooden surface of the oval table where I sat. I knew many runes, and these were what we in the magical community called "squiggles" and "doodles." I should know: I had helped to carve them.

Isabel returned from the back room, smiling warmly and carrying two mugs of tea. She was twenty-five, her skin reddish-brown. Her eyes were almond-shaped, and I knew them to narrow sweetly when she was amused. She wore a shocking bright pink lipstick, the color of a cheeky flamingo. As she approached me, the beads at the tips of her braids clicked together. She was dressed in a loose white blouse and a patchwork skirt that would have looked ridiculous on anyone else, but somehow suited her perfectly. She had a pink shawl draped over the blouse, matching her lipstick.

She set the teacup in front of me, and I took a careful sip from it. It was jasmine tea, and my entire body began relaxing after the Big Dumb Dan incident and the hectic bicycle ride that had followed.

"That tastes great." I shut my eyes and leaned back. "And much needed, thanks."

"How are you doing, Lou?" Isabel asked. She had a deep voice I privately envied. My own voice was too high, shrill when I was angry. A woman with Isabel's voice could get people to take her seriously without resorting to turning themselves into a walking nightmare.

"I'm doing fine," I said lazily and sipped again.

I was stretching the meaning of the word "fine" to its very limits.

In this case, "fine" meant I owed money to one of the worst people in Boston. His name was Anthony Cisternino, but after an interesting and bloody incident in his past, he had been nicknamed "Breadknife." Then, as nicknames tend to do, it became a strange middle name, morphing him into Anthony "Breadknife" Cisternino. Sometimes people called him *ABC*, attaching the sing-song voice as if they were about to recite the entire alphabet. No one did it to his face, though, unless they wanted to be reminded what the *B* stood for.

The debt had been an idiotic mistake—money I'd thought I could easily return in a week. But a disastrous alchemical accident set fire to half my store shortly after I took the money, and the debt remained unpaid, growing each week like a malignant balloon.

I was barely scraping together enough to pay the debt's interest, not to mention the original hefty sum. So Breadknife and his employees showed up every month to collect that interest. It was a visit I did not relish, and it was due tomorrow.

Also, because of this drain on my finances, I couldn't afford to buy new supplies, which meant I was running out. Running out of ingredients, for an alchemist, is generally considered "not fine."

"Totally fine," I repeated. "How are you?"

"Meh." Isabel sipped from her tea. "The internet is killing me."

What she meant was that the online psychic market was slowly running her out of business. People couldn't be bothered anymore to go to a fortune-teller's shop, with all the accessories and knickknacks. They'd just get a psychic on a chat, and get a full reading in ten minutes for a tenth of the price.

Isabel had inherited her skills from her grandmother, and had learned the secrets of the trade from her. Now Isabel had a hard time reconciling what she'd learned from her grandma with the modern version that her clients needed. These days it was less "try to empty your mind and connect with your client's soul" and more "it's really important to get those five star reviews." I'd heard her complain about this before, and I nodded in commiseration.

"Well," I said, picking up my backpack from the floor and unzipping it. "Maybe these will help you get some new clients."

I retrieved three crystals, laying them carefully on the table. They pulsed with an eerie azure light, casting a glow that reflected on Isabel's face as she watched them, mesmerized.

"Oh, Lou," she whispered, picking one up. "These are… beautiful."

I smiled. I wasn't one to toot my own horn, but…

Who was I kidding. Tooting my own horn was one of my favorite hobbies. If there was tooting to be done, you could count on me to be there. Tooting. My horn.

These crystals were perfect. The crystallization process took nearly three weeks, and I had diligently checked their progression each day, making minute corrections to the salty solution. It was a master's work; you couldn't get it from a second-rate alchemist.

"They let you communicate with the dead," I said. "If you're already in tune with the spirit world."

I wasn't a psychic; when I had tried to use them, all I got was a monstrous headache. But I assumed Isabel would fare better.

"Are you going to use them to talk to your... family?" I asked delicately.

Like me, Isabel was an orphan. But despite that, she never ceased talking about her ancestors as if they were living and breathing. She visited them regularly. More than twenty of Isabel's family members were buried in the King family mausoleum. I had been there with her several times myself, when we were younger.

"I don't know." Her face was lost in thought.

I cleared my throat. "Okay! Two hundred each, like I told you." Normally, I'd charge three hundred, but Isabel and I went way back. Two hundred was just enough to cover the ingredient cost.

She hesitated. "Listen hon, I'm having a bit of a cash flow problem at the moment. Can I pay you next week?"

I shut my eyes, cursing inwardly. I should have known. The way she hesitated when she first asked for them, the widening of her almond-shaped eyes as I named the price. I had known Isabel for long enough that it should have been obvious. But I'd blindly followed along, wanting to help a friend.

"Damn it, Isabel," I muttered. "ABC is paying me a visit tomorrow. I need this cash."

"You owe money to Breadknife?" Her eyes widened. "Lou, after all we went through with that bastard—"

"It was an accident," I protested. "I was about to pay him back, but then there was that fire in my shop half a year ago… and things kinda went to hell after that."

"Aw, shit." Isabel muttered.

I nodded and sipped my jasmine tea. It didn't taste so great anymore.

"Listen," she finally said, rummaging in a small purse. "I have a hundred and fifty. So maybe I can buy only one crystal, and pay you the rest later? Would that be enough?" She retrieved a few crumpled notes.

I did a mental calculation. Since I had collected an extra hundred from Ronald, one-fifty would be just enough for ABC. It would mean I didn't have enough for rent, but that was a problem for another day. "Okay." I plucked the bills from her fingers.

"I'll give you a reading, free of charge," Isabel said, her voice apologetic.

"You always give me readings free of charge. Anyway, there's no need, I know my future. It's fucked."

24

She had already retrieved the pack of tarot cards from a shelf behind her. "I'm sure it's not, hon. You're the most resourceful person I know. You'll make it work. Let's ask the cards how you'll fare this month. You'll see—it'll be much better than you think."

I sighed as I watched her deftly shuffling the cards, her nimble fingers a blur. Then she held the deck for me. "Cut it."

I pried the top card from the deck and held it to her, grinning.

"Always a smart-ass," she muttered, taking the card and sliding it under the pack. She picked up the topmost card. "This is your current situation." She flicked the card onto the table.

"Hardly surprising," I muttered as I peered at the Fool. He was walking blithely, approaching the edge of a cliff, holding a flower.

She tapped a long, pink-painted fingernail on the card. "Nothing goes as planned. A situation that seemed straightforward turns out to be slippery. Your plans are foiled, and the best you can do is move along, laughing about it."

"Gee, Isabel, you think? Could you be talking about the money that isn't in my purse right now?"

"The second card," Isabel said, ignoring my tone, "is the challenge ahead of you."

She flicked another card on the table. The Emperor. Sitting on his throne, looking generally pissed.

"A strong, powerful man," Isabel muttered uncomfortably. "One who cannot be resisted."

I frowned at the card. It seemed the same as always, but when the light of the candles flickered, the emperor's scepter looked like a knife, and his face bore an uncanny resemblance to Anthony Cisternino's. I leaned to look closer, and the illusion faded away. My own subconscious playing dumb tricks on me.

"The third card will be your guidance," Isabel said, trying to be cheerful, and flicked the final card.

I glanced at it, half expecting to see Death, and felt a moment of confusion. It depicted an enormous eye, burning with an unnatural flame, green scales around it. It almost seemed as if the card depicted only the eye because there wasn't enough room for the entire creature on it.

"The Dragon?" I asked. "I didn't know that was an actual card."

She stared back at me, her face paler than I had ever seen it. "It isn't," she muttered. "Lou, what did you do to my deck? Is this your idea of a joke?"

"Nothing, Isabel, I swear!"

She picked up the cards, her fingers trembling so hard she dropped the deck. They spilled on the table, their faces up. I gawked at the chaotic spread, trying to make sense of what I saw. I knew almost none of these cards: The Lingering Shadow. The Closed Box. The Secret. Betrayal. Chaos.

My eyes scanned the cards, trying to piece them together, as if they were a picture book. The images were drenched in suffering and fear. There were six different cards depicting Death. Amidst them all, a card with a familiar figure caught my eye: a man in a long trench coat, standing in the darkness. I reached for that card, to look at it more closely.

Isabel snatched it away, and scooped the rest of the cards from the table. "I… I need you to go, hon," she whispered.

"Isabel, what—"

"Please, Lou. Just go."

"Sure." I tried to shake off the uneasy feeling in my gut. Zipping my backpack closed, I stood up. "I told you my future is fucked."

FOUR

I was brooding as I cycled back home, thinking of Isabel's card reading, and her reaction. The cards had surprised her. Which meant either someone was messing with Isabel... or the reading had been spot on.

I had never seen her so scared.

That was saying something. When we were teenagers, our lives were practically laced with fear. We were living on the street, fighting for survival, the cold and hunger constant threats. If it weren't for Isabel's talent for spotting threats in advance, I shudder to think how our lives would have ended.

Finally, after nearly dying of cold one night, Isabel, Sinead, and I realized we had to get off the street. We could let the authorities take charge of our lives, which would mean we'd go back to foster care. Instead we decided to ask Anthony "Bread-knife" Cisternino for help. It's sad to note that we preferred a man nicknamed "Breadknife" to foster care. Unlike in our previous experiences with foster care, Breadknife would let us stay together, would not abuse us, and would feed us well.

In return, we just had to do what he asked.

This turned out to be a raw deal. Breadknife's demands often got us hurt. They got other people hurt as well. The cold and hunger were gone, but the fear remained.

But Isabel had always seemed to withstand fear quite well. At least, until tonight. The cards had spooked her.

I was deep in thought, which is probably why I wasn't on my guard. Or maybe I was just getting soft. Three years before, I would have noticed that there was something wrong a hundred yards before reaching the door of my shop. I would have smelled it, felt the hair rising on the back of my neck, tasted the bitter taste of adrenaline on my tongue. Living under Breadknife's thumb, you had to be always on your toes, had to stay tuned to your five senses and your sixth one as well. But now I was oblivious, music blaring in my earphones, and I hadn't noticed the four thugs until it was too late.

Here is what "too late" looks like: By the time I hit the brakes on my bicycle, two men were blocking the way to my shop, while two more were closing off my escape route from behind. One of the men in front of me held a gun, pointed right at my face.

It was gripped lazily, the one holding it clearly believing a gun in hand gave you complete control.

Hard to argue with that logic, really. Still, no reason to let them feel like it.

His lips were moving. He said something, his face intense. Presumably it was something like "Your money or your life," or "Well, look what we have here," or maybe "Did you ever dance with the devil in the pale moonlight?" Whichever the case, it was all the same to me, because what I actually heard was Taylor Swift singing that she goes back to December all the time. I raised my finger apologetically, and he blinked, his monologue cut short.

"Sorry," I said, removing my earphones. "The music was too loud. Could you repeat that?"

He looked deflated and angry. Perhaps he had practiced his terrifying speech in front of the mirror, imagining the scared look in his victim's eyes. Now I'd ruined the moment, his fifteen seconds of glory as a badass criminal.

While he gathered his thoughts, I took in the situation. One of the thugs behind me was a woman holding a long knife. She wore black pants, black coat, and black lipstick. Cheerful. Her friend was a bit young, and chewed gum like he was making a statement with it. Maybe something like "I like my gum like I like people: chewed up." The two men in front of me were bullies' versions of Laurel and Hardy—thin and short, fat and tall. Laurel, the thin one, was holding the gun. Hardy was unarmed, but really, when your fists were like sledgehammers, there was no need.

"I told my friends here," Laurel grunted, "that a young woman shouldn't be walking alone so late in a neighborhood like this."

"I'm not walking, I'm riding my bicycle."

The loud gum-chewer snickered. The sound of his chewing got on my nerves. Also, I had to admit that, bravado aside, I was scared. The gun pointed at me was no joke. I still had some nightmare cigarettes in my pocket, but it was likely that Laurel would shoot me if I turned into a nightmarish hag, so that was out of the question. My hand began to get hot, uncomfortably so, and wisps of smoke smoldered from my palm. *Damn it, not now.*

Laurel clenched his jaw. "Tell you what, girl. You give us that bag, and your phone, and we let you go on home unmolested. How does that sound?"

I eyed the muzzle carefully, then raised my eyes back to Laurel. He quirked an eyebrow.

"Sounds fair," I said, carefully getting off the bicycle. I leaned it against the wall, then unshouldered my backpack, taking a step toward Laurel, bag held high. He lowered the gun slightly, holding up his own hand.

"Oh!" I took another step forward. "I forgot. My economics essay is in here—I have to turn it in tomorrow, so just let me take it out. You guys don't need it. I mean, it's not like you care about my report on the laws of supply and demand, right?" I opened the bag, rummaging in it distractedly, taking another step toward Laurel. "Not that it's a very good essay, anyway. Probably a C minus at best. My professor is a real asshole; I think he gives pretty girls low grades just so they come and complain to him personally. He's just so sleazy—he makes you guys look like model citizens. Ugh, I swear, I can't find anything in this bag. I don't know why I need so much stuff inside—"

I slammed the backpack into the gun, forcing it aside, and kicked Laurel in what my grandmother would have called his "man-grapes." True to his black and white counterpart, Laurel opened his mouth and closed it without making a sound as he crumpled to the floor.

I let the backpack drop, clutching my silver chain in one hand, a small vial in the other. Holding my breath, I shattered the vial on the floor.

With a sudden hiss, thick gray smoke rose from the broken vial. It enveloped all of us, making my eyes water as the smoke itched at them. Behind me I heard Gum-Chewer and Black Lipstick Girl gasping as they inhaled the smoke. Which was not something they should have done.

It was bottled sadness. Inhaling it evoked—depending on the amount you breathed in—gloominess, melancholy, depression, grief, and, in certain cases, a wave of incapacitating hopelessness.

I took a step back and turned around to face Lipstick and Gum. Gum sobbed and coughed, tears trickling down his cheeks, his shoulders shaking, and I decided he wasn't a problem for now. Black Lipstick Girl's eyes were wet, her breath wheezing from the smoke, but other than that, she was still armed and dangerous. The wave of misery hadn't taken her by surprise. Perhaps sorrow was something she was accustomed to, carried with her constantly. It would definitely explain her fashion taste.

She lunged at me, knife thrust forward. I fumbled backward, not fast enough. It cut my shirt, and a sharp pain shot through my waist. I lashed at her clumsily with my chain, and she ducked. She was crying, the sorrow deep in her, but it didn't dampen her reflexes.

My free hand smoked visibly now, thick tendrils rising from it, and the girl eyed them with fear. I tried to clench my hand, to make the heat dissipate, to calm myself. *Not now, not now, not now...*

It erupted in flames. They licked my skin, up to my elbow, casting a strange orange light on the girl's face. It didn't hurt—the flames never burned me—but once they were loose, they could do irreparable damage. They could kill.

I had to end this quickly before someone died. Black Lipstick was distracted. I swung my chain, the metal links shimmering as they arced in the air. I let go, and the chain twisted and buckled like a silvery snake. It hit the girl, coiling around her, getting tighter, slithering around her wrists. The knife dropped from the girl's hands as she struggled to get away.

Flames licking my fingers, I crouched and turned, searching for Laurel and Hardy. My lungs were bursting, begging for air, but tendrils of the sorrow smoke still circled us. Trying to ignore the pounding in my head, my eyes flickered around, searching. I found Laurel pretty much where I had left him. He was lying on the ground in a fetal position, his eyes staring ahead, his face vacant. The smoke had been thickest near the ground, and he had presumably sucked in lungfuls of it when he gasped in pain. He was completely lost in misery.

But where was Hardy? A man the size of a small moon doesn't just disap—

Something hard slammed into the back of my head. I tumbled forward, hitting the street, the surprise and pain making me gasp, inhaling the bittersweet smoke. I coughed, taking another breath, as I rolled around. Hardy stood above me, looking down. He seemed slightly upset, like a man who's just realized he's going to be late for work. Not so much sorrow as mild discomfort.

Alchemy depended in part on your target. A man the size of Hardy would hardly be affected by my tiny vial.

I wish I could say the same about me.

The sadness started from my lungs, spreading throughout my body. I suddenly felt it, the loneliness that always hovered over my shoulder. The person I loved most in the world had been taken from me five years ago. I hardly had time to meet my friends, had no parents, no family. With Breadknife always in the background, all I could do was scramble to survive. When was the last time I'd had a chance to enjoy myself? To spend some time with people I liked? To fall in love?

Five years ago, that was when. Hugging a tiny human in my arms, kissing her small head, whispering to her that we'd always be together, already knowing it was a lie. I should have kissed her more, held her tighter, smelled her just one more time before they took her away.

I hardly noticed that I was trembling on the street's cob-blestones, sobbing, tears turning everything to a blur. Through a veil of tears, I saw the fuzzy shape of Hardy pick up the backpack that held all my night's earnings, and walk away into the darkness.

FIVE

———◆———

I finally managed to get up from the road, still heaving deep, choking sobs. The four thugs were gone. My silvery chain was discarded on the ground by my bicycle. I scooped it up, and it coiled around my wrist, looping several times, creating an intricate bracelet. My bicycle seemed unharmed, and I righted it and pushed it to my store door, only a dozen yards away. Luckily, my key was in my pocket, and not my backpack. I took it out, unlocked the store, and shuffled inside, carrying the bicycle with me.

All I wanted to do was curl up on my bed in the back room and weep. The thugs had taken my backpack, and with it my money, some expensive ingredients and products, and my favorite coral red lipstick. I didn't have the payment for Breadknife. I was lonely and hurt and…

And still under the effect of the sorrow fumes. I dragged my body, still full of self-pity, to the counter, where a few tiny vials containing a dark brown liquid stood. I unstopped one, drinking it in one quick gulp. It was oily, and tasted like pee. It was the most important tincture in my shop.

The first thing every alchemist learns is: *Always have an antidote.* Alchemy is a delicate process, and prone to accidents. Sometimes you might cook the llama's saliva too much, sometimes you might spill some virgin's tears into a vat of acid. Seriously, don't get me started on what happens when you mix beetle dung with vampire dandruff. And, of course, as was the case now, you could accidentally inhale, swallow, or touch your own concoctions. It could get messy, and occasionally deadly. *Always* have some quick antidotes at hand.

I had more than thirty different cures and antidotes in my shop, but the one I'd just drunk, Margherita's fix-it-all, was the one that usually worked best. It countered most of the poisons and effects created by alchemy magic. The only real drawback was its abysmal taste. I always carried a vial with me. I'd had one on me earlier, but it had been stolen with the rest of my backpack.

I sat down in the chair behind the small wooden counter, letting the antidote take effect. Slowly, the general weepiness and self-pity I felt dissipated. Tonight had been a shit-show, no doubt about it, but feeling sorry for myself would not help, and was something I preferred to avoid. I tended to ignore all the sadness and anger and guilt I felt, bottling them inside me and never letting them out, like any healthy person does. *Let it fester*, that's my motto.

I leaned back into the chair, gazing around me. Tonight's turbulent events made me look at the shop in a new light. The shop was safety. It was my home.

Quite literally, to be honest. I couldn't possibly afford to rent two places, so the front room was the shop, and the two rooms in the back were my lab and my bedroom. But the shop was hands-down my favorite of the three.

It was the size of a small grocery store, and I had installed shelves on almost all the walls, going up to the ceiling. These were crowded with bottles, vials, jars, glass tubes, crystals, herbs, and cloth bags of all shapes, sizes, and colors. There was one window, and a shaft of pale moonlight shone on the wooden floorboards. The shop's electrical light, coming from one dim bulb, wasn't enough to really shine into the nooks and corners of the room, which gave the entire setting an aura of mystery. Though it hadn't been intentional, I liked the effect, and had chosen to leave it that way.

My counter was by the wall directly in front of the door. Though the rest of the shop was crowded, the counter itself was always clean and empty except for a small cash register, and a black bound book in which I jotted down any customer orders I didn't have on hand. My chair had been a gift from Sinead after she'd realized, aghast, that I was using a rusty bar stool. The chair was wooden, with light gray upholstery that already had a slight hollow in the shape of my ass.

Reasonably sure that my fit of misery and sadness had ended, I got up and opened the back door.

A large white shadow dashed at me from the darkness. It barked joyfully, then whined, then barked again, wagged its tail, ran three times around me, and finally, done with the spectrum of canine emotions, sat squarely down, tongue lolling in a permanent delighted grin.

"Magnus!" I said, theatrically raising my hands. "Did you miss me, boy? Did you miss me?"

He wagged his tail, barked, then got up, ears erect. Sniffing, he then ran around me five more times and sat down, which I interpreted as an affirmation that he had, in fact, missed me.

I'd deliberated before taking Magnus in. My list of cons was huge: A dog was a lot of work. I couldn't afford to take care of him. I'd have to walk him three times a day, which was impossible. My tiny shop didn't have room. He would ruin all my furniture. Dogs required attention, and I had no time. I was an alchemist, working with dangerous substances, and he might eat them. This would not be a wise decision.

The pro list was much shorter. It was, essentially: OMG, puppy!

This internal debate had taken place in the street as I'd stared down at the only yellow-white puppy in a large cardboard box. He looked up at me with his trusting puppy eyes.

He wagged his cute puppy tail. He let out one short, soft whine. I was doomed. Not even Margherita's fix-it-all could protect me from his wiles.

I named him Magnus, after Albertus Magnus, the famous alchemist.

Sinead, who knew a thing or two about dogs, told me he was mostly golden retriever. She also warned me that, taking into consideration the size of his snout and feet, he would grow into the dog equivalent of a rhinoceros. Whatever. He was cute, and he loved me unequivocally.

I crouched and scratched him behind his left ear. He narrowed his eyes, his tail thumping like a toppled metronome on the wooden floor.

"Mommy's screwed," I told him, in my high-pitched talk-to-Magnus voice. "Mommy's payment to a psychopathic gangster is gone. Yes. He will flay Mommy alive. Who's screwed? It's Mommy! Yes it is! Mommy's screwed."

I'd become one of those women who call themselves "mommy" when talking to their dog. Sixteen-year-old Lou would have been mortified to see her future self.

Magnus licked my nose in response and then nuzzled his head closer to the scratching hand. He panted in a manner that would have been incredibly disturbing coming from an adult man, but was the epitome of cuteness in a seven-month-old puppy.

I'd had the foresight to walk and feed him before I'd left for my errands, which meant I could get about two hours of sleep before he would jump on the bed, licking me awake to demand his morning walk.

I stumbled into the shower, in a bathroom the size of a broom closet. Negotiating it meant I had to undress in the bedroom, open the bathroom door, and enter sideways, nudging Magnus out with my foot before closing it. Since the room was too small for an actual shower stall, the shower partly sprayed the toilet, which meant I had to wipe it clean afterward. Or, as was mostly the case, forget, and sit down on a wet toilet an hour later.

Rinsing off the sweat and the dirt from lying in the street, I took stock of my options, of which there was exactly one: beg Breadknife to give me a few more days to pay up. We went back a ways; surely he had a soft spot for me?

I prodded the back of my head, where Hardy the goon had hit me, and winced as I touched the bruise. It was swollen, and the pain made me feel slightly sorry for myself again. But this time it was natural self-pity, the type that is sometimes required and can easily be fixed with a shot of whiskey and a good, solid, two-hour night's sleep. Which is what I did.

SIX

I'd hardly closed my eyes before the licking began, morning light shining through the shades of my small bedroom window. I shoved Magnus off the bed, groaning, but his snooze button was eternally broken. He jumped right back on the bed and commenced the licking treatment again. I opened an eye and peered at my phone, checking the time.

"Shit!"

Too late. Too damn late. I lunged from the bed, and Magnus cartwheeled off it in confusion. I was already scrambling at the piles of clothing on the floor—my wardrobe—searching for something that could even vaguely be considered clean and presentable. Shirt. Pants. I could do without socks. I put on my boots still standing, hopping on one leg at a time, nearly crashing to the floor. I checked the time again.

"Shit!"

The leash was nowhere to be found. Magnus occasionally hid it, for reasons known only to himself. I tore through the three rooms in a frenzy, finally locating it under a dress I didn't recall owning. I called Magnus, and he barked with joy and ran over. I tried to fasten the leash to his collar. He kept jumping and barking, his tongue lolling with glee, making it nearly impossible.

"Magnus, sit!" I yelled at him.

Training him was not my strong suit. Presumably, he thought I said, "Magnus, lick my hand and then dribble some pee on the floor in excitement."

Finally, with the leash latched, we both ran at the door, with me glancing again at the time.

"Oh, shit, shit, shit!"

We dashed outside and down the street. My body began to remind me I had taken quite a beating the day before, and that I hadn't slept enough since. My head pounded and the wound at my waist burned. I kept running, ignoring the pain. I could handle physical discomfort, but if I missed her... I needed that glimpse. That one glimpse. As long as I got it, I could get through the day, shitty as it was guaranteed to be.

We ran down the street, took a right, and I slowed down, trying to behave as if I were on a normal daily stroll. My eyes searched for her desperately.

Nothing.

The gray Boston sky rumbled, thick dark clouds promising an oncoming rain that matched the state of my morale. I'd missed her. I had slept too late, thinking Magnus would wake me in time, and I had missed her. And it was already Friday, which meant the next time I would see her would be Monday. A tear materialized in my eye, and I let out a small hiccupping sob. Of all the days to have been late...

And then they appeared, coming around the bend, down the street, and I felt a wave of relief. I hadn't missed her after all.

I strolled casually down the street, just a lady walking her dog. They got closer, and I watched her from the corner of my eye. She chattered incessantly, clutching the woman's hand, smiling—such a beautiful smile.

My brain drank in the details. The ponytail with the purple headband. The pink boots, white stockings, sky blue skirt, white T-shirt with a kitten. That smile. Those eyes. Her lovely, happy voice as they got closer.

"Good morning." The woman who held the girl's hand smiled warmly at me—as she always did, every morning.

"Morning," I said back, as I always did, hoping she could ignore my bloodshot eyes, my hair, the shirt I had put on inside out.

She didn't spare me a second glance. Of course she didn't. I was just another stranger, a woman she saw every morning, walking her dog.

And the five-year-old girl didn't pay attention to me either. Her attention was focused on Magnus. She smiled at him shyly, and hugged the woman's leg as they went by us. I wanted to tell her it was okay, he didn't bite, she could pet him if she wanted, but my voice was gone. Next time. Maybe I could tell her next time.

I drank up her face, her clothes, her smile. Her face became freshly etched in my mind, to remain as it was now, until the next time I saw her.

And then they were gone.

I resisted the desire to glance backward. I couldn't afford to draw the woman's attention, or she might notice some strange details.

Like how they met us every morning on their way to the girl's school. Every single morning.

Like how whenever the girl called her "mommy" as they walked by, I would wince and look away, almost as if I'd been slapped.

Like how her adopted daughter's eyes looked just like mine—large, round, and chocolatey.

By the time Anthony "Breadknife" Cisternino entered my shop, I was on my third cup of coffee, nursing a raging headache, and feeling as if sleeping with the fishes would be a nice relief.

He instantly dominated the room, as he always did, wherever he was. Breadknife had a sort of charm going for him—intense dark eyes, an expression of some deeper understanding of the universe, and a face that had aged incredibly well. His hair was silvery-white and long, reaching almost to his shoulders. Of course, once you knew him well enough, you realized this charm hid a ruthless, violent, and cold individual. You could put all his compassion and conscience in an envelope, and still have room left for a letter.

I'd heard a joke about him once: "How many Breadknives does it take to change a light bulb? Two. One to change the light bulb, and one to kill you for asking dumb questions."

If gangsters had a good sense of humor, they'd be comedians instead.

Following in his wake were two of his scariest goons. Matteo "Ear" Ricci was about thirty-five, sleek, with an emotionless face. He was called "Ear" not because he listened well, but because he was known to bite the ears off people when enraged. Rumor claimed he either ate them later or pickled them and kept them as souvenirs, but I was not one to believe bullshit. When I was a young girl, living with the rest of Breadknife's gang, Matteo had a knack for tormenting all the weak kids, stealing our money and cigarettes, occasionally groping or pinching a girl who walked past him. Whenever I saw him, a flame of hatred instantly kindled in my heart.

The other, Steve O'Sullivan, was my age, and we had originally joined Breadknife's gang two days apart. He was a bit short, his head square; someone had once joked that he was the perfect shape to be a coffee table. Ha ha ha, he was dead minutes later. Steve was the perfect soldier. He had no original thoughts in his flat head, followed orders without asking questions, and was good at hurting and killing. Despite our acquaintance, he showed no sign of recognition when he glanced at me. Not because he didn't know who I was, but because for him, it didn't matter.

"Lou," Breadknife greeted me with a warm smile. "You're looking well! Being a shop owner really agrees with you."

"Thanks, Mr. Cisternino." I smiled demurely, my heart thumping hard.

"Lou, please, how long have we known each other? Call me Anthony. And how are Sinead and Isabel these days? I haven't seen them in so long."

I shrugged, not wanting to drag my friends into the mud with me. "Would you like something to drink... Anthony?"

His eyes locked with mine for a long second, and the charm seemed to seep away from his fixed smile. "Usually when I come here, there's an envelope on the counter. The first thing you tell me is 'Here's your money.' As if you can't wait for me to leave—"

"It's always a pleasure to have you here."

"Of course it is. But today, there is no envelope. And you are very polite and hospitable." He looked around him at the store's shelves, as if wondering if his money was hiding somewhere in the room. "Where is my money, Lou?"

I swallowed. "I'm short."

"Are you." It was not positioned as a question. It was more of a statement, with a veiled threat underlying each syllable.

"I got robbed yesterday. I had it all, but four assholes jumped me... I have a bruise to show for it. They took my bag with all the money I'd made. I have some money in the safe. It was supposed to be for the rent, but maybe I can work something out with the landlord. So it can be an advance, and then next week—"

"An ad-vance." He frowned, as if I had spoken in Klingon. "It really is a terrible world, when a woman can't even go to her home without being jumped by criminals. You know, that shouldn't be a problem for someone as clever as you. I could prevent any further attacks on you. All people need to know is that Lou Vitalis is back with Cisternino, and no one would dare touch you again. I *guarantee* it. I would even forgive this unfortunate debt you've accrued."

I clenched my fist and gave my head a slight shake. *Never again.*

He sighed, as if saddened by the folly of youth. "Well… there is the issue of your monthly payment."

"If you just give me a week… I'll give you all I have right now, and some really expensive products as collateral."

"Products?" He quirked his brow. "So I get a small part of my payment, and a jar full of newt eyes as assurance?"

"I have some crystals that—"

Matteo "Ear" Ricci stepped forward, and with a casual swipe, knocked all the jars from one of the shelves to the floor. Three shattered, a putrid smell rising. I glanced at the spilled liquids, praying none of them contained anything poisonous. Luckily, they didn't. Gripping the counter, I tried to avoid letting my fear show. The blood drained from my face. My hands began to tingle with warmth.

"You know me better than that, Lou," Breadknife said in a low voice.

Magnus yipped from the bedroom where I had locked him, and I prayed Breadknife wouldn't notice. God only knew what this monster would do to my puppy.

"As it happens, I have an alternative," Breadknife continued. "I have a job that needs a professional. It needs the best. It needs you, Lou."

"I don't do jobs anymore, Mr. Cisternino," I said weakly.

"I offer you to come back to my family, and you spit in my face. I suggest an alternative form of payment, and you refuse it," Breadknife said. His eyes were cold and angry flints. "Very well. Steve, get the gas."

Steve turned around and left the shop, slamming the door behind him.

"What gas?" I asked.

"This store is insured, yes? I assume that considering your... flammable occupation, it's insured against fires?"

I remained silent.

"After it burns down, you'll have the money."

We stood in silence. Every few seconds, Magnus barked beyond the door. Steve returned with a large red fuel container. He uncorked it and tipped it to the floor. Gasoline began spilling on the wooden boards.

"Wait," I said.

Steve splashed some gasoline on one of the shelves. Matteo took out a golden lighter, flipping its lid open.

"You should get out of here before it all catches on fire," Breadknife said.

"There's an old woman living above this store," I lied.

"Pity we can't warn her. It would look suspicious if we do."

Steve scuffled around the store, leaving behind him a trail of gasoline that led to the counter. Matteo switched on his lighter, and a flickering flame materialized. He stared at it in fascination.

"Please don't burn my store."

"Will you do the job?"

"I… I can't." I couldn't go back to prison. If I stayed outside, and out of trouble, perhaps one day I could connect with my daughter again. Get to know her. Perhaps I could feel those tiny hands holding mine. But if I started working for Bread-knife again, there were only two ways it could end: with me either behind bars, or dead.

Matteo crouched to set fire to the gasoline.

"Boys." Breadknife's voice changed. It had an edge to it now. "Leave me and Ms. Vitalis alone."

"Uh… are you sure, sir?" Matteo asked, straightening.

Breadknife whipped around, fast as a snake. "Never question me!"

Matteo nodded, his face suddenly terrified. He backed to the door and quickly left. Steve followed.

Breadknife turned back to me. "Normally, I would just burn this store to the ground, Lou. You know that, right?"

I nodded, dumb.

"But I *need* this job done. And you're the only one who can do it."

"I'm sorry, Mr. Cisternino, but—"

"What would your daughter say about it?"

The words died on my lips.

"What would her adoptive parents say, if they knew their daughter's criminal biological mother lived just a few minutes away, and was stalking their adopted child, Tammi?"

My hands were smoldering, and I clenched them, trying to still the flames threatening to erupt. A fire right now, in the gasoline-soaked store, would be disastrous. How did he know? How had he found out? I had been so careful!

"We have only two options, Lou," he said simply. "The first is that you do the job for me, and I forget the debt ever existed. In the other, the shop burns, and Tammi finds out her real mother is a criminal. Her adoptive parents will find out as well. I assume they'll take legal actions to keep you away from her. After all, what parent wouldn't do everything in his power to protect his child?"

My shoulders slumped, and the feeling of defeat made the heat in my hands dissipate. "Okay," I whispered. "One more job."

Magically, the smile reappeared on Breadknife's face. "Fantastic!"

I took a moment to compose myself. Breadknife had shaken me to the core, but I couldn't let emotions cloud my judgment. Steve had left the gasoline canister on the floor. I went over to it and screwed the cap back on it, taking long, measured breaths. When I felt like I was in control again, I turned to Breadknife and asked in an almost cheerful voice, "What do you need me to steal?"

Breadknife peered at me for a moment. "You're an alchemist. Do you know what the Yliaster crystal is?"

I snorted. "Sure. It's an alchemical legend, like the philosopher's stone. Supposedly it can be used to store a soul just before a person dies. It's just another story, a false hope for immortality."

"I have an acquaintance who believes there is a box containing the Yliaster crystal in Boston."

"Your acquaintance is an idiot."

"I suggest that you don't say that again." Breadknife's voice became steely, cold.

I was taken aback. I had never seen him care about anyone but himself. "Okay then. He's not an idiot, but he's wrong. Trust me, there's no such thing."

Breadknife shrugged. "But there *is* a box. Containing a crystal. It took me and my acquaintance a long time to find it, Lou. The box was lost when Troy fell."

"*The* Troy? With Helen and Achilles and the wooden horsey?"

"That's the one. Some think Odysseus himself had found the box and taken it with him—isn't that rich? For centuries, no one had seen it. And then suddenly, there were witnesses. Claiming it had surfaced in a market in Beirut. Sold to its current owner. Stored in a safe. Inside a vault. Which is where you must break into. That's what I want, and what my acquaintance wants. The box with the Yliaster crystal."

"And where *is* this vault? Because I'm not keen on breaking into a bank. I mean... burglary is one thing, but bank robbing..."

"It's not in a bank."

I sighed in relief. "Good."

"It's in Ddraig Goch's mansion."

I blinked, my heart sinking. "Ddraig Goch… the dragon?"

"That's the one."

"But the thing is—he's a dragon."

"Yes."

"Like, one of those fire-eating, ass-kicking lizards."

"That's what a dragon is, yes."

"And you want to steal from it."

"No. I want *you* to steal from it."

I needed a drink, and it was just after ten in the morning. "Can we rob a bank instead?"

"This is the job, Lou. I told you, it's a big one. I need the best."

"You need the craziest."

Breadknife's smile widened, and he said nothing.

"No one *ever* stole something from a dragon and lived to tell about it."

"Well." Breadknife clapped his hands together, satisfied. "You always told me you wanted to be famous."

SEVEN

---◆---

On a one-to-ten scale of difficult-to-break-into, where one is the public restrooms of the nearby McDonald's and ten is the earth's inner core, the Ddraig Goch vault was a solid nine. Although Breadknife thought very highly of my burglary skills, I couldn't do it alone. I needed a team for this one. A team of the very best, and only people I could trust implicitly.

Luckily, there was already one person I trusted more than anyone else in the world, and she was definitely one of the best.

Sinead Byrne was the topmost name in my favorites list. I texted her a quick message.

Where R U?

While I waited for a reply, I rummaged in my bedroom for my handbag. I almost never used it, but my backpack was gone, and I had to make do. Magnus, trying to help, wedged himself between my feet, whining inquisitively, and when I bent down to check under the bed, licked my face with rampant excitement. Trying to ignore his wet communication, I grabbed the strap of my handbag and yanked it out from under the bed, at which point Magnus grabbed it between his teeth.

"Magnus, let go!"

He growled and pulled at the handbag harder, naturally assuming I was playing "tug of handbag."

My phone blipped and I let go of the strap, which resulted in Magnus somersaulting backward.

The screen read *101 Federal Street. 13th floor.*

I glanced at Magnus and asked him in an excited voice, "Where's the ball, boy? Where the ball?"

He barked and bolted out of the room, in his quest to find the missing ball. This gave me time to grab my chewed handbag, toss my phone, keys, silver chain, and a few other necessities inside, put on my raincoat, and leave the room. Magnus was in the shop, his head stuck under one of the shelves, whining as he searched for the ball.

Breadknife had left behind a briefcase that contained blueprints of the dragon's mansion, as well as a summary of the security measures in place for the mansion and the vault. I had no idea how he'd gotten hold of this information, but I knew better than to ask. Breadknife knew people.

I grabbed the briefcase, and left the shop. As I locked the door, Magnus began wailing, realizing my treachery.

The address was only ten minutes away on my bicycle, which would have been a nice ride if not for the rain. Despite my coat, my clothing was developing an increasing sogginess. I hung the briefcase with the documents on the left handle-bar, and it messed with my balance, making me wobble and zig-zag. I cursed myself repeatedly for not taking the bus.

As I rode, the houses around me slowly shifted into office buildings, which grew taller and taller as I got closer to the address Sinead had sent me. When I reached it, I checked my phone twice, just to make sure I was in the right place.

101 Federal Street was the Lebron James of buildings. As I stared up at the endless wall, my neck slowly creaked from the unnatural angle I was imposing on it. What the hell was Sinead doing *here*?

I pulled open the glass door and entered the shiny, lavish lobby. Feeling very much out of place with my informal attire and wet hair, I shuffled past the front desk to the elevators. There were six of them, and I entered one, pressing number 13.

I had no idea which office Sinead would be in, and when I got off the elevator, I gazed around me, rummaging in my handbag for my phone. Then my eyes landed on the formal writing etched on one of the glass doors, and I instantly knew I had found her.

I went over to "Friedman and Co.—Hippopotamus Hunting Trips."

The interior of the office was old-school, the furniture mostly dark wood. A young secretary eyed me as I walked inside.

"Can I help you?" she asked.

"I'm looking for…" I hesitated, suddenly guessing my friend was using a fake name.

"Are you Ms. Vitalis? Lou Vitalis?" the secretary asked.

"That's right."

"Ms. Dubois is expecting you. Second door on the right."

I strode down the hall toward the second door, where the name "Sinead Dubois" was stenciled on a plaque. A murmur of conversation came from inside. I knocked on the door.

"Come in," Sinead's chirpy voice called.

I opened the door, slid inside, and closed it behind me, gawking.

Sinead sat behind a huge oak desk, dressed in a white button-down shirt and a black skirt, a pair of fake glasses on her nose. Her long, smooth, beautiful red hair was tied in a businesslike updo. The desk in front of her was mostly clean, aside from a monitor, a pile of pamphlets, and a small brass statue depicting a man standing with one foot on what looked like a dead hippopotamus.

In front of her sat a plump man with a pink face, lanky hair, and spots of sweat under his armpits. He glanced at me, then back at Sinead.

Sinead smiled at me. "Lou! Come in! Mr. Dickson, this is Lou, the famous hippopotamus hunter I told you about."

He studied me, frowning. I gave him my best hippo-hunter face. I sat down in the one free chair, putting the briefcase on the desk.

"Nice to meet you," I told Mr. Dickson. "Um… I take it you are considering one of our trips?"

"The premium trip!" Sinead said. "Mr. Dickson wants the real deal."

"Oh, good." I smiled at him with respect. "There's none better. Do you have a hunting rifle?"

"A rifle?" His eyes widened in outrage. "I was told—"

"The premium trip, as you recall," Sinead interjected, giving me a look, "employs custom-made spears."

I blinked, taking a full second to recuperate from the outrageous stupidity in front of me. "Custom-made spears. Of course—how could I forget."

"Mr. Dickson has a very strong right arm," Sinead added. "He played baseball in college. Best pitcher in his team."

I nodded, satisfied. "Oh, good! But let me ask—are you up to the trip? Physically?"

"Of course!" Mr. Dickson puffed his chest. "I'm in the peak of health."

"Did he get a medical certification?" I asked Sinead.

"Not yet," she answered. "I thought that, for Mr. Dickson, we could make an exception."

"We need it, Sinead. The insurance company demands it, no exceptions."

She sighed mournfully. "Lou is right. You'll have to get a medical certification. We have a specialist; I'll set a meeting. There's a small advance fee."

"Of course." Dickson nodded. "*If* I decide to take this tour..."

"What date are you two discussing?" I asked.

"Mr. Dickson wants to go on the November tour," Sinead explained.

"Well, we can't do that," I said sharply. "It's full."

"What?" Dickson squeaked.

"It's not full!" Sinead protested. "We have five places left!"

"The Smith family booked it this morning. Didn't you check your email?"

Sinead gave me a disappointed head shake for using the name "Smith," which showed a lack of imagination on my part. "Oh, damn. I'm sorry, Mr. Dickson. Perhaps we could interest you in a later date?"

"I can't! I told you, my vacation is in November!"

I lowered my voice. "What if... No. Never mind."

"What?" Dickson asked.

"It's nothing. Except... well, one of our clients is still unsure. She told me she'd call today, but if you book now, we can give you her spot. She doesn't look like hippopotamus hunting material to me anyway. And I'm the expert. She doesn't have your..." I paused, searching my mind for any trait he might have that could conceivably help with hunting hippos. "Stamina."

"All right! I'll book now!" The urgency and excitement in his voice was somewhat pitiful.

"Fantastic!" Sinead clapped her hands together, and began to outline the registration fees, the medical exam fees, the insurance fees, the personal spear customization fees... My mind wandered as Mr. Dickson signed a bunch of forms, gave her his credit card number, and accepted a pamphlet titled "The Ultimate Big Game—Hippopotamuses." It showed a man grinning and holding a spear above a clearly Photoshopped hippo.

Mr. Dickson finally left, his eyes unfocused as he presumably imagined himself standing above his slain hippo. Sinead and I sat in silence as we listened to his footsteps receding, the office door closing behind him.

At which point Sinead burst out laughing. I joined her—there was no other option. Sinead had a laugh more infectious than the flu—joyous, full of life. Her eyes crinkled as she teared up.

"Your face!" she wheezed. "When I said 'custom spear'! Oh, god, that was priceless!"

"Where do you find these people?" I shook my head in disbelief.

"I started prowling hunting groups on Facebook."

"And when poor Mr. Dickson comes here in November? What happens then?"

"He'll find an empty office space, and will realize our website has disappeared without a trace, as well as his registration fees. And don't you try to make me feel guilty. The man came here to book a hunting tour of *hippos*. I asked him if he would be interested in hunting pandas next year and he didn't even flinch. 'Poor Mr. Dickson' my ass." Sinead had her own dubious moral compass, but I really wasn't one to judge.

I surveyed the room. "Is this scam even worth it? I mean, the office space must have cost you a fortune."

Sinead nodded mournfully. "And renting the furniture, paying the receptionist, managing the website… I admit, it's not my best venture. But it's a lot of fun."

I nodded distractedly, recalling the reason for my visit.

"What's up, Lou?" Sinead asked, her face becoming serious.

"I need your help," I said. "I'm in a bit of trouble. I need a team for a job."

Her eyes widened. "A job? I thought you were done."

"I was. But I didn't have the money to pay Breadknife's monthly interest, and… he knows about my daughter, Sinead. He threatened to expose me."

She whistled. "Bastard."

I nodded. "That's been well established. I have no way around it. I have to give him what he wants."

"If he's got leverage on you, he'll never let it go. As long as he can twist your arm with the knowledge about your daughter, you're fucked."

I knew that. "I'll worry about that later."

"What's the job?"

"I need to break into the safe in Ddraig Goch's vault. There's a box inside that Breadknife's client wants."

There was a moment of silence as Sinead digested this.

"I just need your contacts, Sinead. I don't want you to risk your life for—"

"I'm in, Lou."

I felt a wave of relief, intermingled with guilt. What was I dragging my friend into?

"So where do we start?" she asked.

I gestured at the suitcase. "I think to begin with, we should find out what we're facing."

EIGHT

S inead and I sat in the large meeting room of Hippo-potamus Hunting Trips, blueprints and papers strewn all over the table. We had been drinking espresso as the day drew, and the table was littered with empty cups. The caffeine made me jittery, which didn't mix well with my anxiety about this job, and with my overall tiredness. It was almost midnight, and my eyes were blurry from reading and rereading the summary, and examining the mansion's layout bit by bit. The blueprints were scribbled with notes in both our handwriting. Some were short informative sentences, like *air conditioner ducts too narrow to move through* or *motion sensors here*. Others were somewhat less informative, such as *fuck this security cam* and *motherfucking big lock*.

We peered mournfully at the mess.

"This doesn't look good, Lou," Sinead finally said.

"It's not the best, I agree."

"See there?" Sinead pointed. "That's… bad."

"Right, and this." I tapped the large blueprint. "Terrible."

"And this."

"Argh. I mean, how paranoid can you be. And there's this, of course."

"This really isn't good, Lou."

"It definitely isn't good."

"Maybe if we look at it like that…" She turned the blueprints upside down and we stared at them for a few seconds.

I shut my eyes. "You've made it worse."

We sat in silence for a while.

"Well, the upside is that if we break into the vault, crack the safe, and manage to leave alive, we'll be very rich," Sinead muttered. "What with the dragon scales."

According to the notes, there were six dragon scales in the safe. Saying that dragon scales were valuable was a bit like saying the crown jewels could fetch a nifty price. Dragon scales were more than just rare—they were powerful items, each storing a portion of the dragon's magic. Dragons were, for obvious reasons, quite stingy with their scales, which meant that six scales could potentially make us very rich. Or, if the dragon caught up to us, very dead.

"You'll have to fix your flamey-hands problem," Sinead said.

"I don't have a problem," I objected.

"Lou… you can't break into the dragon's vault if your hands keep bursting into flames every time you get a bit emotional. People whose limbs are on fire are sorta conspicuous."

"Don't worry about it. It hardly ever happens."

Sinead rolled her eyes. "You told me it happened *yesterday*. Look, it's not a big deal. Just figure out a potion that will make it go away."

"It's not that simple," I muttered. "I… can't. I tried."

What Sinead called my "flamey-hands problem" was a result of an alchemical accident involving phoenix blood a few months before. Coincidentally, it was the same accident that had burnt my store down, and resulted in my inability to pay Breadknife back. I couldn't figure out how to fix it, and it definitely made life complicated. Sinead was right. Heists usually involved hiding in the darkness, or blending in with a crowd, things that became quite difficult when your fingers were happily blazing like twin bonfires.

"Okay. I'll fix this," I said.

"Good." Sinead smiled in satisfaction. She'd been hassling me about the "flamey-hands problem" ever since it had begun, like a nagging mother. She'd been worried I would eventually light my hair on fire.

I changed the subject. "We'll need to find a way around the dragon's senses."

Sinead's face crumpled. This was the worst bit of the information Breadknife's notes had summarized. Dragons, it turned out, had a special affinity with their lair and hoard. When someone stepped into a dragon's lair, the dragon immediately knew about it. Even if it was miles away, it would sense the intruder. In our case, the dragon's lair was his mansion, which meant we couldn't enter the mansion's premises without the dragon being instantly aware.

Even worse, supposing you did manage to enter a dragon's lair without him noticing, once you touched the dragon's treasure, it would instantly feel the intruding hands on its hoard. It would rush to stop you. And dragons moved *fast*.

So, in essence, we had to figure out two things: how to get *in* without the dragon noticing, and, once we got in and stole the safe contents, how to get *out* before the dragon turned us into crispy bacon.

"We should probably look for a sorcerer."

Sinead was definitely right. A sorcerer could help with these problems. The only problem was that sorcerers were a nasty bunch. The reason was simple—sorcery was dark magic, and that tended to attract a certain type of person. Even if they were fantastic to begin with, the magic slowly warped them, changed them, peeling off their humanity, leaving behind a diseased soul. It's hard to maintain a good nature when demons constantly whisper in your ears. There were exceptions, of course, but they were few and far between.

"You'll have to call Estagarius." I sighed. He was the only sorcerer we ever really worked with.

"He's dead, Lou."

I gawked at her in shock "No! Really?"

"Died two months ago, haven't you heard? Cancer."

"He was such a nice old man," I said sadly.

"You called him pompous and unbearable!"

That was true, but when people died on you, adjectives morphed, becoming slightly more positive. "He was a pompous and unbearable nice old man."

"That's a lovely eulogy. You should send it to his wife."

"Who then?"

Sinead thought about it for a second. "There's a new guy. Kane Underwood. He has a good reputation."

"What does that even mean?"

"Probably that he's never been caught drinking blood in public, or cackling with his hands raised high as lightning flashed behind him."

"Oh, good."

"I can't think of anyone else."

"I'll check him out," I muttered.

Sinead leaned back, putting her feet on the table. "Don't you have a puppy?" she suddenly asked. "He's probably pissed all over your house."

I shook my head. "I texted Isabel earlier. She took Magnus for a long walk."

"That's nice of her."

"Isabel is good people."

"We'll need her. You know that, right?"

"Yeah."

"And we'll need a hacker."

"A hacker who can handle magic." I tapped the notes.

"Fine, I'll ask around."

"And I'll talk to this guy Kane."

Sinead groaned and massaged her forehead. "So… you, me, Isabel, Kane, and hacker. That's five. Do you think it's enough?"

I considered it. "Yeah," I finally said. "I think it's a job for five people."

NINE

K ane Underwood's office, located on the second floor of a dinky building in East Boston, was not what I expected.

There were no shelves stacked with leather-bound tomes in the room; no raven, cat, or lizard staring at me, eyes unblinking. The office was also lacking in ancient ceremonial daggers, weird mysterious masks, and arcane glowing glyphs.

It had a small wooden desk, littered with pages, some torn or crumpled. A brimming ashtray and a half-full whiskey bottle acted as paperweights. There was a tall metal filing cabinet in the corner of the room, and another ashtray, also full, sat on top of it. The office was dimly lit by one bare lightbulb, but even in this murky light I could see the fine layer of dust that settled in the corners of the room. The place smelled richly of clove and pine. And it was empty.

I took a step forward and glanced at the papers on the table. It was a bizarre mix of unpaid bills, yellow crumbling parchments scrawled with dark blotchy ink, diagrams of circles of power doodled on napkins, and various takeout menus. Mesmerized by this assortment, I leaned closer to inspect one of the scraps of paper, when I heard footsteps behind me. I turned around, and was taken aback at the sight of the man standing in the doorway.

"I know you!" I said. It was the guy I'd met in the street two nights before. He was dressed in the same dark trench coat, and had the same smug face. The coat and the smugness were probably permanent fixtures.

He quirked his lips in a tiny smile, and stepped inside the room, brushing past me. He put a plastic cup of coffee on the desk, and then shrugged off his trench coat, hanging it on a nail in the wall. He sat on the chair behind the desk, and leaned back, folding his arms. "You're the dream peddler," he said. "Sorry, I didn't know you were coming, or I'd have brought a cup for you too. What brings you to my office, Ms. Lou Vitalis?"

I was thrown off by the fact that he knew my name, and found myself opening and shutting my mouth like a goldfish. The fact that this guy managed to consistently throw me off my guard vexed me. Finally recovering, I blurted, "Are you Kane Underwood?"

"Yes, I am. Pleased to see you again, Lou." He said my name strangely, as if tasting the way it felt on his tongue. His green eyes never strayed from mine. "How can I help you?"

"What were you doing that night, in the street?" I asked.

He took a sip from his cup and fished a pack of cigarettes from his pocket. Placing one in his mouth, he motioned at the only other chair in the room. It was by the corner of the desk, and had a layer of dust on it. I brushed it lightly, and sat down. Kane lit his cigarette with a dented metal lighter. He inhaled, blew the smoke sideways, and looked at me thoughtfully. "Working," he finally answered.

I let the word hang in the air. The smoke from his cigarette carried the same scent of clove and pine that lingered in the room. It was a rich fragrance, unlike any cigarette I had smelled before. "Working at what?" I finally asked.

"Something I was hired to do."

"I need to know what it was, to know if I can trust you."

"Well." He sighed sadly. "I guess you won't be able to trust me."

That didn't satisfy my curiosity, but it did satisfy my need to know he could keep a confidence. Most sorcerers could; you don't get far in the sorcery world if you blab.

"I need a sorcerer," I said.

"You found one." His green eyes twinkled. "What for?"

"For a difficult, dangerous, confidential job."

He took another puff from his cigarette. "People don't come here when the jobs are easy, safe, and widely known. Before I take on a job, I need to know the details first."

"I need to break into a vault. It's very well protected. There are some wards, runes, probably a curse or two."

"Where is this vault?"

"We can discuss that later."

"Who does it belong to?"

"Later."

"What's in it?"

"Later."

"Then what can we talk about right now, Lou?"

"I want to know if you're the man for the job."

He smiled and stubbed out his cigarette in an ashtray. "So this is a job interview? Okay. You want to ask if I'm the man who will break into a well-protected vault whose location, contents, and owner I don't know? No. I'm not that guy. That guy sounds like a moron, and I'm not a moron." He took another sip of his coffee. "I really feel shitty that I can't offer you anything. Do you want to go downstairs? There's a nice café there."

"It's fine," I said. "Look, what I want to know is if you're good at what you do. If I can trust you. If—"

"Does this look like a face you can't trust?" He gestured at his scruffy unshaven cheek. "What's the job? And what are you paying?"

There was no way around it; I had known it when I came to his office. He was right, only a moron would agree to a job without hearing the basic details. "I want to break into the vault of Ddraig Goch."

He put down the coffee cup and cleared his throat. "Well, you weren't kidding about difficult and dangerous."

"There's a box in the safe my client wants," I explained. "I only need the box. The rest of the safe's contents can be split between the members of the crew. There should be six dragon scales inside."

He digested this. The mention of dragon scales didn't seem to have an impact on him. I was beginning to suspect I'd have to find someone else.

"How many members in the crew?" he asked.

"Five, including me and you."

"Six dragon scales divided by five people? Who gets the extra scale?"

"We'll worry about that later."

"Who are the members of this crew, aside from you?"

I shook my head. "That's as far as we go. I'm not risking their lives, in case you decide to go snitching on us to Ddraig Goch."

"You think I would snitch?"

"I don't know you."

"That's true, but you know what?" He took out his cigarettes again. "Snitches get stitches."

"Is that some sort of ancient sorcerer rule?" I tried to catch a glance of the cigarette pack. It wasn't a brand I recognized. There were Chinese letters on its face.

"More like an ancient public-school rule."

"So? Can you do it?"

"I don't know. I never broke into a dragon's vault before."

"No one has."

He drummed on the table for a bit, thinking about it, occasionally taking a drag from his cigarette. Finally, he stubbed it out in the ashtray, adding to the quite impressive amount of cigarette butts and ash in it. "How do you intend to overcome the dragon's senses?" he asked.

"We had a few ideas," I answered slowly. "But they depend on your capabilities. How good are you?"

He leaned forward, a strange smile curving his lips. "Do you want me to demonstrate my powers now? Pull a rabbit out of my hat? Saw a lovely young woman in half?" The air crackled, making the hair on the back of my neck stand. His eyes flickered to black, their darkness mesmerizing.

"You don't have a hat. And I'm not letting you near me with a saw."

He snorted in amusement, and the strange tension in the air dissipated. His eyes morphed back to green. "What do you want me to say, Lou? That I'm the best sorcerer to walk the earth since Merlin? I'm better than most. But I can't perform miracles."

"Can you cloud the dragon's senses?"

"No."

I nodded, unperturbed. "Can you teleport us into the vault?"

"No…" He hesitated. "Teleportation spells are quite common, but they require immense power. You'd need a magical object that can focus that power. And those are very rare. Do you have something like that?"

"Probably not," I admitted.

"Can you get one?"

"I'll check, but I doubt it."

"Then I can't teleport us into the vault."

"Okay… but suppose you had one, could you teleport us?"

He shrugged. "I'd have to do some research, but yeah, I think I could."

"Can a dragon scale be your magical object?"

He blinked in surprise. "Yes. But the dragon scales are *inside* the vault."

"Right." I folded my arms. "So assuming we're able to enter the vault, open the safe, and retrieve the dragon scales… you could teleport us away?"

"It would destroy one of the scales."

"Luckily, we have one to spare."

He grinned. "You're full of surprises, Lou Vitalis. You already knew what I would say when you entered my office."

"I had some assumptions." I returned his smile. "So would you be able to do it? Teleport us out of the vault? Somewhere safe?"

"Maybe. Probably."

I smiled in satisfaction. One of our two problems was solved. We had a way *out*.

"But that raises the question, are *you* capable of doing this?" Kane asked. "No offense, but last time we met, you didn't exactly inspire trust in me. And you seem young."

I bristled. "What does age have to do with it?"

"With age comes experience. You're asking me to risk my life on this—quite frankly—almost suicidal job, and I would feel better if I knew you were an experienced hand."

I was prepared for this. "Did you hear about the break-in into the cult of Dra'akthol's inner sanctum eight years ago?"

He grinned. "Of course. It was hilarious."

"It was." I relaxed in my chair, feeling in control. "Their sacred blade was taken, along with several arcane items."

"That's right, and the burglar wrote *Dra'akthol sucks donkey balls* on the altar."

"It was actually *Dra'akthol sucks* dirty *donkey balls*."

"Are you going to tell me that was you?"

"One of the items stolen was a chain."

He nodded. "The chain of Apollonius."

I took the chain out of my handbag, and placed it carefully on the table. He stared at it, then leaned forward to touch it.

The chain coiled and lashed at his fingers. He pulled his hand back quickly.

"Careful, it bites," I said, and touched it. It circled around my wrist, and I could almost hear it hissing in outrage.

"*You* have the chain?" I had the satisfaction of seeing him surprised for the first time.

"Yup."

"Do you know what it can do?"

"It can thwart bicycle thieves really well."

"You use the chain of Apollonius as a... bike lock?"

"I usually do. Though right now it's locked with a regular lock, because I thought you might want to see some proof that I know what I'm doing."

He considered this. His cigarette went out, but he didn't seem to notice.

"Okay," he finally said. "I'll do it."

I tensed. He didn't seem particularly interested in the dragon scales, so why would he agree to risk his life on this heist so quickly? I considered getting up, telling him I'd changed my mind, that he wasn't what I was looking for.

But Kane was the best choice. The only choice.

"Good," I said. "So... now we need to seal the deal."

"I'm sorry?"

"I wasn't born yesterday, Kane Underwood. When I work with sorcerers, I *always* seal the deal with blood. It's the only way we can really trust each other," I said. "We both cut our hands, and squeeze them together. We bind our hands with white silk. We swear an oath of loyalty as the silk slowly turns crimson. Then we untie the knot, and lick the mixed blood from each other's fingers."

I savored his stare of bafflement.

Finally, he cleared his throat. "Lou... are you fucking with me?"

I grinned at him. "Maybe a little."

"Okay then." His lip quirked in amusement, his eyes twinkling. "That was fun. Now let's talk some more about our dragon vault."

TEN

◆

"I'm not sure I understand what you want me to do." Isabel frowned.

We were in her shop, drinking tea. She'd been more than happy to join our crew. Dragon scales were rumored to enhance psychic senses, and that was something she just couldn't refuse.

"My hands," I said. "They burst into flames sometimes." I opened my right hand and concentrated on it. On cue, a flame rose from my palm, dancing merrily.

"I know. Because you played with phoenix blood."

"I wasn't playing, I was working with it. It's a very volatile material. The thing is, I can't always control it."

She eyed the flickering flame. "Looks like you're doing fine, hon."

"Sure, because I'm relaxed right now. But when I'm angry or scared, it can go off without my control." I clenched my fist, the flame disappearing.

Isabel raised her eyebrows. "That's quite a problem. Good thing you don't drive. The way some people behave on the road... There was this one asshole this morning—"

"Right." I hurriedly interrupted her. Isabel was the most relaxed and patient person I knew. But thirty seconds behind the wheel turned her into a frothing, screaming madwoman. I once saw her get out of her car, intent on smashing all the windows of a vehicle that had parked diagonally across two parking spaces. I really didn't have time for one of her road-rage rants. "The thing is, I need a way to control my emotions. You have relaxation techniques, right? You said you have to be completely relaxed to glimpse the future."

"Well... yes. I've studied and practiced them for years. Mediation, guided imagery, self-hypnosis, dream walking—"

"Awesome! I need something quick. A sort of crash course. Relaxation 101. How to relax for dummies."

"Quick?" she frowned. "How long do we have? Months?"

"Well..." I thought about it. "Preferably... two, three days?"

"You want me to impart all I learned—"

"Not all you learned," I interjected. "Just some quick breathing techniques. You know? To get me all nice and relaxed and not in a burning sort of mood."

"So we have three days—"

"Not whole days, really. Something like an hour every day."

"Three… hours. To teach you self-relaxation."

"Let's start now, shall we?" I said brightly.

She sighed. "Okay, fine. Maybe I should put on some soothing background music before we begin."

"Well… it's not like I'll have soothing music in the dragon's vault, right?" I pointed out. "If anything, there will be screaming alarms and police sirens. Better do it without the music."

"Fine." She sounded irritated and pretty far from relaxed. "I want you to close your eyes… not that hard. Just close them. Loosen your muscles a bit. Start taking deep steady breaths. You sound like you're hyperventilating. Slow down… you don't need to breathe so hard. You don't get points for volume, Lou—"

"How long should the breaths be?"

"How long?" She sounded confused.

"Like… two seconds in, two seconds out? Three seconds? I'm good with recipes."

"Relaxing is not a recipe. Just… breathe in, breathe out. Yes. Something like that. Good. Now I want you to focus on your toes."

"My toes?"

"Stop talking. From now on you don't talk. Focus on each toe. I want you to imagine feeling the muscles in your toes relax."

The muscles in my toes. Up until now I'd never even known I had muscles in my toes. It sounded perverse. Could someone train their toe muscles? Could they work them out in the gym? I bet Jason Momoa had really muscled toes. I bet he could lift weights with them.

"Feel them grow lax, liquid, completely dormant."

I had a million things to be doing right now. I needed to start scouting the dragon's mansion. And we had to find a hacker who could crack the dragon's security systems. There were some potions I had to make. Did I have the ingredients? I began to tally a shopping list of what I needed. I could probably get Breadknife to pay for the ingredients. Maybe I should buy some extra stuff while I had an expense budget.

"Lou, you have to concentrate."

"I am concentrating!"

"Hon… open your eyes."

I did, feeling sheepish. Isabel smiled at me, her face looking a bit sad. "I've known you for a long time, hon. You have a mind that races like a speeding train. It's full of whirling ideas, and plans, and inspirations. I've seen you think on your feet so fast, it left me breathless."

I blinked, surprised. I'd never thought of myself that way, and definitely hadn't imagined Isabel did.

"But to truly relax you have to think much slower. I could almost *see* your mind racing right now. You have to focus on this one, tiny part of yourself, and push away all other thoughts. Do you think you can do that?"

"I… I can try."

"Okay. So first, when you close your eyes, I want you to focus only on my voice."

I shut my eyes, and began breathing deeply again.

"I want you to *feel* each breath as you inhale. Focus on your lungs, follow their rhythm."

I focused on my lungs. Breathing in and out. In, and out.

"Good. Now, focus on your toes. Feel the muscles relaxing."

She made me focus on each toe, then on my ankles, my knees, my thighs, feeling each muscle grow soft. Her voice—that deep soft voice—lulled me, made me feel mesmerized. Slowly, my breathing slowed, and I sank into a calm stupor.

"Now, focus on your stomach. Feel the muscles in it relax, the tension dissipating…"

A question crept into my mind. It had been there all along, waiting for me to pause for a moment, to really think.

Breadknife knew there were six dragon scales in the safe, but he hadn't demanded even one. Only the box with the crystal.

It seemed so unlike him. It was as if the scales were almost irrelevant compared to the crystal.

What if it *was* the Yliaster crystal in the dragon's vault? Could I really discount that so quickly? What if the Yliaster crystal existed? If it did, it would definitely be more powerful than a dragon scale—a crystal that could hold souls.

But if that was true, it could mean something even more sinister. The Yliaster crystal could trap a soul. Could that be what Breadknife's client was really after? Did they want me to steal a soul for them? If they did, whose could it be? What did they want with it? Could I really hand over someone else's soul?

"Lou?"

I sighed, and opened my eyes. "Sorry," I said, dejected. "The thoughts just popped up."

Isabel patted my hand. "Don't worry about it. You did much better than I thought you would. Want to try again?"

I shook my head. "Not tonight. Tomorrow."

Perhaps by tomorrow, I would manage to push the troubling thought of the trapped soul out of my mind.

ELEVEN

The sun broke through the morning clouds, illuminating the sky in the sort of crisp magical light that was perfect for picnics, walks in the park, and surveillance.

Ddraig Goch's mansion was located in the so-rich-you-could-never-afford-to-live-here town of Weston. Less than a mile away, on a green-grassed hill, stood another mansion, which belonged to a lawyer who knew Breadknife through ways best left unexplored. Since he was currently on vacation, he had agreed to let us use the place. It was anyone's guess what dirt Breadknife had on him that made him so complaisant.

By sheer luck, due to a combination of topography and aggressive gardening, there was one bedroom on the top floor of the lawyer's mansion that had a direct line of sight to the premises of Ddraig Goch's home. And this was our base of operations. The room enabled us to maintain a constant surveillance on the mansion's personnel, slowly figuring out the shift changes of the security guards, what time the gardeners showed up and left, the exact path of the patrol routes… anything that might be important.

Through the twin lenses of my binoculars, I looked at Ddraig Goch's home for the first time, making small notes on the blueprints that were spread on the king-size bed by my side. The bed was inviting, the bedsheets tightly spread and clean, the mattress possessing that perfect balance between soft and firm.

Sinead and Isabel had taken the night shift, and now it was my turn, with Kane as my shift partner. I'd showed up at six in the morning to relieve my friends, who were blurry-eyed and cranky, as expected. I'd asked Kane to show up at seven-thirty. I felt a bit tense about spending a long day with him, and I wanted to have a bit of time to myself before he arrived, to settle into the relaxed atmosphere of a long, eventless day.

As I waited, I practiced breathing steadily, and relaxing the different muscles of my body. I had to be able to control my emotions by the time we broke into the dragon's mansion. I couldn't let the entire job be blown because my hands suddenly decided to combust.

When does a house stop being a house and become a mansion? Is it a simple matter of number of rooms? Six rooms means it's a house, eighteen means it's a mansion? Or maybe it's the size. If it takes a few minutes to cross from one side to the other, it's definitely a mansion. Or it could be style—the expensiveness of the furniture, the intricate carvings framing the doors and windows, the serving staff roaming the halls.

Ddraig Goch's mansion had left those distinctions far behind. It was one-hundred-percent mansion, and inching its way toward being a palace.

The front lawn was immense, a bright green carpet of carefully mowed grass. At the edges grew enormous red maple trees, their leaves creating an explosion of orange, red, and pink. Towering above the garden was the mansion itself, a light-brown three-story structure spotted with arches and ancient-looking windows and terraces. An enormous porch, large enough to contain my entire apartment, protruded from the third floor. A greenhouse sat on the roof of the mansion, its glass panes clean and translucent, a myriad of strange plants growing inside.

I had stared at the blueprints of the mansion for hours and knew the layout well, but the place still took my breath away.

The sound of footsteps coming up the stairs made me lower the binoculars and glance at the time. Twenty past seven.

He was early. A second later, Kane appeared in the doorway, a smile on his face, holding a Starbucks bag.

He set the Starbucks bag on a tasteless mahogany dresser that stood against the wall by the door. "It's the first time I spend a whole day with a woman in a bedroom, and all she wants to do is peep at the neighbors."

"How long did it take you to think of that quip?" I asked, raising the binoculars again and looking through them.

"About ten minutes. My quick wit doesn't really show up until noon." I heard the bag rustle as he rummaged through it. "I didn't know how you drink yours, but you struck me as someone who likes her coffee strong."

"You were right," I said. I still held the binoculars to my eyes, but I heard his soft steps on the carpet and smelled the strong scent of coffee. I lowered the binoculars and took the cup from him. "Thanks."

"I also got us some muffins." He sat on the edge of the bed, moving aside the blueprints, and his leg brushed against mine accidentally. He had taken off the trench coat. Underneath he wore a white T-shirt that accentuated the width of his shoulders. His face was lit by the sunlight filtering through the window, and his grass-green eyes seemed to shine. It took me a few seconds to realize I was staring at him, almost mesmerized, and I pulled my eyes away, doing my best not to blush.

"See anything interesting?" he asked.

I blinked, my tongue suddenly tied. Oh—he was talking about the mansion, not about his face.

"Uh… nothing we didn't know about beforehand. Take a look." I removed the binoculars' strap from my neck, handing them to him. He leaned forward to look out the window, and I shifted my chair slightly to give him some space.

"Oh, wow," he muttered. "That's a big-ass mansion."

I sipped from my coffee, and determined that Kane had pegged my taste perfectly. Black coffee, strong, bitter, perfect. I felt almost tearful with gratitude.

"What else do you see?" I asked, my voice flat and innocent. I needed to know this guy was the real thing. Was he an actual sorcerer, or was he just a guy who thought it was cool to mutter in Latin?

He took a few seconds to answer, and when he did, his voice had an edge. "There's an aura of magic shimmering from all the windows. It's well hidden; whoever cast it was a master. I assume it's some sort of ward."

I nodded with satisfaction. I couldn't see the aura myself, but I knew it was there. It had been mentioned in Breadknife's notes. The fact that Kane could see it indicated he had a sharp third eye, a good sign of his powers.

"The windows are all warded against intruders," I said. "Anyone who tries to enter or leave through them dies. Anyone who breaks them dies."

"Dies of what?"

"Does it matter?"

"Just professional interest. Is it a heart attack? Does it make your brain explode? Does it make you combust? Turn you into a toad?"

"Turning into a toad isn't dying."

"Fine. Do you turn into a dead toad? I just want to know how powerful the magic is."

"I don't know. It's a ward that kills you," I said testily. "Maybe it disintegrates you, maybe you die of sniffles. The point is, it's terminal. You die. Cease to be. Can you break the spell?"

"It depends." He kept looking through the binoculars in concentration. "Maybe. Yes, I think so. With enough time. But whoever cast the spell would instantly know it's been broken."

"That's not good. We don't want to alert anyone."

"Then we're not entering through the windows." He lowered the binoculars and glanced at me. "There's no spell on the front door."

"There's no spell on the back door either." I leaned toward him and took the binoculars from him. His eyes lingered on mine for a moment, and I met them, my gaze steady. Then I drew back, and put the binoculars back to my eyes, looking at the doors. "The problem is, there's always guards stationed by the doors. No one enters or leaves without their permission."

"We'll have to take care of that."

I shook my head unhappily. He was right, of course, but I preferred to avoid it if possible. I could think of a myriad of ways to take care of the guards, and all of them posed risks I didn't want to take.

Kane got up and fetched the muffins. They were still warm, and I snagged the chocolate chunk one, leaving the walnut muffin for Kane. In this world's vicious food chain, I am chocolate's natural predator. We ate our muffins in silence, and then Kane pulled out his strange cigarette pack. He put a cigarette in his mouth, but I quickly leaned forward and plucked it out.

"No smoking here."

"Seriously?" He seemed outraged.

"We had very clear instructions. We're guests here, after all." I rummaged in my purse and took out a pack, which I handed to him. "Here. I made these some time ago. Smokeless cigarettes."

"What, like vaping?"

"No. These are actual cigarettes, but the smoke dissipates once you expel it. No smoke, no smell, no problem."

He lit one suspiciously. Its tip glowed bright green as he inhaled, a strange quirk of the magical tobacco I'd created. He breathed out, the smoke instantly disappearing.

"These taste like ass," he said.

"Well, they're a bit old, I guess," I admitted. "But it's real tobacco, so you still get the lung cancer and stains on your teeth."

"You should find a job in marketing." He took another drag from the cigarette. Despite his complaint, he didn't seem about to stub it out. He used his empty coffee cup as an ashtray, puffing on my handmade cigarette with a thoughtful look in his eyes.

"So…" he said, five minutes later, the cigarette gone. "Now what?"

"Our shift is just starting." I smiled at him. "Learn to appreciate your quiet time with me. We'll be here for ten more hours."

"*Ten?*"

"Isabel and Sinead were here all night. You got the better shift, trust me."

He groaned, got up, paced the room. Sat down. Got up again.

"Try taking off your shoes. It'll make you feel more comfortable," I suggested. "Make fists with your toes."

"Fists with my toes?"

"It's a *Die Hard* reference."

"Oh. I never saw that movie."

I gaped at him, incredulous. "You never saw *Die Hard*? The best Christmas movie ever made?"

"*Die Hard* doesn't sound like a Christmas movie."

"Come on! 'Now I have a machine gun, ho ho ho'?"

"I have no idea what you're talking about."

I shook my head in disbelief and raised the binoculars to my eyes. The guards at the front gate waved a black car inside, and I noted its license plate number in the logbook while Kane removed his shoes and socks. I glanced quickly at his feet. They were large, much larger than mine. When he sat on the bed, our bare feet were quite close. I had a sudden urge to slide my foot up his ankle, and that, in turn, led to other images flickering in my imagination.

We kept at it for a few hours, exchanging the binoculars between us, sometimes talking, sometimes remaining silent for long stretches. This was the main reason for the shared shift. There was no real rationale to have two people here—one would have been enough, especially during the day, when staying awake was less of a hurdle. But I wanted us to get to know each other better, to cement us as a team. When push came to shove, we would need to rely on each other, and be able to predict each other's actions.

What do people who spend long hours together talk about? We discussed our taste in books and movies, which hardly intersected. I read thrillers and mysteries; he read literary books about the struggle of everyday life. I liked action movies and rom-coms; he preferred science fiction and fantasy. Finally, we found one movie we both agreed was fantastic— *Cool Runnings*, about the Jamaican bobsledding team, which we'd both seen as kids.

He told me about his sister and her gift for playing the viola, stunning the room into silence with her craft, everyone around her listening with rapt attention. When she'd finish the piece she was playing, she'd inevitably smile in an embarrassed, innocent way, as if she was flustered that everyone had listened to her play that silly tune for all that time. When I asked him if she still played, he muttered that she'd been hospitalized, and refused to discuss it further.

I told him about my own childhood, before my parents died, all my recollections positive and bright and happy. I had no bad memories of my parents. I'm sure they occasionally shouted at me for no reason, or acted in ways that, as a child, I found annoying. But those moments had been erased by time and by life in foster care. And every good memory—every picnic on the beach, every night curled in my mother's arms, every day I was sick and my father took care of me—they had all become chiseled into my mind, a source of comfort.

He asked what happened to them, and I said shortly, "They died when I was eight."

I guess neither of us felt close enough to discuss the darker moments of our history.

For lunch, we ordered from a nearby restaurant that delivered. I had oven-cooked salmon with garlic, and Kane had a medium-rare steak.

"Who's paying for all this?" he asked, chewing.

"Our employer."

"Very generous of him."

"Trust me. Generosity is very far from his mind." I picked up the binoculars, scanning the mansion for the hundredth time. "Once we're inside, we need to be able to open the vault door. It has a keycard lock, a combination lock, and is also warded by a set of runes called… Södermanland Futhark?"

"It's Fu*thark*, not *Fu*thark."

"God, you're like an old, unshaved version of Hermione. Do you know how to counter them?" I took another bite of the salmon. It was perfect, still a bit juicy, melting in my mouth.

"Yes. And those kind of runes are easier to break without alerting the person who inscribed them. You see, runes, unlike wards, aren't constantly maintained by a sorcerer. They're inscribed, and then they just—"

"I know the difference between runes and wards, thank you. No need to mansplain it to me."

"Right." He grinned. "But I can't break combination locks and keycard locks."

I nodded. "That's not up to you. Ddraig Goch's security chief has a keycard, and knows the combination. So we'll have to find a way to get to him."

"Like what?"

"Every man has a weakness. Maybe he's having an affair and we can blackmail him. Maybe he has crippling gambling debts that we can use. Maybe he's addicted to heroin. There's always something. We'll find it."

"You sound very sure."

"This isn't my first rodeo."

For dessert I opened my brand-new backpack, retrieving a bag of M&Ms and two Snickers bars. In retrospect, eating those was a mistake, as both of us were jittery afterward—not an ideal state for an additional five-hour shift of surveillance. I tried to pass the time by coming up with ideas of how to infiltrate the mansion without going through the front or back doors. They quickly became more and more ridiculous, as my sugar-addled mind hopped from tunneling, to blasting our way through, to me dueling the dragon one-on-one.

And then my eye caught a movement somewhere unexpected. A section of the greenhouse wall suddenly moved, opening, and a gardener walked outside. I pressed the binoculars harder into my eyes. I hadn't noticed a door there at all.

The gardener fiddled with the greenhouse's door, making sure that it remained open. Then he lit a cigarette.

"Look at that." I gave Kane the binoculars. "There's a door to the greenhouse. The blueprints didn't note that."

"The door's not warded," Kane muttered, looking carefully. "So we might be able to get in through there."

He returned the binoculars. I glanced through them again. No door handle, no lock. How would someone on the roof open it? The gardener had intentionally left it open while he was smoking.

"I wish we could see how it's opened from the outside," I muttered. "There's probably a hidden button somewhere."

"Watch the gardener," Kane said. Then he began to murmur under his breath, a string of syllables I didn't catch.

"I *am* watching the gardener. But the door's open." I gritted my teeth in frustration.

Kane's voice rose as he chanted, the words strange and arcane. The mystical energy in the room crackled against my skin.

"Kane… what—"

And then suddenly the greenhouse door, hundreds of yards away, slammed shut.

"Did you do that?" I whispered.

"Yeah." He breathed heavily. "God, I hate telekinesis. It always leaves me itchy and dry all over. What's the gardener doing?"

"Mostly… swearing at the door," I said, watching as the gardener paced to and fro, shaking his fist angrily, shouting at the door as his face grew red. Finally, he retrieved a phone from his pocket and called someone.

A few minutes later, a woman dressed as a maid opened the greenhouse's door. She and the gardener exchanged a few words, and the gardener walked inside, closing the door behind him.

"He had to get someone to open the door for him," I said, disappointed. "No way to open it from the outside."

Still. It was unguarded, and there were no wards. If only we could get someone to open it for us...

The sun slowly set, plunging the mansion's lawns into darkness. Only some lamps, few and far between, lit the main path to the front door. I could still see the front gate, and an occasional silhouette moving across one of the mansion's windows, but that was it. My eyes were tired, my forehead throbbing. Then, just as I was about to pass the binoculars to Kane, the front door opened, and a man came out. He strode to the gate and began talking to the guards. His manner was unmistakable—the manner of a superior.

"This is probably the security chief." I handed the binoculars to Kane. "This is the guy who has the keycard and combination to the vault. His name is Maximillian Fuchs."

"Sounds very German." Kane watched him for a while. "Looks full of himself."

I took back the binoculars, ingraining his face in my memory. I regretted not getting a camera with a zoom lens. It would have been handy to have this man's picture.

The security chief went around the yard, inspecting the walls, probably verifying that nothing blocked the security cameras. Then he marched back into the mansion, closing the door behind him. His movements had been sleek, sharp, and fast. Even after he disappeared, the guards on shift seemed more alert, as if his presence had jump-started their motivation.

Nothing much happened after that. I was tired of watching the mansion, and was already trying to decide if we needed to keep up the surveillance for much longer. I checked the time. We had thirty minutes until Isabel came to take the next shift. I handed the binoculars to Kane.

"Here, watch them. I want to shower."

"Seriously?"

"My bathroom back home is as cramped as a broom closet. I want to be able to shower in comfort for once."

I went into the bathroom, which was as large as my entire bedroom, and took off my clothes. I stepped into the shower and turned on the hot water. The water pressure was violent and constant, unlike the shower back home, which alternated between dribbling and spurting water as if spitting at me. I let the powerful current of water wash the tiredness from my body. I found a shampoo bottle that smelled of lavender, and washed my hair twice. Finally, my skin practically pink, I turned off the water and stepped out, dripping over the rug on the floor. I grabbed the large towel, dried my hair and my body, and wiped the steam off the mirror to take a long look at myself.

A refreshed, wet Lou Vitalis stared back at me from the reflection. I smiled at her, then looked around for my bag, which was nowhere in sight.

I'd left it in the room.

Groaning, I wrapped the towel around my body, tying it carefully. Then I slipped out of the bathroom.

Kane blinked as I crossed the room, clad in a towel, my wet hair plastering my face. Ignoring him, I bent to pick up the bag I'd left by the side of the bed.

The knot I'd tied broke free, and the towel's edge flopped loose. Cool air breezed against my ass and my right boob. Squeaking in horror, I fumbled at the towel, my bare nipple standing to attention in the cold. I just managed to keep the left part of the towel flattened to my body, hiding my feminine charms, though probably not as thoroughly as I would have wanted. My left breast was well hidden, but given that it was quite similar to the right one, Kane could probably deduce its general shape. Finally, I managed to grab the corner of the towel and quickly covered myself, feeling all the blood rushing to my face.

Kane studiously gazed out the window, the binoculars pasted to his face. I would have liked to assume that my performance had been lost on him, but the amused smile that he failed to hide hinted otherwise.

My cheeks crimson, I hurried to the bathroom, where I quickly took off the traitorous towel and put on a pair of jeans and a dark green T-shirt. Then, retrieving a comb from my bag, I hurriedly brushed my hair a few times, giving it a semblance of order.

I strutted from the bathroom, trying to look as if I couldn't care less about my impromptu show.

"Oh look," Kane said, still looking out the window with the binoculars. "It's almost a full moon tonight."

TWELVE

———◆———

"No one told me hunting hippos was part of the plan," Kane said.

We sat around the large table of the HHT meeting room. Kane peered, fascinated, at the paperweight that decorated each table in the office complex—the man with his foot on a hippo.

"We're not hunting hippos," I said.

"Good. Hippos are dangerous."

"Can I start the presentation?" Sinead asked.

I blinked. "What presentation?"

"The PowerPoint presentation I made."

"You made a… PowerPoint presentation? To explain how we intend to break into the dragon's vault?"

"Lou," Sinead said patiently. "I'm the CEO of Hippopotamus Hunting Trips. How do you think I got to where I am?"

"You printed a bunch of business cards that said so."

"That's true. But it's also because of my amazing organizational skills. Now hang on, let me figure out how this works."

It took a few minutes to connect the projector to Sinead's laptop, and when she finally succeeded, the screen on the wall displayed the words *The Plan for Breaking into Ddraig Goch's Vault*. A small smiling dragon stood in the bottom left corner, with a tiny orange blaze coming from his mouth.

"Catchy title," Kane quipped.

"I wanted it to be clear," Sinead said. She hit a key and the slide changed, the new one titled *How to overcome the dragon's senses*. There was that green dragon again at the bottom, with crudely painted squiggly lines emanating from his head. Sinead's graphics skills were giving me a migraine.

"What dragon senses?" Isabel asked.

"A dragon knows whenever someone enters his lair," I explained. "It's the way they're wired. So once anyone places a foot in Goch's mansion, he knows. He can sense their aura or something."

"Can we confuse his senses with magic or anything?" Isabel asked.

"No," Kane and I both said together. I gave him an irritated look, and then added, "Think of the lair as an extension of the dragon's body. No matter what we do, he'll know when we enter."

"Then we should break in when he's far away. That way, by the time he gets back—"

"Ddraig Goch hasn't left Boston in the past twenty-two years," I told her. "In fact, he rarely even leaves his mansion. He doesn't like to be far from his hoard."

"Happily," Sinead interjected, "we can work around it."

"Right," I said. "In six days, there's a large banquet in Ddraig Goch's mansion. At least a hundred people are invited. He'll be expecting a bunch of people in his mansion that evening, so it won't matter if we show up. Also, he won't be sleeping."

"Don't we *want* him to be sleeping?" Isabel asked, almost on cue. "Usually that's when burglaries happen, right?"

"Dragons sleep *in* their vaults," I said. "And they often sleep for days. We want to make sure he's awake when we break in—awake and busy mingling with his guests, away from his vault. Of course, we need to get invited to that banquet."

"How do we do that?" Isabel asked.

"I'm working on getting Lou onto the guest list." Sinead smiled proudly.

"Well, not the guest list exactly," I pointed out. "Sinead's trying to get me a job as a waitress at the banquet. I'll be our man on the inside."

"Okay," grunted Kane. "So you're a waitress. Congratulations. How do the rest of us enter the mansion?"

"We're hoping we can hack the dragon's computer, get another name onto the guest list," I answered.

Kane raised an eyebrow at Isabel. "Are you a hacker?" he asked. "Because these two just spent ten minutes hooking a computer up to a projector. They don't strike me as hacker material."

Isabel looked offended. "I hardly know how to turn on a computer," she said with the strange pride technophobes sometimes display. She studied each of us in turn, and then added sharply, "There's no hacker here. Aren't we missing a crew member? I was under the impression there should be five of us."

"That's explained in slide number seven," Sinead complained. "You're all ruining my presentation."

"Our fifth member is in a bit of a pinch," I mumbled.

Sinead rolled her eyes. "That's Lou's delicate way of saying he's essentially a dead man."

"Why?" Kane asked.

"His name is Harutaka Ikeda," I answered. "And he's—"

"That's an interesting coincidence," Kane interrupted. "Because I heard the Shades recently caught someone by that name in their sacred library."

"That's our guy," I said cheerfully. "Silly Harutaka. Always getting himself into trouble."

Isabel stared at me, biting her bright bubblegum-colored lips. "Lou, the Shades will execute him. No one is allowed into their library."

"That's why we need to get him out," I said. "The Shades are keeping him in one of their warehouses. They'll hold his trial during the next full moon."

Sinead clicked frantically through her slides until she got to one that said *Step 3—Saving Harutaka from the Shades*. There was a hand-drawn man, painted black with a deranged red smiley face—presumably her attempt at drawing a Shade.

"The next full moon is tomorrow," Kane said.

"Right. And they'll probably execute him immediately after."

"Just throwing an idea out there." Kane folded his arms. "Maybe, instead of messing with a deadly cult, in addition to breaking into a dragon's vault, we just find an alternative crew member?"

"We can't," I said. "The server's security has been magically enhanced. We asked around. Harutaka's the only one who can handle that."

"But the Shades..." Isabel muttered.

"Not the nicest group of people," I agreed mildly.

As cults go, the Shades were definitely one of the creepier ones. Like many before them, the Shades wanted immortality—and they'd actually found it. It just required one simple exchange. They relocated their souls from their bodies into their shadows. Shadows never got old. Shadows never died.

Strangely enough, their bodies stayed attached to their shadows. After all, with no body, there can be no shadow. Except now, the shadow made all the decisions. It thought and spoke and moved, and the body followed it and mimicked its actions like a... well, like a shadow.

The Shades were unnerving. Their human bodies were blank, empty things, as if they were in a coma, except they moved around, puppeteered by the shadows. It was also impossible to know what went on in their minds. Once they turned into shadows, their desires and motivations became unclear. Who knew what a shadow wanted, what it craved? But one thing was quickly established—they really didn't like it when people entered their sacred library. People who did that always turned up dead. People like Harutaka.

"I talked to some people," Sinead said. "The Shades are holding Harutaka in a large warehouse located in Malden. We know that there's very little electronic security. Most of the security is composed of patrols and guards."

"Even one Shade is enough to stop us," Kane pointed out. "They're rumored to be hellishly strong, and I don't think they can be hurt."

"We only need to temporarily disable the Shades," I said. "We need darkness."

In complete darkness, there were no shadows. Several eyewitness accounts claimed that when a Shade's shadow disappeared in the dark, the body froze. It would start moving again once the light returned and the shadow reappeared. That meant that there was a common thread between Shades and four-year-olds: Both were afraid of the dark.

"There are six spotlights around the warehouse." Sinead clicked to a slide with a detailed diagram, displaying a map of the warehouse from above. "And inside it's lit by rows of strong neon lights."

"Tonight should be a cloudy night," I said. "And the moon rises at two a.m."

"Twelve minutes past two," Isabel interjected automatically.

I grinned at her. Naturally, the fortune teller knew the movements of the celestial bodies much better than I did. "So the plan is simple. We kill the electricity to the warehouse and its vicinity. All the Shades go to sleep. We break in, take Harutaka, get out. Easy-peasy."

"Won't it be a bit... dark?" Kane asked. "What with us killing all the lights?"

"I'll make us some night-vision potions," I answered. "We'll be able to see just fine."

"One hitch with the plan is that the Shades have a generator which instantly kicks in when the power goes out,"

Sinead said, pointing at a square in the upper right corner of the diagram, where it said *Spare Gen.* "The Shades didn't want to be at the mercy of the power company."

"Right," I said. "So one of us—that would be Sinead—will go and sabotage the generator, while Kane and I kill the electricity and get Harutaka."

"What about me?" Isabel asked.

I smiled at her. "You sit safely a mile away in a heated car, gazing into your crystal ball. Let us know if anything is about to go very wrong."

THIRTEEN

I sat with Kane in his car, waiting. The air was tense and silent, the stillness before the storm. I clenched my fists, breathing, doing my best to keep my fear at bay. I glanced at Kane. If he was worried, it didn't show. He seemed to be deep in thought.

"What's on your mind?" I asked, more as a distraction than anything else.

"Just thinking of my sister. I haven't visited her for a while."

"In the hospital? What's wrong with her?"

He glanced at me, and for a moment it seemed he might answer. Then he looked away.

"Okay, guys," Sinead's voice buzzed in my ear. We all had Bluetooth earphones, set up to a conference call. "I'm nearly at the location. So drink up."

I fished for the two vials I had in my pocket. I had already given Sinead her own vial. I handed one to Kane. Our fingers touched for a second, and a sweet chill ran up the back of my neck. I gritted my teeth. Now was really not the time to be unfocused.

I unstopped my vial and drank its contents in one quick gulp. It tasted like battery acid. My tongue prickled slightly after swallowing, and my throat felt scratchy.

"Mmmmm, yummy," I said, looking at Kane.

He stared at the vial doubtfully.

"Go on," I urged him. "It will take ten minutes to work, so we should get a move on."

He drank it and winced. "Ugh. I think there's something wrong with mine. My throat feels weird."

"It's just the basilisk venom in it."

"Ha ha, you're hilarious."

I glanced at him, quirking one eyebrow, and he blanched in surprise. "You're serious? There's basilisk venom in this?"

"Just a bit. It won't kill you."

He smiled wryly and looked out the window.

He had worn the same trench coat tonight, and a black shirt and black pants underneath. I wore a similar outfit—a black sweater and black leggings. I had also put on my dark boots. My hair was swept back in a haphazard ponytail. I quickly checked my gear for the hundredth time: lockpicks, a tiny flashlight, a small switchblade. My chain was looped around my wrist, and I had a small gun in an ankle holster, which I prayed I wouldn't need. Shades couldn't be hurt with bullets, anyway.

"I'm near the shack with the generator," Sinead said. "No guards here. Are you guys in position?"

We were, and my eyes automatically went to our target. An old-looking utility pole stood across from the car, on the sidewalk. It was the one that fed power to the entire area around the warehouse. "Yeah," I answered. "We're here."

"Cool," Sinead said. "Just waiting for your juice to kick in, Lou."

We didn't want to kill the light before we could see in the dark. I glanced at my watch. It was a quarter past one. We had ample time before the moon rose.

"Do you know this guy, Harutaka?" Kane asked.

"Not really. Just stuff I heard. He's supposedly incredibly talented, but weird. We never needed a hacker of his caliber on our jobs."

"Did you do a lot of those *jobs*?"

I shrugged. "Some. Sinead, Isabel, and I all worked for the same guy, and he occasionally sent us to break into rich people's houses."

"This guy... he's ABC, right?"

I glanced at him, surprised. "I wouldn't call him that to his face. But yeah. Anthony 'Breadknife' Cisternino."

"How did a sweet girl like you end up working for an asshole like him?"

I blushed, feeling both a bit giddy and irritated. "I'm not a *sweet girl*. And he may be an asshole, but for a teenager living on the street, he was one of the only options left."

"It must have been hard."

"Working for him? Not at first." I thought back to that first year. "When I joined Breadknife's gang, I hated myself. After almost six years in shitty foster families, I felt like I was nothing, that I was worthless. That the only point to my existence was the tiny check my foster parents got from social services every month for taking care of me. As if they were doing it well enough to get paid."

I swallowed, suddenly swamped by bad memories. I shook them off. "Breadknife can spot talent. And he saw it in me. Something I didn't know I had. He began teaching me how to pick locks, how to sneak, to climb walls. We would go together on hikes in rich neighborhoods, picking targets together, planning the jobs. It was like a sort of father–daughter quality time. I actually loved it. I was happy."

Why was I talking so freely? It must have been the basilisk venom in my potion. It often reduced inhibitions.

"What happened then?" Kane asked. His voice was soft. He leaned toward me, listening raptly.

"People got hurt," I said. "I began to find out about small things. A maid was blamed for one of my jobs, and got fired. She was a single mom. Had the cutest son…" My voice faded away as I recalled the son's face when I'd spied on them. Tired and hungry. "Then it turned out a bracelet I stole had belonged to a man's dead wife. Our fence sold it back to him for ten times what it was worth, because Breadknife knew the value of love and grief. I started hating it. Then I made a mistake." I swallowed, recalling the police cars surrounding me, the cops shouting at me to lie down on the floor. "I got arrested. Spent a year in jail."

I didn't add the rest. That a few weeks after the arrest, during a medical checkup, I found out I was pregnant.

"When I got out, I knew I had to stay out of prison. So I left Breadknife and his gang."

"Just like that?"

"Just like that. I was eighteen, and could fend for myself." I was leaning forward as well. Our faces were just a few inches away. I pulled back slightly, trying to regain my composure. "What about you? How did you end up as a sorcerer?"

"Sometimes," Kane said, "I ask myself the same question. But if I look back, it almost seems like I had no other choice."

He breathed slowly, and his eyes had a faraway look. His face suddenly seemed so beautiful and sharp. I saw every detail—his unshaven cheeks, his long eyelashes, his firm jaw.

It was all much clearer than it should have been in the dark. The potion was working.

"Sinead," I said, turning away. "I think the potion is kicking in. What's your situation?"

"It's definitely kicking in," she answered. "But we'll have to wait a bit. A patrol car just stopped nearby the shack with the generator."

"What are they doing?" I asked worriedly.

"Just talking. I think they're taking a break."

I glanced at my watch. One thirty-five. "Isabel," I said. "Do you see anything?"

"Everything looks clear so far," her soft, low voice hummed in my ear. "The future is calm. There's love in the air."

I blushed. "Hardly. We're just talking."

"I wasn't talking about you two." She sounded amused. "There's another couple somewhere. They're in love. I see it in the tea leaves and in the cards. Tonight is their special night."

"That's very nice, but what does it have to do with our job?" I asked.

"I can't control what I see, Lou," she answered. "I drank three cups of tea already, and that's the only thing I see in the leaves. Lust and love."

There was a moment of silence.

"I really need to pee," she added. "All that tea..."

"Uh... guys?" Sinead said. "I think I know what Isabel is talking about. The cops in the patrol car? They're going at it."

"Seriously? Don't they have a job to do?" I felt outraged. Part of it was jealousy.

"Yeah. It's kinda hot. The guy is really muscular, and he just took off his shirt. And... Oh, damn, he just tore off two buttons from the girl's uniform. She didn't even notice."

"Sinead, can you just go kill that damn generator?"

"They're parked practically on the shed's door, Lou, sorry. But the rate they're going, it won't take long. I think these two have been fantasizing about it for a while... There we go, her hand is in his pants. You go, girl!"

I rolled my eyes, and glanced at Kane. He watched me with a half-smile, a roguish glint in his eyes, and for a moment I suspected he was trying to imagine us in the same situation. Then *I* imagined it, and had to look away quickly.

"You guys should see this," Sinead said. "Dude, you can't swallow her entire boob, your mouth isn't big enough."

"Sinead, this is really distracting."

"The tea leaves are very suggestive," Isabel said.

"Isabel, maybe we should make some tea-leaf porn." Sinead giggled. "We'd make a fortune."

I checked the time again. One forty-two. We had thirty minutes before the moon rose. But we had an even more urgent problem. "Listen," I said. "The potion won't last for much longer."

"What? You didn't say that earlier," Sinead complained.

"I didn't think it would be an issue. But we have only about twenty minutes more, depending on body mass. Kane probably has less time. And we can't drink more of it, because the basilisk venom will kill us."

"Well, what do you want me to do, Lou?"

"Can you just sneak in while they're distracted?"

"Well, the girl is straddling the guy, but he's looking right past her into the street, and the shack door is in front of him. And I have to pick the lock. I mean… they're definitely busy, but I'd say burglarizing the place in front of them is really testing their dedication to fucking."

"Damn!" I muttered.

"What's that?" Kane asked, pointing ahead.

Though it was dark, I saw everything in sharp detail, as if it were the middle of the day. A man shambled toward us, his movements sporadic, limbs jerking strangely. My heart sank.

"Maybe it's just a drunk," Kane said.

"It's not," I muttered. "It's a Shade."

FOURTEEN

—◆—

If you look at the body of a Shade as it moves, it seems to shamble. Its features are lax, empty, its movements jerky and strange. But if you watch the shadow that the body casts, you see a man moving smoothly, quickly, with catlike grace. Because it's actually the shadow that moves, not the body. For the Shades, the shadow casts the body, not the other way around.

When the Shade came closer, it was easy to see the face of its body. One eyelid was shut, the other open, the eye vacant. The mouth drooped, a trickle of saliva hanging from it. Facial features cast almost no shadows, and were useless to the Shades. Over time, the face of a Shade's body lost its semblance of humanity completely, marking it for the empty shell that it was.

It moved toward us purposefully. Perhaps to investigate the unfamiliar car, parked close to their warehouse. Or perhaps it sensed Kane's magical aura. Or perhaps he was turned on by our shadows. Whichever the reason, we didn't want it to get close.

"Sinead," I said weakly. "We need the power down now."

"It's okay." She was breathing hard. "I'm getting there."

"Did the cops drive away?"

"No, but the windows are fogged completely. They can't see a damned thing. I hope not, at least."

The Shade was about fifteen yards from us.

"How long?" I asked.

"Damn this lock!" she muttered to herself. "A few more minutes."

"I'm not sure we have that long."

"Delay him." Kane unlocked the door. "I'm going for the power cable."

"But I'm not in position yet!" Sinead said urgently.

"Better get in position, then," Kane answered sharply, sliding out of the car.

I opened the door on my side, leaping out. It was cold outside, much colder than inside the car, and it almost felt like the chill radiated from the Shade as it got closer. Behind me, Kane muttered in an unknown language, and the hair on the back of my neck prickled as the magical energy around us shifted, focusing around him. I moved toward the Shade, intent on intercepting it before it sensed what Kane was doing. If it hadn't already.

Up close, the Shade's face was even more horrifying. Ugly sores pocked the right cheek, and the closed eye leaked some sort of yellow goo. The shadow didn't care about the body's condition. It was just a body, after all.

"Excuse me!" I called. "My husband and I got lost. We were looking for Franklin Street? Our friend is having a baby shower tonight, and we really don't want to be late."

Kane's voice rose as the energy crackled around him. Above us, I heard the staticky sound of electricity, and I saw blue sparks flashing from the utility pole. In one ear, I heard Sinead say "Got it!" as she managed to pick the lock of the shack.

The Shade opened its mouth to speak. Its head faced sideways, but its shadow faced my own, and its lips moved clearly as its voice echoed. *What are you doing here?*

The voice didn't come from the Shade's body's larynx. It came directly from the shadow, and it almost felt as if it were my own shadow that heard it, and not me. Trying to overcome the bubbling terror in my chest, I smiled blithely and said "Well, I'm Martha, and this is my husband, Gussy. And like I said, we're looking for our friend's baby shower. Perhaps you know her—"

The shadow pointed straight at Kane, the body mimicking the movement, pointing randomly in the air. *What is he doing?*

"Oh, you know, just getting directions from our friend on the phone."

The Shade froze, and then, with a hiss of anger, it lunged for Kane. I leaped at it, colliding with its body, my shadow intermingling with the Shade's own shadow. We fell to the floor, the force of the jolt making me bite my tongue painfully. The Shade screeched in fury, and threw me off, its power immense. I tumbled and landed roughly on the road, hitting my shoulder, and a hot blazing pain jolted down my arm.

Kane's chanting was a roar in my ears as the spell hit its climax, and I heard the crackling of electricity. The air filled with smoke as something exploded up above us. As I got up, I saw the Shade running for Kane, hands outstretched— then all the lights in the street suddenly went dark, and we plunged into blackness.

The sky was cloudy, hiding the stars, and the lamps around us had all died. There was still an inkling of light, but not enough for the Shade. The body froze mid-run, its hands stretched toward Kane.

"Well," Kane said. "That was—"

A sudden loud mechanical sound filled my ear. It emanated from the Bluetooth earpiece, and I could hear Sinead cursing in the background. It was the generator, kicking into life.

Down the street, a spotlight flickered to life. Then another. Shadows materialized on the ground. And the Shade came alive. Screeching, it crashed into Kane, slamming him into the smoldering utility pole. It opened its mouth wide—seemingly *too* wide—as it brought its jaw closer to Kane's face. Kane tried to push the thing's forehead away, to keep that mouth away from him.

I ran at them, my chain unraveling from my wrist and dropping into my outstretched palm. I slung it over the Shade's head, pulling against its neck and shouting, "Angustus!"

The chain reacted to the spell word, its links shrinking, biting into the Shade's throat. I pulled hard, trying to haul it away from Kane. It twisted, the huge mouth snapping at me. It was inhuman, a mouth free from the limitations of a jaw bone, the teeth filed to sharp points, yellow and brown with rot, the smell overpowering—

"Got it!" Sinead said victoriously in my ear, the generator coughing and dying in the background. The lights died again. The Shade went limp as darkness swallowed its shadow.

"Jesus," I muttered.

"Lou, your hands!" Kane barked.

I saw the plumes of smoke rising from my fingers. "Oh, shit."

"Breathe, Lou," Isabel said. "Breathe and relax."

I tried, but my breaths were too fast and shallow. The heat built in my palms, and I knew they were about to erupt in flames. A fire would be catastrophic right now, casting us in light, waking up the Shade. I tried relaxing my muscles, one by one, but my mind was whirling, muscles trembling from the adrenaline and effort, the struggle with the Shade. To my horror, a small flame began to dance on my right palm. I clenched my fist, but the flames snaked through the cracks between my fingers, my hand a flaming fist of light.

Then suddenly Kane stood between the flaming hand and the Shade, his body blocking the flickering light. He was entirely silent, his eyes meeting mine, as he gently grasped the wrist of my burning hand, bringing it closer to his body, hiding the blaze. It danced inches from his chest, but he showed no fear, no discomfort. Instead, he wrapped his free hand around my shoulder and pulled me toward him, his body hiding mine. My head spun and I lowered my face, letting my forehead touch his chest, focusing on that sensation of intimacy. After a few seconds, his fingers intertwined with mine, and I realized my hand was no longer blazing. The fear and anger I had felt had been replaced by other emotions.

"Everything okay, guys?" Sinead piped in my ear.

I cleared my throat and pulled back. "Yeah. We're going for Harutaka now. You can join Isabel, or go back to peeping on the cops."

"Can't see a damn thing through those car windows," she muttered, sounding irate. "These guys fogged them up completely."

"Let's go," I told Kane.

He was pale; the effort of the spell he had cast had clearly sapped his strength. But he nodded at me, and when I began jogging down the street toward the warehouse's door, he matched my pace.

The warehouse was a few hundred yards away from us, and my pace was fast. We had lost all our wiggle time and then some, because of the lover cops. But really, it was me. I was rusty. I should have known there would be some sort of hurdle, should have prepared for it, should have been ready to compensate. I couldn't afford mistakes like these when we broke into the dragon's vault. Everything would have to go flawlessly.

"Isabel?" I breathed hard. "Anything interesting?" The dark streets were deathly quiet. Even with my sharp night vision, it felt as black as coal.

"Nothing new," she said, her voice calm, almost sleepy. It was impossible to read the future under pressure. She had to stay relaxed, serene, even when things got hairy. She was breathing steadily, probably going through her relaxation techniques, at which I had failed so miserably. "But you should hurry. The moon will be up soon. And I *really* need to pee."

The warehouse door was up ahead, and for a minute my heart skipped a beat as I saw the looming figures around it. But they were all completely still, frozen by the utter darkness that enveloped them. The Shades were dormant.

Kane stumbled by my side, almost falling, and cursed.

"You okay?"

"I can hardly see," he whispered sharply.

"The potion is wearing off. It's your body weight."

"Are you saying I'm fat?"

"Look out!" I grabbed him and pulled him sideways just before he ran into an erect, dormant Shade.

"Damn it," he muttered.

"Here, take my hand." I grabbed his palm. It was warm, and when he felt my touch he tightened his grip. For a moment I just focused on that touch, on our feet, running fast on the hard cobblestones. But the warehouse towered ahead, and I forced myself to focus, to sharpen my senses.

There were three Shades standing still by the door. The closest one towered high above us, over eight feet tall.

"What the hell is that?" I muttered.

"Shadow body manipulation," Kane said, breathing hard. He pulled his hand from mine, now that we had stopped running. "The Shades can do that. You know how your shadow is huge if the light hits it from a certain angle?"

"Sure."

"Well, apparently Shades can use that to warp the shape of their body as well. If their shadow is constantly bigger than the body, the body stretches. They become giants."

I swallowed. We were only a few yards from the door, and I stared up at the enormous giant. The word *stretched* was right. He didn't look like a large man, suitably proportioned. It was as if his body had been distended upward, his head a narrow oval, its features transfigured and twisted horribly, one eye lower than the other, the mouth twisted in a permanent, creepy, one-sided smile. I felt like an icy drink had been poured down my shirt as I gazed at him.

But it stood completely still, as did the other Shades. I crept over to the door, and tried the handle. The door didn't budge.

"Locked." I inspected the lock. It wasn't particularly complicated, and I could pick it in five or six minutes. But by that time, Kane would be entirely blind in the dark, and I might start losing my night vision too. And the moon was about to rise…

I knew what I had to do, but for a moment I just stood still, mustering the courage. Then I edged toward the giant Shade.

"Lou? What are you doing?"

"Hang on," I croaked, my throat dry. I glanced up at the giant, then down. His clothing was torn in places, but his pants still had several pockets. And through one, I saw the outline of a key chain.

I edged closer, the Shade's smell hitting my nostrils. It was the smell of sweat and filth and rot, of a body that was no longer maintained, no longer groomed. After all, it was just a body. I slid my hand into his pocket and touched the key chain. Then, one of my fingers brushed against something warm. His skin.

The pocket was torn, and my finger had gone through, touching his inner thigh. It felt rubbery and... wrong. Almost like it was stretched too tight. I imagined his body, expanded by the Shade, the skin stretching to its limit. Would my touch be enough to punch a hole, as if it was a sheet of plastic? My mind filled with the image of the rotting meat underneath that skin. Feeling sick, I pulled my hand out of the pocket, clutching the keychain. Then I peered up into his face.

For a moment, I almost screamed. His eyes were staring back at me. But the body still remained completely inert.

And yet... something was alive in those eyes. They weren't empty and blank. There was an emotion there. Pain, and desperation, and horror.

Suddenly I had a terrifying thought. What if someone was still in that body? Someone trapped in a puppet, completely controlled by its shadow? Only now, with the shadow gone, perhaps he could almost break free.

Almost.

It didn't move. Only its eyes seemed alive. Tormented. Begging for oblivion.

I tottered backward, bile rising up my throat. I couldn't throw up, I *couldn't*. If I threw up, I would probably lose my night vision, and I needed it. I forced myself to breathe deeply, tears in my eyes, and turned to the door. The keychain had only two keys on it, and the first one slid in and turned easily.

"Are you okay?" Kane whispered.

I shook my head sharply, but said nothing. I didn't trust my voice.

The warehouse was large and windowless. It was even darker inside it than outside. I could glimpse several still figures inside, none of them moving. There was one large shipping container, locked with a padlock on its far side.

"That's where Harutaka is," I croaked, pointing at the container.

"What is?" Kane asked. "I can't see anything in here, it's too dark."

"There's a shipping container. Come on, I might need your help." I took his hand.

"You're trembling," he said.

"I'm fine. Come on." I led him inside.

We circled around the still Shades, and I avoided their eyes, terrified I might see that same trapped gaze there.

The padlock on the container was heavy, and would take effort to pick. I tried the second key on the chain, but it didn't fit. Carefully, I tapped the metal surface of the container.

"Hello?" I said.

"Yes!" a muffled voice answered from inside. "I'm here!"

"We're here to get you out. Do you know if there's a key to this lock?"

"I didn't even know there was a lock," the voice said.

I looked around. I could search the Shades in the warehouse, but it would take some time, and I couldn't be sure any of them had the key. After all, the giant had the key to the warehouse, but not to this padlock.

"There's a padlock here," I told Kane. "Can you blast it open?"

He considered it. "Not without creating a lot of light," he finally said.

Light would reanimate the Shades, and I wasn't keen for that to happen.

"Okay, I'll handle it."

I knelt in front of the padlock and fished my lock-picking kit from my pocket. I unrolled it and squinted at the tools. It was getting really hard to see. I felt them with my fingers, finding the small tension wrench and the curvy pick. I turned to the lock and tried to insert the tension wrench into it, but it was almost impossible. I couldn't see the keyhole, could hardly see my hands. I tried to feel the surface of the lock, searching for the keyhole, but my fingers were numb from the cold, and my palm trembled slightly.

"Fuck!" I spat.

"What is it?" Kane asked.

"I can't see the lock. Hang on."

I rummaged in my pocket, finding the last vial. I pulled it out and unstopped it.

"What are you doing?"

"I need to see." I took a quick swig of the potion. Just half. Enough to see... and hopefully not enough to kill me.

"Didn't you say more basilisk venom would kill you?"

"Only pussies are afraid of a little basilisk venom," I muttered, waiting for the potion to take effect. "Uh... I might need some help when we make a run for it."

My body was already under the influence of the potion, and it took only a minute for my vision to sharpen enough so I could see the keyhole again. I inserted the tension wrench into it, applied a bit of pressure, then slid the lockpick inside. I was pretty sure there were five pins in the lock. I began fiddling with the pick, trying to find the sweet point for the first pin.

"Harutaka?" I asked.

"Yeah?" the muffled voice answered from inside the container.

"My name is Lou Vitalis. I'm here to break you out."

"I'm much obliged."

"In return, I want you to help us with something." I felt the first pin catch. On to the second one.

"Well, I'm hardly in a position to refuse."

"I agree. Don't worry, you'll like it." I began feeling nauseous. The venom, taking effect.

"Lou, there's something in the tea leaves," Isabel said. "Something… bad. It's unclear. A bad man, maybe two. I'm pretty sure it's two… no… hang on. I'll try to get a card reading."

"No pressure," I mumbled, feeling the second pin catching. Number three now. "Harutaka, I just want to make sure. You know how to counter Danann runes, right?"

A second went by. "If I say no, will you leave me here to rot?"

"Well, I don't want to sound heartless." Number three done. On to number four.

"Yeah, I know how to counter Danann runes. Piece of cake."

Isabel cleared her throat. "Lou, it's definitely on its way. It's a shit storm. The cards aren't happy."

I wasn't happy either. "What's on its way?"

"Two Shades. Or one. I'm not sure. But they're angry."

"It's dark here. They shouldn't be able to move." The fourth pin clicked. On to number five. The hand holding the tension wrench shook slightly, numb. If it shifted even a bit, all the pins would drop, and I'd have to start all over again. I gritted my teeth, trying to focus.

"Harutaka, can you walk? Are you tied up?"

"No, I'm not tied up, I can walk."

I wasn't sure I could. My feet felt weak, and a chill was spreading in my body. I couldn't sense my toes. I wanted to vomit. "Okay, better get ready to run once we open this. Kane, I'm about to get this lock. Be ready to open the door."

"Lou, whatever you're doing, you need to get it done!" Isabel sounded panicky. The calm, serene voice was gone. That probably meant she could no longer read the future.

The fifth pin clicked and the tension wrench swiveled, turning in the lock. The padlock loosened, dropping to the floor with a loud clang, and I turned away and vomited loudly, coughing and spluttering.

I heard a loud metallic creak as Kane fumbled over me at the door, pulling it open.

"Thanks!" Harutaka's voice was clear now. "I was sure I was about to… Oh fuck, what's that?"

"Gods!" Kane whispered.

I turned around, horrified to see light beams in the dark warehouse. And then my eyes drew to the source of the light, and I gasped.

One or two Shades, Isabel had said, and she wasn't wrong. It was both.

Shadow body manipulation, I instantly knew. When two people stood closely behind each other, their shadows mingled to create one shadow with four hands and two heads. And the

Shades had found a way to use that and morph their bodies together. This *thing* was a monstrosity, its four arms protruding at weird angles from its deformed body, its heads half connected to each other.

It held flashlights in two of its hands, the beams sweeping the warehouse, casting light on the still Shades. And they began to move.

"The flashlights!" Kane barked. "Get the damn flashlights!"

The monstrosity shambled toward us as the rest of the Shades slowly turned around, hissing, realizing their prisoner was getting away. Kane began to mutter in his otherworldly language, raising his hand as he did so. The thing ran at us, and a faraway part of me noted that it scrambled on four human feet.

A large, azure orb of magical energy shot from Kane's fingers and hit one of the flashlights. It exploded in the thing's hand, taking off most of its fingers. The creature didn't even flinch, the discomfort of its body irrelevant. It kept running for us, was almost upon us. In my peripheral vision I saw the other Shades closing in, surrounding us.

I went for my ankle holster, pulling out the small Glock. I aimed at the light, and began to shoot. Spots danced in my eyes, which had been primed for the darkness. The light from the flashlight was blinding, almost impossible to look at, but I kept my eyes straight ahead, my finger pressing the trigger again and again, feeling the jolts, the explosions loud in my ear.

And then a shot hit the flashlight with a clang, and it went out, plunging us into darkness. I was half blind, but could still see the forms of the Shades coming to a halt. The monstrosity kept going, inertia pushing it forward. It tumbled on its four legs, crashing two inches from me, one of its heads hitting the cement floor with a wet, sickening crunch.

"We need to go," I said weakly. My throat felt swollen, and I could hardly breathe. "The moon is about to rise."

Kane knelt by my side, fumbling for me. "Can you stand up?"

"Sure." I tried, but collapsed, groaning, my muscles feeling like jelly. "Maybe not. Can you help me?"

He felt for me, brushing against my waist, which might have been nice if not for the fact that I was dizzy, nauseated, and possibly dying. Then, to my surprise, he lifted me in his arms, standing up straight. I could feel his muscles under his trench coat. He was strong—much stronger than I had thought.

"Walk straight," I mumbled, and he began to walk. "A bit to the left... no, that's too much... that's right, straight ahead."

In the land of the blind, the half-dead girl with the dancing spots in her vision was queen.

He strode through the door, past the giant, and onto the street. I was groggy, feeling as if I was in a dream. Something large and white glimmered in the sky.

"Oh look," I mumbled, half asleep. "The moon is up."

A loud roar of anger rumbled behind us, and Kane began to run. Perhaps I should have been scared, but the jerking movement of my body just made me sleepier, and all I could think of was that one of Kane's hands was under my ass, and that he really was very strong.

And when I heard the screech of the car, and Sinead shouting, "Get in!" I let myself lose consciousness.

FIFTEEN

◆

The licking on my face was insistent enough to rouse me from my deep sleep. I struggled against my attacker, pushing his snout away before he licked me to death.

"Bwargh! Go away!" I said weakly.

Magnus barked happily in response, and placed a paw on my chest. Then he panted suggestively in my ear, sneezed, barked again, and left.

"Oh good, you're awake," I heard Sinead say.

I opened my eyes slightly, the light of day piercing through my skull like a hot poker. I was in my bedroom, Sinead standing in the doorway, holding a glass of water. I whimpered pitifully as my headache intensified.

"Here." She put the glass to my lips and tipped it slightly. I took a few sips. It was cool, and felt like heaven was sliding down my throat. She let me drink some more, then set the glass aside.

"Thanks," I croaked.

"You're welcome."

"What happened?"

"Well, Kane and Harutaka came out of the warehouse just seconds before the moon rose. Kane was carrying you in his arms, which is something guys should do more. The Shades gave chase, but Isabel and I picked you all up and drove off. Then, once we were far enough away, we pulled over and I checked your vitals. Kane said you poisoned yourself."

I nodded, and immediately regretted it. My head felt like someone had filled it with rocks.

"Your breathing was a little shallow, and your pulse just a bit high, but it seemed like you'd be fine, so they dropped us here. Then I cleaned you up and put you in bed."

"You also undressed me, apparently," I muttered, feeling under the blanket.

"Your clothing had vomit and dirt on it. You don't want that in your bed."

"Thanks." I straightened a bit, my movements careful and slow. I reached for the glass Sinead had placed on my night table, and drank the rest of the water. I placed it back and looked at her. She was dressed in clothing she'd taken from my closet, a black T-shirt and a pair of blue leggings. Her hair was wet, as if she had just showered. She must've stayed here all night.

Licking my lips, I tried to smile at her. "We did it. Go team."

"Yeah, go team. The big job is still ahead of us, you know."

"I know. Did you talk to Harutaka? Will he work with us?"

"He's actually excited about it. He's really weird."

"The guy was caught in the sacred library of the Shades. I'd say him being weird is an understatement." I sniffed my hand. "My hand smells like dog drool. And so does my arm. In fact, my entire body smells like it has been licked thoroughly by a dog with poor dental hygiene."

"Magnus insisted on administrating his own treatment for basilisk venom overdose. I tried to shoo him away, but your dog is relentless."

"That's him. What time is it?"

"It's half past two."

"At night?"

"Of course not. In the afternoon."

"Oh." I blinked as the timeline swam together in my mind. I was planning to tail Maximillian Fuchs, the dragon's security chief, this evening. "Why the hell didn't you wake me up sooner?"

Here's what happens when you jump out of bed while recuperating from basilisk venom overdose: Your head explodes.

Your feet buckle. Your body, half entangled in the bedsheets, falls sideways on the floor. You say, "Argh." And you wish you were dead. At least, that was my experience.

"Because, honey, you almost killed yourself with your damn concoctions, and I wanted to give you time to recuperate," Sinead said sweetly, looking down at me.

Magnus ran into the room and barked excitedly. Determining I was under attack from my bedsheet, he lunged at it heroically, tugging it with his teeth while growling ferociously. It ripped, and he stumbled backward, careening into the bed. He did three victory laps around me, his barks loud and sharp, painful to my tender brain. Then he quirked his head at me, confused by my lack of enthusiasm at his triumph, and licked my nose.

Sinead helped me get back in bed. "Honey, you're staying in bed today. And probably tomorrow."

"But Maximillian Fuchs—"

"I'll tail Fuchs. We're doing this together, Lou, you know that, right? You don't need to do everything by yourself."

"But you can't. You need to get me that waitress job," I said weakly.

"Already done." She grinned at me proudly. "And I didn't even have to leave the room."

"Seriously?"

"Yeah. You remember Fred?"

"The guy you used to date? The one you dumped when you found out he has a mole on his—"

"Yes. So Fred has this cousin. It's not a cousin, exactly... what do you call it if someone is married to your cousin?"

"I think it's still a cousin."

"Okay, so Fred has this cousin, who goes bowling every week in that place in Brookline. What's it called? It's on the tip of my tongue."

"I honestly don't care. Get to the point."

"It's going to drive me insane all day. It starts with a P. Anyway, one of the guys he bowls with—they're really close, it's like this tight-knit group of men. And one of them is... get this—in the Secret Service."

"That's... nice."

"So Secret Service guy apparently knows a lot of important people, and he—Lucky Strike!"

"What?"

"The bowling place."

"That doesn't start with a P."

"How is that relevant?"

"How is *anything* you just said relevant?"

"I'm getting to it, sheesh! So this guy—the Secret Service guy, knows the owner of the catering company that's serving the dragon's banquet. And Secret Service guy gave him your name after he got it from Fred's cousin, who got it from Fred, who got it from me."

"That's amazing."

"I already updated the rest of the crew. They were here earlier."

"In here?" I asked, aghast. The thought of Kane and Harutaka seeing me unconscious in my bed was horrifying. I tried to imagine I was like Sleeping Beauty, lying pale in my bed, my hair and makeup looking perfect, just waiting for a prince to show up and kiss me awake. But I knew the truth. I snored slightly when I slept. My hair was always a mess. Sometimes I drooled.

"Relax! Do you really think I'd let them in your bedroom? We sat in your store. I told them they couldn't come back here, because you were naked in bed."

"Wonderful," I said, somewhat sardonically.

"I used the word *naked* several times when talking about you. Kane seemed interested. You can thank me later."

"Okay." I pressed at the bridge of my nose with my fingertips. "So… what did you discuss?"

"Harutaka said he can definitely hack into the security server in the complex. Once inside he'll be able to see everything that's going on, and he'll have access to the banquet's guest list."

"Oh, good."

"But he needs someone to hook him up from the inside."
I groaned.

"Which is totally fine, because you'll be able to do it in a few days, right? The catering staff all need to show up the evening before the banquet, to help set things up. I figure that's your opportunity."

"And what do we do until then?"

"You rest and get better from your basilisk venom overdose. And I'll tail Maximillian Fuchs, and figure out what's his deal."

"Just be careful."

"Yes, mom, who overdosed on basilisk venom and nearly got eaten by creepy Shades. I'll be careful."

SIXTEEN

R ecovering from the basilisk poison took me three days, which translates to seventy-two hours, and those seventy-two hours were actually four thousand, three hundred, and twenty minutes. Time *crawls* when all you can do is shuffle slowly to and from the bathroom.

Sinead and Isabel brought me food, and Isabel also took it upon herself to walk Magnus, who was confused by my dormant state. Kane called once to check how I felt, which gave me a warm fuzzy feeling that I found worrying. The fact that I was *attracted* to him was no big deal. The fact that I seemed to *feel* something for him could mean trouble. I knew from painful experience that falling for someone during a job could end very badly.

The leftover venom in my system gave me some strange dreams. One night I dreamed I was breaking into Ddraig Goch's mansion, except it looked like school, and the dragon was my math teacher. He caught me sneaking in and incinerated my clothes with one fiery breath, leaving me nude in front of the entire class. In another dream I was in prison again, but Kane was my cellmate. I tried to dig us a tunnel so we could escape, but I only had a spoon, and Kane kept taking it away, insisting that he needed it to eat his pudding.

I used most of my endless hours awake in bed to practice on what Sinead called my "flamey hands problem." I would shut my eyes and start breathing deeply, focusing on each body part in turn, relaxing it, directing my complete attention to those muscles. When Isabel dropped by, she'd coach me, her deep voice instructing me to concentrate on my feet, my ankles, my thighs, going all the way up to my head.

The problem was, I invariably lost concentration, my mind chasing any random detail it snagged upon.

"I can't even concentrate in my bed," I grumbled. "What will happen during the job? There's no way I'll be able to relax when the shit hits the fan. And you know it will. No plan survives contact with reality. And I *can't* have my hands randomly going fwoosh."

Isabel bit her flamingo-pink lip. "Maybe we've been going about this the wrong way," she said. "We were trying to get you to relax."

145

"Because fear or anger is a big no-no."

"That's my point. Maybe we just need you to focus on another feeling. Switch gears in your mind. Happiness, sadness, nostalgia, love… those emotions are fine, right? I think that's what happened that night with the Shades. You were focused on Kane instead of your fear."

"I was not! I just, uh… I got it together, that's all."

"Uh-huh. Well, anyway, doesn't it sound like it could work?"

I thought about it. "Maybe, yeah. I can make some condensed emotion pills. That way, whenever I feel scared or angry, I could just swallow a happiness pill or a sadness pill and—"

She took my hand. "Or, for once, you can avoid abusing your body with your concoctions, and just use regular human emotions, Lou."

"Well, sure, if you want to ruin my fun," I muttered.

"Let's try it now. Close your eyes and focus on a memory. Something that evokes happiness. Something vivid."

I shut my eyes, and it came almost instantly. Pink boots, purple skirt, red coat, and pigtails. Clutching her adoptive mother's hand, half-walking, half-skipping, and talking nonstop. That bright excitement in her eyes as she thought of something new, the way she happily jumped with both feet into a puddle, splashing water, shrieking in laughter. And me, watching her from the corner of my eye, holding Magnus' leash, yearning for her attention.

I wasn't sure what I felt right then, but it was definitely powerful, and it wasn't fear, or anger.

So I trained on focusing very hard on vivid thoughts. A memory of my mother's smile. The feeling of my first kiss. More memories of my daughter—fragmented and much shorter than I wanted.

And, occasionally, thoughts of Kane. The way he grasped my wrist and pulled me to him. The sensation of him picking me up, carrying me in his arms out of that warehouse. His green eyes, staring into mine.

Sinead kept giving me the details of her nights tailing Maximillian Fuchs. He seemed to leave around nine every evening, choosing a different bar each time. All the bars were high-class joints, which Sinead enjoyed describing in her half-mocking, half-jealous manner. Maximillian spent his time there buying women drinks, talking to them. Every night he ended up leaving with a different woman, going to her place. He'd stay there for about an hour, then leave.

"So... he likes women," I finally said after she told me about her third night of tailing him.

"He likes *a lot* of women. And he isn't exactly the snuggle-until-morning type. He fucks and leaves, Lou. Every time. And he doesn't seem to get out of the mansion during the day. But I have some good news. He has a type."

"What's his type?"

"Tall, pale, elegant. Two of the women were red-headed, the third blonde. All three were ravishing, but in an old-fashioned way. Long dresses, huge cleavage. One of them had a French accent; the second was *definitely* British; the third I think was German. So I think he's into aristocratic European women." She waggled her eyebrows. "Know anyone who matches this description?"

I looked at her innocently. "Ravishing and elegant? Doesn't ring a bell. All the people I know are kinda crass and ill-mannered."

"That's…" She thought about it for a moment. "That's actually probably true. But if I wanted, I *could* be an aristocratic European lady. May I introduce—" she changed her accent and tone— "Baroness Fleurette van Dijk."

"What's that ghastly accent?"

"It's Dutch."

"It sounds like you're trying to poop."

"Well, who's crass now? I'm still working on the accent. Anyway, once Harutaka hacks the servers, he can add Baroness Fleurette van Dijk to the guest list. I'll enter the banquet, use my feminine wiles to woo Maximillian, and have a drink with him."

"Then, while you two are drinking, you can drip some truth serum into his wine." I warmed up to the idea. "You get the combination from him, pick his pocket for the keycard, and voila! We're in."

"It's a fantastic plan! Or, as the Baroness van Dijk would say, *fantastisch*."

I flinched. "Awesome, just please work on that abysmal accent."

I inched slowly across my bedroom, my body not yet entirely healed. The floor was icy cold, and each barefoot step ran chills up my spine. Twice I had to stop because Magnus blocked my way, mouth open wide, tongue lolling. His face indicated that he was ready for a walk, and that he assumed I was ready as well. My dog was cute, but intelligence wasn't one of his stronger traits. I opened the door to my lab, and slammed it behind me before Magnus could slither inside. He whined and scratched at the door, but I ignored him. The lab was the one room that was off-limits.

Across the room, the counter where I did most of my work lined the wall. All my tools were there—some classic ancient alchemy tools, others more modern, because I tried to move with the times. There was a copper mortar and pestle standing next to a high-powered blender. My retort—a glass container with a long mouth pointed at a downward angle, like an overweight giraffe drinking—lay on a three-legged iron stand above a small gas grill. I had rows of empty tubes, pots, vials, bottles, pans… all waiting to be used. The rest of the lab consisted of shelves, trunks, and cupboards containing my ingredients. Those used to be full, but lately I'd been running out, and many of the jars that lined the shelves were empty.

Installed in one wall was a small safe, containing my most prized possession in the entire world. The safe had a combination dial, and even a skilled burglar would find it almost impossible to crack. But knowing how devious a dedicated burglar could be, it was also etched with various runes that would hopefully keep anyone but me away from the safe's contents.

I crossed the room to the safe and unlocked it, the mechanism's ticking echoing in the silent room. I pulled the safe door open, and, ignoring the gun and the meager amount of cash inside, I removed the false bottom. Underneath was a book.

It was thick and leather-bound, the pages yellow and brown with age. Engraved on the cover with spidery letters were the words *Tenebris Scientiam*. It was a book assumed long gone by sorcerers and alchemists alike. People had been looking for it for centuries, claiming to have seen it, or to have acquired a page of it. And it was in my possession.

The memory echoed in my mind. The sad, serious voice. *Your mother left something for you, Lou. Something important.*

I took it out, placing it on the counter, and opened it carefully, treating the pages with the utmost care. The first time I'd handled it, a page crackled and broke between my clumsy fingers, and I had cried for hours at my carelessness. Since then, I had coated all the pages with a special oil to strengthen them, and I flipped the pages as if I were touching a delicate butterfly that might flap its wings at any moment.

The *Tenebris Scientiam* was, for all intents and purposes, a cookbook.

It wasn't for delicious chocolate cakes or three hundred exciting recipes for paleo. No, this book was for alchemists, and it contained recipes and instructions for some very nifty potions discovered by hundreds of scholars over decades. Unfortunately, like paleo recipes, most tasted like crap.

But the things they could do! Enhance senses, change a person's shape, heal, kill, distill emotions, manipulate reality. The possibilities were endless, provided you had the right ingredients. Which is where the problem really started. Because the local 7-Eleven did not have hydra venom, or the blood of a martyr, or mistletoe cut on a night when Mercury occults Uranus. Ingredients were expensive. Sometimes impossible to acquire. And I was running out.

I flipped the pages carefully until I reached a recipe I had already made several times: a truth serum. I read the instructions, though I knew them by heart. It required, among other things, a crystallized angel tear. Or, in accountant's terms, it required nine hundred seventy-five dollars, which is what one of those tears cost, last time I purchased one. I had only one, and the thought of wasting it made me sick. But you can't make an omelet without breaking some eggs, and you can't get a combination key without spiking Maximillian's drink, so waste it I would.

I walked over to one of the shelves and picked up a jar labeled in my own almost illegible handwriting: *Cryst. Angel Tear.* It had one small crystal in it, its color a sparkling silver. I put the tear in the glass retort and lit the flame underneath. The tear itself was highly poisonous to humans, but when distilled, I could extract its essence. I wasn't sure exactly what it contained—perhaps God's own DNA, or distilled holiness, or maybe just the condensed essence of a whiny angel. But regardless, the essence could compel truth, if used correctly. Which was what I needed here.

While the tear distilled, I went back to my cookbook and skimmed the instructions again.

Something thumped loudly behind me. Probably a client knocking on the shop's door. I ignored it. The "closed" sign should have been clear enough on its own.

I took a bit of earth from the old country (a.k.a. England) and the shell of a bluebird's egg, and crushed them together with my pestle. My sharp grinding movements aligned themselves with the rhythm of repeated knocks on the door. Finally, exasperated, I put the pestle down. I returned my cookbook to the safe, and locked it up. I verified that the gas flame wasn't burning the angel tear, and that the essence was distilling nicely. Then I went to the shop door and unlocked it, preparing myself to shout at the persistent customer.

It was a short Japanese man, his hair the color of cinnamon, and a cheerful smile was plastered on his face. It took me a moment to recognize him. Last time I had seen him, it had been pitch-dark, and I had been vomiting.

"Harutaka!" I remembered I had told Sinead to ask him to come over.

"Yes!" he answered, his voice carrying a mild accent, and a tone of excitement. "You are Lou Vitalis, who saved my life four days ago."

"You can just call me *saved my life*," I said, and then, at his confused look, added, "Sorry. It was a joke. Not very funny. Not funny at all, really."

"A dad joke," Harutaka said helpfully.

"Yes, thank you. Come in."

I moved aside, and he entered the shop, looking around in wonder. Magnus barreled into the room, barking excitedly at the new visitor. Harutaka bent his knee, crouching to look at my dog, frowning in a serious manner.

"That's my puppy, Magnus. He's very excitable."

Harutaka smiled at the dog. Magnus barked again, wagging his tail, and licked Harutaka's face.

"Magnus, no!" I rebuked him sharply. "I'm sorry. He really likes you, apparently. Usually he doesn't lick anyone except me and his…" *balls*. "Uh… anyone except me."

"Maybe that's his way of saying hello," Harutaka suggested, and then, to my astonishment, he stuck out his tongue and licked Magnus' face.

My puppy was overjoyed. He ran all over the shop, knocking down a stool and a coat rack, then jumped at me, his eyes clearly asking me if I saw what had just freaking happened.

"I have dog hair in my mouth," Harutaka said, standing up.

"That's what you get, apparently," I muttered. "Oh shit, the tear!"

I dashed back to my lab. To my relief, the tear hadn't burnt yet. I quickly turned off the gas, inspecting the jar with the distilled essence. It condensed on the glass surface, a silvery fog speckled with tiny spots where the liquid materialized. It looked good.

"Can I come in?" Harutaka asked behind me.

Panicked, I glanced at the counter, where the cookbook had been, but then remembered I had put it back in the safe. Aside from it, I didn't keep any secrets in my lab. "Sure, come in. I have to prepare some stuff. But close the door, don't let Magnus in." A wave of dizziness hit me and I leaned on the counter, breathing heavily. My dash had drained what little energy I had.

"Are you all right?"

"Yeah. Still a bit sick from that night. But I'm getting better." I slowly shuffled back to the mortar and pestle, a wave of nausea roiling in my stomach.

"So." I began to crush the earth and the eggshell again. "Sinead said you're willing to help us."

"Of course." Harutaka pried a dog hair from his mouth. "After you saved me, it is the least I could do."

I smiled, amused. "Don't bullshit me, Harutaka. You're not doing this out of a sense of debt. You're doing it for the dragon scales."

"Can it be both?"

"Sure, whatever floats your boat."

"Then I would say it's about twenty percent sense of debt, eighty percent dragon scales."

I put the crushed powder in a sieve above a copper pot, and began wiggling it back and forth. The powder that filtered through the sieve's holes and scattered inside the copper pot was brown and thin. "What were you doing in the Shades' sacred library anyway?"

"I was searching for shadow magic runes."

"Did you find any?"

"The books were all blank," he said.

"Well, I guess the Shades don't read the books, right? They read the books' shadows." I tossed the few pebbles and eggshell particles that remained in the sieve into the trash. Then I poured some water into the copper pot.

"That's very true… What are you doing?"

"What does it look like I'm doing?"

"It looks like you're preparing mud."

"That's pretty much what it is," I agreed. "But it's a special mud. Soil from various countries and eggshells of different birds form the baseline for many potions. Just like flour and eggs are often the baseline for cakes."

"I see."

I put the pot on the gas and stirred it occasionally. "But you must have known the books in the library would be empty. And you still went there."

"I may have found a way to read the shadows of books myself," he said carefully.

"That's impressive. So did you find what you were looking for?"

He didn't answer. I kept stirring the mud in the pot, not pressing the point. What he had found in the Shades' library was his business, but I had a different question in mind. "When we broke in, I got the sense that there's someone... trapped in one of the Shades' human bodies."

"Did you?" he asked. He sounded innocent enough, but I began to suspect Harutaka didn't divulge knowledge easily. He knew what I was talking about, I was almost sure of it.

"These cult members. They get recruited to their cult, and they're told that their soul is transferred to the shadow, leaving the body as a sort of empty husk. But that's not what happens, is it?"

"I think not."

"What actually happens is they summon something that *takes control of their shadow*. And they're left stuck in their body, while the shadow moves it around, like a puppet."

"It's a demon," Harutaka said. "I don't know which."

I shivered, remembering the desperate stare of the Shade when our eyes met. Pushing the image away, I turned the gas off, letting the bubbling mud cool a bit, and then poured some of it into a glass tube. I went over to the shelf, taking a dried mushroom from a jar and a small bone from a leather bag. I dropped them both into the tube. Then I picked up the jar with the distilled tear, where the silver liquid slowly formed in the bottom, and dripped three drops into the solution. The entire thing bubbled and frothed. Harutaka hissed in surprise. The color of the mud slowly shifted until it was golden, and glowed with a strange light.

"What is that?" he asked.

"A truth serum," I said. "We're going to use it to compel the mansion's security chief to tell us the combination to the vault door."

"And what else?" He seemed suddenly very excited.

I blinked. "What do you mean?"

"While he's under the effect of the serum, he is compelled to give us the truth, right? Why not ask him the big questions? Is there a god? Do we determine our fate, or is it pre-destined? What is true happiness?"

"Um… it just compels him to tell us what he knows. Not all the truth in the universe."

"Oh." His face fell.

"We could get him to divulge his sex kinks, if it'll make you feel better."

"I do not think it will."

I poured the liquid from the tube into a small copper vial, and corked it. "Sinead said you need my help to hack the server," I said. "I'm going to the mansion tomorrow evening, so I'll be able to hook you up."

"Take this." He pulled a chain from his pocket. A black stone was attached to it, with a single rune in dark red. The tip of a USB stick protruded from it, almost hidden.

"What is that, exactly?"

"It is a magical USB stick."

I stared at him. "Seriously?"

"Very seriously. This is what I do, Lou. I write code, and magical runes, and I bind them together."

I took the USB stick from his hand. A constant hum of magical power emanated from it. "What's that?" I asked, pointing at the rune.

"Chaos," he said, his tone simple. But he stared at me intently, as if the word meant something more.

"Okay," I said. The chain was necklace-length, and I draped it around my neck. "So what do I do with it?"

"According to the blueprints Sinead showed me, all the rooms in the mansion are connected to the central heating, except for one."

I nodded hesitantly. I remembered noticing it when we were poring over the blueprints.

"That should be the server room. It is kept cool because of the computers in it."

"How do you know it's not the pantry?"

"Because it's not adjacent to the kitchen." He raised his eyebrow. "You're very weird, Lou Vitalis."

"*I'm* weird. Right. Why would there be a whole room of servers?"

"Trust me," he said. "For the security this dragon has, he needs some strong computers. I want you to go to that room, and just plug the USB key I gave you into one of the computers. I'll do the rest."

SEVENTEEN

For the first time in many days, I woke up feeling almost like myself. I was walking Magnus, who was beside himself with joy at my recovery, when my phone rang. It was Kane.

"Hello?" I held the phone in my left hand, pulling the leash with my other hand while Magnus barked at a squirrel as if it was his lifelong nemesis.

"Lou! How are you feeling?"

"Better, thanks." I tried to sound cool and professional, failing miserably.

"Glad to hear it. Are you walking your dog?"

Magnus stretched against his leash to the point of choking, his barking almost deranged with fury. This squirrel was clearly the source of all evil, and had to perish. The squirrel watched

Magnus with the jaded boredom of one who had seen all the dogs, and found them lacking. I tried to pull Magnus away. "Yeah. There's a… squirrel."

"They're the worst. Listen, can I drop by this morning?"

"Why?"

"I have the teleportation spell all figured out, but I need to practice it. I've never cast it before."

"Don't you need a dragon scale for that?" The squirrel turned away in disgust and hopped up the tree. Magnus whined, the chance to save the world from this vile presence forever lost.

"To actually teleport, sure. But I can practice the chant, the alignment of the mystical energy. I need to see if I can get the focal point of the arcane force to center on our combined entities—"

"Is this some sort of sorcerer's techno-babble?"

"Of course not." There was a pause. "Maybe. A bit. Basically, I need to train at casting the spell on both of us."

"I need to be in the mansion this evening, Kane." Magnus raised his leg and peed on the tree the squirrel had escaped to. He seemed satisfied with this outcome of affairs. He'd managed to have the final word. Or pee. Whatever.

"I know. I'll be out of your hair by noon, okay? And I'll bring brunch."

"You could have started by saying that. See you in a bit."

"Where can I draw a circle?" Kane asked, looking around my shop.

"I'm sorry?" My hair was a bit damp from the quick shower I'd taken. I told myself I hadn't showered because Kane was coming over—I'd showered because I wanted to feel fresh. And if I wore my blue shirt with the nice cleavage, and my tightest-fitting jeans, it was because I wanted to dress nicely. It had nothing to do with Kane.

When he entered the shop, he paused for a long moment to look at me. His eyes lingered on my chest for a bit, and when he finally tore his eyes away, there was something hungry in his gaze.

Then he pulled a piece of charcoal from his pocket, and began looking at the floor of my shop in a way I didn't like.

"I need to draw a circle to focus the energy. That's how the spell works."

"Then maybe we should have practiced it in your office. You're not drawing anything on my floor, mister."

"It's just charcoal. It washes off."

"Will you be the one doing the washing?"

He sighed.

"Fine. Just draw it anywhere," I muttered.

Kane crouched in the middle of the shop and outlined a circle on the floor with his charcoal, about two feet in diameter.

He then retrieved a long, silvery needle from his coat's lapel, and pricked his finger with it. A large droplet of blood materialized. He let the drop fall on the circle's perimeter, intoning an arcane chant slowly. The circle seemed to glow with a faded orange light. He squeezed his finger, and additional drops of blood dripped on the charcoal marks. The hair on the back of my neck prickled as the mystical energy in the room began to converge around us. Magnus whined behind the bedroom door, where I'd shut him to prevent him from interfering with the spell. He sensed something was going on.

"Okay." Kane stood up, putting the charcoal in his pocket. His fingers were smudged with black. "What I want us to do is stand in the circle. I'll cast most of the spell, focusing the energy on our bodies. I just want to make sure it can work on both of us."

"Will it hurt?"

"No. The energy can feel a bit... ticklish at first."

I peered skeptically at the circle. "It's awfully small. You're teleporting us together?"

"Yeah." He looked at me in surprise. "Isn't that the plan?"

"But... can't you draw one circle for each of us?"

"No."

"Is it possible that it'll merge us? Like in *The Fly*?"

"What?"

"In the movie. *The Fly*. Jeff Goldblum invents a teleportation device, but when he uses it, he doesn't notice there's a fly in the device with him. The machine merges their bodies together, and then Jeff slowly becomes a man-fly—dribbling acid on his food, skin peeling—and he's all yucky."

"I didn't see it. It sounds ridiculous."

"The movie is much better than it sounds. The point is, will I slowly become Lou-infused-with-Kane after your spell? Chain-smoking and wearing outdated coats?"

"Maybe I'll become Lou? Constantly looking for trouble and spouting snarky remarks?"

"I can think of worse fates. Anyway, I'm not that snarky."

"And my spell will not merge us into one body. Right now, it won't even teleport us, I need the dragon scale to do that. It'll just tickle a bit, and you'll feel the magical energy accumulating in your body. There's no reason to worry. Please stand in the circle."

I entered the circle. Kane stepped in as well, and I had to shuffle a bit to give him room. We were standing very close to each other, our bodies nearly touching. My heart began to beat faster, my throat feeling dry.

"Don't touch the circle with your feet," Kane murmured, his eyes closed in concentration. When his sharp eyes were shut, he seemed much softer, almost defenseless. I stared up at his face as he began to chant, his lips inches from my face. He was a foot taller than me, and if I leaned forward, I could press my ear to his chest, my head nestled under his unshaven chin.

My skin felt as if something was prickling it lightly. The mystical energy of the spell surrounded us as Kane's arcane chanting grew louder. My hair hovered around me, as if an unseen wind blew through it. Kane's voice dominated the room, strong, deep, commanding. A voice that could change reality, twist the laws of physics, manipulate the fabric of space and time.

And then he stopped, and gazed down at me.

His eyes glowed, their green color shining at me, exuding power. "I think it worked," he said. The air throbbed strangely as he spoke. His body crackled, as if infused with static electricity.

"What's going on?"

"The mystical energy of the spell accumulated in our bodies, but the spell remained unfinished, so it wasn't released." His voice echoed in my ribcage, in my heart, my stomach, between my legs. "It should take a few minutes to dissipate."

I tried to convince myself to step away from the circle, to let the energy leave my body in peace. But the rush in my body, the warmth, the pulse of power and need was almost impossible to resist. Instead of taking a step back, I put a hand on his chest, feeling the energy coursing between us, two bodies connected together. His heart thrummed underneath my palm. I felt his breath quicken as he wrapped his arm around me, pulling me closer. His scent, clove and pine, was everywhere, and I breathed it in huskily, licking my lips.

My other hand found its way under his shirt, sliding up his back, enjoying the feel of his skin. He leaned forward and my lips parted, meeting his halfway, my tongue finding his. At that moment all I wanted, all I needed was *more*.

He grabbed my ass with both hands and I coiled one leg around him. Half lifting me, he took a few steps forward, pushing me against the counter. I pulled off his trench coat hungrily, consumed by a desire to feel his skin on mine. My shirt rose, my stomach pressing against his, and his hand sank into the waistband of my jeans, only my panties between his fingers and my body. I could feel the warmth in my chest and my face, my legs tightening around him. The touch of his fingers was tantalizing, brushing against that thin soft fabric, tracing its edges, touching the skin of my inner thigh.

And then I pushed him away. He stumbled back, his eyes widening in surprise. I quickly vaulted over the counter, to keep it between us, not trusting myself to keep away from him.

"I'm sorry," I blurted. "I can't. Not now."

He nodded hesitantly. "Okay." His voice still had that sexy, otherworldly thrum, though it was fading.

"I don't hook up before jobs. It complicates things." *It ends badly.* "I need to be focused tomorrow. I can't afford to be distracted."

He cleared his throat. "That's fine. I didn't anticipate the effect of the spell's energy on us." His eyes had stopped glowing. The energy had dissipated.

"Right," I said, my voice hoarse. "It was just the energy. That's all."

EIGHTEEN

———◆———

As I approached Ddraig Goch's mansion, I felt inconse-quential, tiny. I had previously seen this house from afar, and it had seemed big. From here, it was colossal. If I needed a reminder that the being I was stealing from was infinitely greater than me, here it was. I was living in the back-room of a shop, my bedroom just large enough to contain my bed. Ddraig Goch lived in a modern palace. I wouldn't have been surprised if I'd learned it was surrounded by a moat, complete with crocodiles.

The outer wall was vast, reaching five or six yards above my head, its top crowned with iron spikes. The burglar in me instantly examined it for handholds, for weaknesses. Of course I could climb it, but I easily spotted two security cameras.

And even if it weren't for those, as soon as anyone hopped over the wall, Ddraig Goch would know about it. Dragons and their lairs.

I touched my necklace, verifying that the small black rock with the USB plug Harutaka had given me was still there. Sometime during the evening, I would have to sneak away and find the server room to plug it in. I shivered in apprehension at the prospect. My palms began to warm up, and I forced myself to breathe deeply, and think of my daughter, chasing the fear away.

There were two armed men at the entrance gates, both looking at me with a mask of boredom as I got closer.

"Name?" one asked.

"Bethany Holt," I said, giving the name Sinead had secured for the waitress role. Bethany Holt was a girl we both knew; she had been in Breadknife's gang. She was one of the nastier people there, always searching for ways to bully the kids around her. She had homed in on Sinead, who'd unfortunately had a serious acne problem when we were sixteen, calling her the most unimaginative name available—pizza face. One memorable night, we filled Bethany's bed with pizza sauce and Vaseline, and there was much rejoicing. We were a sophisticated bunch.

He checked his papers, then took a cursory look at the fake driver's license I produced. Finally, he nodded at me, and I walked past the gate. For a second, my skin tingled strangely, and I wondered if it was Ddraig Goch's senses as they sniffed at the stranger in his lair.

A group of young men and women stood a few yards away on the paved walkway to the entrance. They were looking around them, with expressions of awe mixed with nervousness, at the vast expanse of lawn that served as the front garden. It was already dark, and it was almost impossible to see the far ends of the garden; the darkness swallowed it. I pegged the group to be the rest of the waitstaff. One of them, a slightly older guy with an air of self-importance, strode toward me. He had a long cucumber-ish face, with hair that seemed like someone had doodled it with a black marker on his scalp. He had a large bag on his shoulder.

"Bethany Holt?" he said.

"That's me."

He glanced at his wristwatch, his lips twisted in displeasure. I had arrived three minutes late, and apparently this was his way of letting me know of his dissatisfaction. After a second or two of staring at his watch pointedly, he let out a long breath through his nose. It was probably part of the entire charade, but his sinuses were quite clogged, and the end of his breath was a soft squeak. He reddened and eyed me with anger, as if this was my doing. I made sure to remain perfectly composed, and did my best to remember the squeak's exact pitch for when I told Sinead about it later.

"Right!" he said. "Now that you're *finally* here, we can start."

I joined the rest of the staff, and he stood in front of us, hands clasped behind his body.

"My name is Jonathan Roth, and I am the banquet captain," he said. "The banquet's guests tomorrow evening are *very* high class, and will expect a certain standard from the people serving them."

He looked at each and every one of us carefully and then sniffed, as if we were all lacking in the quality that was expected by those important people. "To that end, we will discuss some basic rules."

Thus began the long list of Jonathan Roth's rules. I zoned out after rule three: Ladies are always served first. Instead of listening, I began mentally listing the security measures I spotted around me. Inside the garden I could spot three more security cameras, and I guessed there were more hidden within the mansion's walls. We'd known about their existence, of course. We would be monitored at all times once we entered the mansion. Even if they didn't sound the alarm as we crept through the hallways, they would be able to look through the stored footage later and identify us. That also meant that today, when I went to plug in Harutaka's USB stick, I would probably be visible on the security monitors.

A man was patrolling the walls, carrying a submachine gun, and I was willing to bet that on the night of the banquet there would be more. Trying to enter the grounds over the wall would be suicide. No. The only way inside would be through the front gate, as guests or staff.

The group around me was moving, the monologue apparently over. Jonathan led us down the path and through a back door to the kitchen. It was huge, and already teeming with cooks and smells that made my stomach grumble. He gave an explanation of the various dishes we would serve during the banquet, and pointed out a few of the chefs' names. Two of them had won on some reality cooking show. One owned a Michelin two-star rated restaurant. Jonathan let that sink in for a moment. Once he had ascertained we were suitably impressed, he led us to the dining room. Or dining hall. Or dining stadium. Whatever you called *that*.

It was an enormous hall, lined with round tables, the wooden floor polished to a high gleam. There were several huge windows along one wall, and the entire space was lit by a chandelier that probably cost more than my entire store. A double door stood at the far end, leading, I knew, to the lobby. Another armed guard stood by the door. The tables were covered in tablecloths, but were not set yet. That, Jonathan explained, was what *we* were there to do this evening.

"It's important you get this right. I will be making sure that each seat is set correctly. If you mangle it, I will make you do it again. Here's the order. Dinner plate, with a salad plate on top. To the left, dinner fork, salad fork, and napkin, in a classic three-point fold. If any of you doesn't know what that is, please let me know and I'll have you escorted from the premises." He laughed, or I think that was what he did. It was a wheezy, slightly deranged kind of sound, ending with a snort and a slight squeak from his malformed nose. One of the young waiters followed suit, giggling slightly, marking himself as the group's ass-licker. The rest of us stood silent.

"Okay." Jonathan cleared his throat. "Dessert fork above the plate. To the right we have dinner knife, teaspoon, and soup spoon. I want an inch and a half between each utensil. If you need a ruler, feel free to ask for one."

By the time he finished his explanation, Jonathan's armpits were visibly wet. As the waiters milled around the room, starting to set the tables, I saw him open his bag and retrieve a fresh shirt from it. It was a garment bag, which he had obviously brought with him, expecting this problem. Jonathan's squeaky nose was accompanied by a sweating problem.

I couldn't spot the security camera, but that was no surprise. Inside the mansion, the cameras would be well hidden. I hazarded a guess that it was in the chandelier. There would be more, all over the mansion. The blueprints didn't note where the cameras were installed, but Breadknife's notes made it clear that every hallway and every room was well monitored. The security room was near the lobby, and it was a safe bet that a guard was positioned there at all times, scrutinizing the security feeds.

I eyed the guard by the door. He was a slight complication, but not one I hadn't anticipated. I'd just have to be careful and fast.

I went over to one of the carts with the cutlery, and began to set one of the tables, copying the actions of an experienced waitress nearby. I didn't really know which was the salad fork and which was the dinner fork, nor any of the other cutlery names. But I was more than capable of giving them my own names. Papa fork went by baby fork, to the left of the dishes, while mommy fork went above them. Mister knife and his two girlfriend spoons, big mama and little minx, went to the right. Folding the napkin took a bit of work, but after a few attempts I got it right. By the third place setting I was a professional, and even got an appreciative grunt from Jonathan as he went past.

Looking around at the very slow progress, I determined it would take about four hours to get the entire hall set to Jonathan's standards. I decided to make my move about halfway through the evening, when the drudgery and repetitiveness of the job would make everyone in the room inattentive.

After fifteen minutes of cutlery fun, the double doors opened, and the unmistakable Maximillian Fuchs marched inside. Even without our earlier surveillance, I would have immediately pegged him as the man in charge. The hair at the back of my neck prickled at the sight of him, though I couldn't pinpoint the exact reason. He was very tall, his face pale and sharp, his eyes dark. His hair was a shock of white, but not the white hair of an old man. More like the white of a blank page. He wore a dark blue suit that seemed timeless—a suit that a man could wear in the thirties, or today, and radiate the same amount of authority and importance.

He stood motionless, inspecting us as we worked in silence. No one joked or laughed or talked under his scrutiny. Everyone knew instinctively to remain quiet and professional. I began imagining that his eyes were following me in particular. Was it possible that he could sense something was off about me? My palms began to heat up, and I focused on memories of Christmas with my parents, opening gifts early in the morning, shrieking with joy as they stood above me, smiling. My breathing became steadier, my heartbeat slowed.

All he did was stand and look at us. I couldn't shake the feeling that something was very, very wrong with the man, but I didn't know why. I kept waiting for him to leave, but he didn't. Finally, I decided I couldn't wait any longer. I would have to sneak out with Maximillian looking.

Jonathan was ranting at one of the waitresses, who had mixed up her mommy fork and baby fork. I interrupted him mid-rant.

"Excuse me, where's the bathroom?" I asked.

He motioned impatiently at the double door with the guard. "What hovel did you work in before you came here?" he shouted. "Was it Kentucky Fried Chicken? What sort of amateur does that?"

I walked away, approaching the guard by the door. I clutched my stomach slightly and winced. "Hey," I said, my voice slightly tight. "Which way to the ladies' room?" I felt Maximillian glancing my way, and tried to ignore his look.

"Just go out to the lobby, first door to the right," the guard answered, his face sympathetic.

"Thanks." I grimaced, clutching my stomach a bit tighter, and opened the door, closing it behind me.

Okay, I'd definitely established my need to go number two. That meant I had about ten minutes before the guard began wondering where I was. I glanced at my watch. Nine fifteen.

The lobby was grand and spacious, but I had no time to waste gawking. Was there a man in the security room, watching me right now? I was almost sure there was. After all, a single waitress roaming the hallways was something that stood out.

I felt in my pocket for the vial I had with me, and palmed it. Then I wandered around a bit, as if searching for the bathroom, checking behind a few doors, carefully staying away from the actual bathroom. Finally, I beelined directly to the door of the security room and opened it.

A middle-aged guard sat there, and as I had thought, he was studying a row of monitors, one of which displayed me, standing by the doorway. He swiveled his chair and looked at me balefully.

"Oh, sorry!" I said. "I was looking for the bathroom?"

"Does this look like the bathroom?" the man asked impatiently.

"I'm really sorry."

He stared at me, but I didn't budge, wearing my slightly confused expression. I used the time to watch the monitors, trying to figure out the locations of the security cameras.

Finally he sighed. "Just across the lobby." he sighed. "White door. You can't miss it."

"Thanks, sir," I said.

He had already swiveled away.

My thumb flicked open the vial hidden in my palm. I quickly upended it into a trashcan to the side of the door, holding my breath. The few drops of liquid dribbled into the can, and I could already glimpse the fumes rising. I left the room, closing the door behind me. Then I went to the bathroom.

The vial had contained a sleep draught. Not a lot—I didn't want the security guard to fall into a deep sleep. It would be too suspicious if he was found later. No, I just wanted him to be drowsy enough to be unable to focus. Even if he noticed me in the monitors later, he would remember I was the dim-witted girl who went to look for the bathroom, and would be too sleepy to care.

The potion should work in about two minutes, but he was a bit fatter than I had planned, and I decided to give him three minutes. I put on my Bluetooth earphone, and connected to the voice chat.

"Okay, almost there," I said. "Just waiting for the dude in the security room to nod off."

"Good," Harutaka's voice piped in my ear. He sat in the nearby lawyer's mansion with his laptop, waiting.

I counted the seconds, checking the time. Twenty past nine. Good enough. The guard in the security room should be fighting to keep his eyelids open by now.

I left the bathroom, and opened one of the doors. It led to a hallway I knew well from the blueprints. I strode down the corridor, ignoring the doors to my left and right, until it branched. I took a right, and walked to the end of the corridor. To my left was a door, which led to the server room.

I opened it, slid inside, and closed it behind me.

It was *cold* here, and dark. Blinking lights revealed there really were several computers. Harutaka had been right. I approached the closest one and checked behind it, using a small flashlight to shine a dim light on its surface. There was an available USB port amid the spaghetti of wires attached to it.

I suddenly hesitated. "Listen... I'm in the server room. I can plug your USB stick in one of the computers. But if I leave it plugged in, someone might find it later."

"Don't worry," Harutaka said, sounding amused. "No one will find it."

"Okay," I muttered.

I removed the USB stick from my neck, the strange black stone that covered it feeling warm. The red rune pulsed slowly, like a strange heartbeat, almost as if it sensed the proximity of the computers. I plugged it into the port.

"Okay, it's in."

"Give it a minute."

I waited, hopping from foot to foot, hoping the guard in the security room really was nodding off. Then, the rune in the stone began to glow brighter. Its red color changed to orange, then white, emanating a blinding bright light. I squinted at it in astonishment. Then the stone and the rune seemed to liquefy, crawling through the USB port into the computer, disappearing from sight.

The room sank back into darkness. The USB port was empty. The stone had vanished.

"Holy shit." I wheezed.

Harutaka cackled in my ear. "Cool, huh? Okay, give me a moment—I'm connected, and already breaking the walls.

Some nice security here, nothing earth-shattering. Oh, is that an actual cyber demon? I thought those were extinct..." There was a sudden sound of static, and a spark flashed from one of the computers. "Well, maybe now they are. Just a few more seconds... There! I'm inside."

"Okay, can I leave?"

"Just a second, let me see... there we go. I have eyes on you now. You can wave."

I waved.

"Hey! I can see you!" Harutaka sounded drunk.

"Awesome. Can you see the dude in the security room?"

"Yeah. He's barely awake. Keeps shaking his head."

"Can he see me?"

"Well, if he looks at the monitors, sure. But hang on, I'll fix that." A second later he said, "There. I killed the security footage around you. Just for a few seconds. Enough time for you to get back to the rest of the catering staff."

I went out the door, and began striding quickly down the hall.

"This is so cool," Harutaka buzzed in my ear. "I have almost full access to all their files. I'm going to have a party with... Shit! Stop! Go back! Someone's coming your way!"

But it was already too late. A guard rounded the corner, and as our eyes met, his fingers tensed around the grip of his submachine gun.

NINETEEN

We stood frozen for a fraction of a second and then I marched over to him, my face twisting into an expression of fury.

"Excuse me?" I said loudly. "What is the meaning of this?"

He blinked, surprised. "I'm sorry?"

"This!" I pointed at his right boot, where the tip was slightly scuffed. "You were all told to keep your boots in good shape. Is this how you maintain your uniform?" I hoped fervently that the security staff was large enough to account for unfamiliar people.

"Uh… I shined the boots last week. I thought—"

"You must shine them Every. Single. Day. You should know that by now."

Harutaka's voice whispered in my ear. "Okay, I have the personnel file open. The photo here matches him to the dot, he's our guy. According to the file, he's called Gavin Pollard. And you're in luck. He was hired only two weeks ago. He probably knows nothing about anything."

"You're that new guy, right?" I placed my hands on my hips. "Mollard?"

"Uh... Pollard. Yes, ma'am."

"Okay, Pollard. Since you're new, I'll give you a break. But you better shape up. This is not a job at mall security. This is the real deal. This is Ddraig Goch's mansion. You know that, right?"

"Last week he was docked a day's pay for not cleaning his gun," Harutaka murmured.

"Of course, ma'am, I..."

I grabbed the submachine gun and lifted it to my eye, peering into the barrel. My heart hammered hard with the thing pointed straight at my face.

"Looks like you're learning to maintain your weapon, at least," I said. "Don't want last week to repeat itself, do we?"

"No, ma'am."

"Look, Pollard, I'll level with you, I talked with your shift captain..."

"Frank Lowe," Harutaka said.

"Lowe," I continued. "He said you look promising. And I trust his judgment. But if I ever see you walking around here with your boots looking like that again, you're out. You got that?"

"Yes, ma'am."

"Okay." I took a deep breath, realizing that if he saw me rejoining the serving staff, all would be lost. "For the rest of the shift, I want you to stay out of sight. There are people here preparing the dining hall for tomorrow, and I don't want the state of your boots to disgrace us. So go patrol the southern wall until they're gone, understand?"

"Yes, ma'am. I'm really sorry."

"Just don't let it happen again, Mollard."

"Pollard. Yes, ma'am."

He scuttled away. I glared at him darkly until he disappeared, and then let out a long, relieved breath.

"That was amazing," Harutaka whispered.

"Amazingly stupid," I muttered. "We should have checked to see if anyone was coming before I walked back. Any other surprises?"

"No, you're good to go."

I quickly marched back, logging out of the chat and removing the earphone from my ear. I glanced at the time. Nine thirty-two. Damn it. I had been gone for seventeen minutes. Just as I was about to reach the door of the dining hall, it swung open.

Maximillian Fuchs stood in the doorway, close enough to touch.

"Oh," I said. "Uh… you startled me."

His eyes burrowed into mine. Could he see through my disguise? My palms began to itch with warmth, and I desperately tried to think of my daughter. I lowered my eyes and tried to walk past him.

He moved slightly, blocking my path. Leaning forward, he inhaled deeply through his nose. Creepy.

I raised my head, meeting his gaze while thinking of Tammi, her smile, the way she skipped to school.

"Can I go back?" I asked, making sure to maintain the meek tone of the subdued waitress.

He looked at me for another second, then smiled. His teeth were impeccable, as white as snow. "Of course." He moved aside.

I brushed past him and entered the dining hall, relieved. The guard eyed me, quirking his eyebrow. Right. I'd been gone for seventeen minutes.

"So much better," I said. "You know how it is, sometimes."

He nodded with uncertainty, but his face didn't strike me as particularly suspicious.

Jonathan Roth was less amiable. "Where the fuck were you?"

"Lady problems," I informed him shortly.

"Oh." His eyes widened. "Listen, tomorrow is the banquet, and you can't just disappear—"

"It's okay," I said. "The first day is the worst. I sometimes need to change tampons every thirty minutes. Ugh, I'm so bloated. But tomorrow—"

"Okay, okay!" He waved his hands in panic. "Just… don't disappear like that tomorrow."

Say the words "bloated" and "tampons" to a man, and he dissolves. I smiled politely and returned to setting the tables.

The evening seemed to stretch out forever. My nerves were shot after the near thing with the guard in the hallway, and all I wanted to do was leave. But the tables seemed endless, and Jonathan Roth was true to his word—he made people set the same place over and over until they got it just right. As the hours ticked by, almost the entire catering staff became united by our shared hatred of the nasal-voiced banquet captain. When he turned his back to us, we commiserated with the time-honored tradition of pantomiming to each other motions of strangulations, of cutting throats, of legs kicking his butt. Middle fingers were raised. Eyes were rolled. I earned a lot of love by doing very precise imitations of the way he strutted, my face wearing the same pompous expression he had. And, like kids in a classroom, whenever he turned around to see what the giggling was all about, we were all intently busy with the cutlery, lips pursed in concentration. As the evening progressed, his armpits began to acquire matching sweat spots and he had to change shirts again. How many identical shirts did he have in there? Three? Four?

At a quarter past eleven, the final seat was arranged. Jonathan gave us a speech he presumably thought would be motivating. He told us to get a good night's sleep, that there would be no room for mistakes tomorrow. Most of the staff stared at him numbly, his words meaning nothing. But I took them to heart. There really would be no room for mistakes tomorrow. When I broke into the vault, even the smallest mistake could be fatal.

TWENTY

—◆—

My school education had been sporadic, dotted with long stretches of absence over the years, but I still remembered what it was like to wake up on the morning of an important test. The eyes open, seemingly into another normal day, the brain still trying to rewire the pieces together, a layer of blissful ignorance. And then the realization hits you. It's today—the math test, or English test, or whatever test. A test that could determine your future—scientist, or coal miner? Businesswoman or crazy bag woman? There is always a feeling of unpreparedness, and a sense that something will go wrong. You'll be late for the bus, or won't find the classroom, or you'll have to pee in the middle of the test. An impending sense of doom.

When you wake up on the day of breaking into the vault of a dragon, it's like that—only a hundred times worse. My gut felt as if I had swallowed a ten-pound barbell, and it dragged everything down with it. My mind began racing with all the things I still needed to do before tonight, and with all the possible things that could go wrong. These were endless, and all resulted in me and my friends dying horribly. I began wondering if there was a way to avoid it all. I half-convinced myself I could kidnap my daughter and fly to Mexico—not an ideal solution, sure, but better than being burned alive by a raging dragon, right?

Magnus pattered around me as I shuffled around in my bedroom, getting ready. Those who say that dogs can sense how we feel have never met Magnus. He was obliviously cheerful, nipped at my feet, tripped me twice, and was generally unhelpful. Finally, I grabbed the leash and left with him.

We reached the street that my daughter crossed on her way to school. We were a bit early, and walked back and forth several times as we waited for her to make an appearance, Magnus glancing at me with exasperation.

And there she was. The crushing weight of the day lifted momentarily as she skipped down the street, wearing her pink boots, a purple dress I was pretty sure was new, and a bead bracelet on her right wrist. She was talking to her adoptive mother, Jane, asking something over and over. But Jane was distracted by her phone, and didn't answer. For a second I was outraged. How dare she ignore my daughter like that? It was her job to raise her! I would never have been busy on my phone while Tammi talked to me.

But of course, I had done far worse. I had given her away, and this woman had raised her to be a wonderful, happy child. And now I'd also let a dangerous gangster find out about her. In the better-mommy contest, I came last, and I probably didn't even deserve a participation award.

As they went past, she hugged Jane's leg tightly while Magnus stretched his leash, sniffing at them. I opened my mouth, trying to tell her it was fine. He didn't bite. But nothing came out.

"Can she pet him?" Jane's voice startled me.

"Uh… sure." I looked at her and quickly glanced away before she noticed my eyes. "He doesn't bite."

"Want to pet the doggie, Tammi?"

My daughter glanced at her mom, and then at Magnus. Then she gave a hesitant nod, and stretched out one hand, the other one still hugging Jane's leg. She touched Magnus' head, and he wagged his tail and licked her fingers. She giggled, pulling her hand quickly back.

"I used to be afraid of dogs," Jane told me. "When I was a child. I don't want her to be the same."

"You're doing a good job," I said hoarsely.

She smiled at me warmly. "Okay, come on, Tammi, let's go. Say goodbye."

My daughter stared up at me. "Goodbye," she said shyly.

"Bye, Tammi." I waved.

They walked away.

My daughter had talked to me. I called her by her name. I was overcome by waves of gratitude, and new strengths. I was ready to kick some dragon ass.

Or at least, sneakily break into his vault.

To keep away from Shade hunters, Harutaka was staying at the mansion we used for surveillance. We had decided to neglect mentioning that fact to anyone concerned. I called Kane, asking him to meet me there, to go over some final details before the job.

I took an Uber to the mansion, the driver mercifully quiet for the entire ride. He gave me a sly look as we got there, probably deciding that I was the owner's current lover.

Harutaka sat in the dining room downstairs, his laptop on the table, the monitor's light illuminating his face in an eerie neon blue. The room was dark, the blinds pulled down. I flicked the light on. He squinted and peered up at me. He had a pair of earphones in his ears, and he removed them, unplugging them from the computer.

"Lou!" he said. "Shouldn't you be sleeping?"

"It's nine in the morning."

"It's tomorrow already?"

I folded my arms. "You never went to sleep?"

"This security system is fascinating! So many different encryptions, so many loopholes and dead ends and small traps. It's clearly the work of several different people, who weren't allowed to see each other's work. That way, no one has the lock to this strongbox. It's a great way to avoid someone hacking from *inside*. But it also leaves tiny cracks and holes for someone like *me* to use."

"So you hacked it, right?"

"Well… most of it. There are still some parts I don't have access to. I'm currently trying to get access to the mansion's electricity and lights. It's all automated."

His fingers glided across the keyboard, making a strange sound—not so much typing, but more like a whirring, the sound of keys tapped fast enough to buzz like bees. I sat next to him and glanced at the monitor. He typed a set of incomprehensible instructions, but the weird part was that some characters were not in the English alphabet. In fact, they weren't in any language I recognized. One of them, which repeated several times, matched the rune on the USB stick I had used the day before.

"Are those runes?" I asked.

"Yes." He nodded, his fingers never pausing their dance. "A lot of their files are encrypted by 256-bit AES keys. I could just try to brute-force through them, but it would take too long."

"How long?"

"Well..." He glanced at the time in the bottom right corner of the monitor. "It's now seventeen minutes past nine in the morning. Brute-forcing these encryptions with this computer would take about... enough time for the sun to become a red giant. Humanity would be extinct, and we'd be late for the banquet."

"Okay. Not brute force, then."

"No." He shook his head sharply. "That's why I use chaos." He pointed at one of the runes.

I scrutinized the character representing the rune. It seemed to almost pulse on the screen. The letters around it occasionally shimmered, as if just their proximity somehow affected them. I knew I was watching nothing more than pixels on the screen, but I couldn't shake the feeling that what I witnessed was somehow a form of magic. Not the magic that Kane performed, channeling mystical energy through his body—a different form of magic, infused with technology.

Harutaka laughed his small, strange laugh. "People think chaos is just a mess," he said. "But it isn't. There is beauty in chaos. There are magnificent patterns. And there is possibility. When dealing with chaos, there is always a chance to beat the odds. And when you use the right runes, this chance can become almost a certainty."

The front door opened and Kane strode inside, carrying a tray of three Starbucks cups. Same trench coat, same smile. But there was something behind that smile now, and his eyes slid away from mine. Despite my efforts to avoid complications, it was clear that things between us had changed. "Hey guys. I brought coffee. Lou, here's your extra strong coffee."

"Oh, god, you're a life saver."

"And Harutaka, you wanted… black coffee with two chai tea bags and a pump of caramel?" Kane gaped at the man with a mixture of horror and fascination.

"Yes! Thank you!"

"The barista asked me to repeat the order three times. She seemed quite shaken."

"That is the general response I get in Starbucks," Harutaka admitted. "And they always spell my name wrong on the cup."

"They mangle everyone's names," I said.

"I have a cup collection at home. There's one where it's Harutacka with a *ck*, and one where it's Harutaha. And of course, Harukata. I even have one where they spelled it Rokaka."

"You have a complex name for Americans."

"Rokaka! That's not even close!"

Kane gave him the cup, and he sipped from it and licked his lips happily. Mine was the same as last time—perfect.

"There," Harutaka said with satisfaction. "I can turn the lights on and off now."

"There are more important things," I pointed out. "What about the guest list?"

"I changed it last night," he answered. "I added Baroness Fleurette van Dijk to the guest list, as well as her butler and her personal assistant."

"Fantastic." That would allow Sinead, Kane and Isabel to enter the mansion's premises tonight. Harutaka would stay behind, monitoring us through the security cameras. "And the invitation?"

"I found the file with the invitation document, and sent it over to Sinead."

"Good job." Sinead would be sure to make a perfect forgery of an invitation for Baroness Fleurette van Dijk.

"I also deleted all the video footage of your little foray last night, overriding it with footage from the middle of the night. Oh! And I checked the guard shifts—our friend Gavin Pollard was supposed to be on shift during the banquet, so I changed it. You won't run into him."

"Good thinking. Did you manage to access the vault door?" I asked.

He paused and looked at me. "The vault door is not connected to the main security server. I can't get to it."

"Damn it. That means Sinead still needs to get the keycard and the password from Maximillian Fuchs."

"I don't like that part of the plan." Kane frowned.

"That's not the question," I said, a bit coldly. "The question is—can you think of a better plan?"

He didn't answer.

"The advantage is that by that point, if something goes wrong, we can still leave unharmed, and figure out a different way to break into the vault."

He gave a small nod, conceding the point.

I turned to the hacker. "Harutaka, are there personnel files in the dragon's servers? Maybe we can find something Sinead can use."

Harutaka tapped some keys, and a small personnel file opened with the name "Maximillian Fuchs" on top. It had no image of him, only a physical description. Height: six feet; white hair, dark brown eyes. There was scant detail beyond the description. He had been hired seven years ago, and his current title was "security chief." No CV, or anything else.

"Do we have to enter through the vault's door?" Kane asked, clearly still bothered by the plan. "How does the dragon enter the vault? He sleeps there. Surely you saw him enter and leave it."

Harutaka shook his head. "I checked the footage. He doesn't enter through the door. And there's no security cameras inside the vault, so I don't know what entrance he uses."

"I saw no other entrance in the blueprints." I frowned. Something else nagged at the back of my mind.

"Dragons are magical beings," Harutaka said. "Perhaps he shifts into another dimension. Perhaps he shrinks to the size of an atom and flies through the wall. Perhaps he turns into gas."

"I can try to hypnotize Maximillian if Sinead can't pull off the seduction trick," Kane said. "But hypnosis can't make a man do something he doesn't want. And I assume he won't be ecstatic about opening the vault door for us, so—"

"Why does it have his description in the file?" I asked, interrupting him. "Don't you think it's weird?"

Harutaka shrugged. "I guess that's how the dragon likes his employee files."

"Are there descriptions for the rest of the employees? A photo would be simpler, right? Yesterday, you told me you matched that guard's face to a photo in his file."

Harutaka hesitated, then clicked the mouse a few times. Gavin Pollard's file opened, with an image of his face on top. It had no description. Harutaka opened a few more files. All had images.

A feeling of dread filled my gut. "I knew there was something wrong with him when I saw him," I muttered. "Can you show us the footage from the dining hall yesterday evening? About eight p.m."

Harutaka got busy doing as I asked. I sipped my coffee, my anxiety rising. To distract myself, I said to Kane. "The coffee is perfect, thanks."

"You're welcome."

I wanted to say more, but couldn't find the words. And besides, I wasn't about to talk about the day before with Harutaka there. So I bit my lip, and took another sip, my eyes glancing away from Kane.

"There," Harutaka said.

It was a video feed of the dining hall. I could spot parts of the chandelier at the edges of the image. Just as I had suspected, the camera was hidden in it.

All the waiters—including me—were setting the tables, and Jonathan Roth was strutting around pompously, but I couldn't see Maximillian Fuchs.

"Fast forward a bit," I said.

He did, and it ran quickly. We watched until nine p.m. without Maximillian making an appearance.

"Rewind," I muttered. "Slower."

He did. After a while, I leaned forward, gripping my chair. "Stop."

He paused the image.

"See there?" I pointed at the screen. "Where that waitress dropped the plate? It fell but didn't break, which was a huge relief. Those plates probably cost more than a hundred bucks each."

"Okay," Kane said. "So? Is there a significance to the plate?"

"When the plate fell, Maximillian was in the room," I explained. "I remember, because I thought he'd say something. But he didn't."

"Is he standing somewhere outside the camera's range?"

"He's standing right there." I pointed at an empty spot on the screen. "I'm sure of it."

"There's no one there, Lou."

"Something was wrong, I knew it even then," I muttered. "See how clean and polished the floor is? You can see the tables and us reflecting in it. But you know what? I think Maximillian cast no reflection. Not in those huge windows, either. That's what I noticed, subconsciously. That's why he felt so wrong. And that also explains why we can't see him in the footage, and why there's no image of him in the personnel file."

"Because cameras can't take his picture," Kane said slowly. "He's a vampire."

I nodded. "And that means we can't pick his pocket—he'll notice it. And we can't trick him into drinking truth serum. Vampires drink nothing but blood."

TWENTY-ONE

———◆———

I had less than ten hours to come up with an alternative plan, or our chance to break into the dragon's mansion tonight would be blown.

Harutaka had gone to sleep in the bedroom upstairs, leaving me and Kane in the dining room alone. I fiddled with my empty Starbucks cup as I tried to figure out what to do.

Now that we knew Maximillian Fuchs was a vampire, his nightly excursions to pick up women suddenly took on a much darker aspect. He was picking up his dinner. I doubted he killed them; he probably only drained as much as he needed. Vampires who killed their prey didn't survive for long. The vampire community was small and tight, and policed its own. A vampire who killed his food endangered them all, which meant he had to go. But still, I doubted that these women Maximillian picked up knew what they were getting themselves into.

Could we use it? Maybe one of these women would help us somehow? Could they know something about him? Or they might serve as a distraction—barging up into the banquet, throwing accusations…

No. I couldn't see how that would help us, and I was leery of using anyone else for this job.

"You want to discuss it?" Kane asked. He stood by one of the dining room windows. He'd opened the blind and was gazing out at the garden.

"Discuss what?"

"The plan. Obviously we need to change it a bit."

"I'll think of something."

"We can think of something together," he suggested, turning to face me. "Brainstorm it. Throw ideas into the wind. No idea is too dumb to consider."

"Fine. Sure. What do you have in mind?"

"We could force him to open it," Kane suggested.

"How exactly?"

"With a holy symbol. Or garlic. Threaten to drive a wooden stake through his heart."

"That's a dumb idea."

"I don't think you understand the whole brainstorming concept."

"Vampires don't really fear holy symbols, and they have no problem with garlic, you know that as well as I do. Besides, we're burglars, not fighters. I doubt if even the five of us together could overcome one vampire."

"What about running water? Vampires can't cross running water."

"So what do you want to do? Dig a canal?"

He walked over to the table and grabbed the chair adjacent to mine, sitting down. "I'm just thinking out loud. Why are you being so hostile?"

"Because we're screwed, that's why! There's no way we can beat a vampire. Maybe if we had a week to plan… but the banquet is tonight. And Breadknife knows what we're planning. He knows tonight is the night. He'll show up tomorrow morning at my door, wanting his box and his Yliaster crystal, and I'll have to tell him, 'sorry, dude, but it turns out that a vampire got in our way, no hard feelings, right?' And then he'll burn my shop and… and…"

Kane grabbed my palms, squeezing them lightly, his grass-green eyes looking into mine. I stopped rambling, lost in the depth of his gaze, feeling a sudden warmth in my stomach. I took a deep breath.

"Sorry," I muttered.

"*Breadknife* is our client?"

"Yeah." I already regretted blurting that. "He just wants the box with the Yliaster crystal, nothing else. You don't have to worry about that. Breadknife is *my* problem."

"I see. And we're talking about *the* Yliaster crystal? The one that can contain souls?"

"You've heard of it?" I tried to laugh it off, but it came out as a strange gurgle. "I doubt the Yliaster crystal is real. It's a box with a crystal inside it."

"But Breadknife thinks it's the Yliaster crystal?"

"It really doesn't matter, okay?"

"Okay." His fingers slid along the back of my hands, rubbing them in a soothing motion. "Then let's figure out how to handle this vampire problem."

"How?" My breathing became husky. I wanted him to keep sliding his fingers up my hands forever. I wanted him to go higher, up my wrist, my arm, to my neck.

"Maybe we don't need to beat the vampire. Maybe we can figure out how the dragon enters his vault and use *that.*"

"Harutaka is right, dragons are incredibly powerful. It could be anything. Maybe he can teleport. Or move through walls. Anything is possible. It might take days to find out how he does it."

"I think we might have to try, Lou. Vampires can't be easily tricked. They are faster and deadlier than almost anything.

They can smell the fear in our blood. They want nothing that we can offer them. We can't tempt them with lust or bribery or gifts—"

"Smell the fear in our blood," I repeated. I snatched my hands from his, trying to clear my mind. "They *do* want something from us, Kane. Something we all have. Blood."

"Lou, no offense, but if you're thinking of offering that vampire a goblet of your blood, spiked with a little truth serum, I think you might be disappointed by the result. Vampires are not known for their stupidity."

I was only half-listening to him, my mind whirling with possibilities. "I think I have a plan. But I have to get to my lab and start working. There's no time to lose."

TWENTY-TWO

—◆—

B y the time I finished preparing the potion, my body was drenched in sweat. The lab was more than just stuffy. The alchemical reactions my preparations created exuded heat and steam, and the air was almost hazy with warm fog. A single vial, containing a sticky, dark red fluid, sat on the counter.

I checked the time and spat out a curse. It was half past five. The banquet started at eight, and I had to be there at seven sharp.

My hair, clothing, and even my skin stank from alchemy.

I smelled like a mixture of ammonia, ripe cheese, and the weird tobacco my great-uncle used to smoke in his pipe after Thanksgiving dinner. I couldn't go to the banquet smelling like that; I would be fired before I even stepped through the gate.

I dashed to the bedroom, Magnus chasing me and barking in excitement. Cursing and repeatedly glancing at the time, I shrugged out of my shirt, pants and underwear, throwing them all in a stinking crumpled pile. Magnus stepped to the heap of clothing, sniffed at it, then commenced rolling in it, eyes closed in glee. Given that my dog had a penchant for rolling in roadkill carcasses, that wasn't a great compliment on my current odor.

Okay, shower. I opened the door, stepped inside, closed the door behind me while leaning against the wall, one foot pushing Magnus out. I turned on the water and adjusted the temperature to "fires of hell." Only water close to boiling would wash this stench away.

I'd had the foresight to braid my hair before I began working, so I only needed to shampoo it three times to get the stink out. I scrubbed my body until it was red and raw. Then I got out, toweled myself, wrapped the towel around me, and went out to the bedroom.

I had picked the outfit for the evening beforehand, and it was spread out on my bed. Black shirt and pants, dark boots, a brown belt with a silver clasp. It was well suited for both a waitress and a bona fide burglar. The pants' legs were tailored to be wide and loose. After putting them on, I grabbed the ankle holster with my small Glock and slid it onto my left ankle. My lockpicking kit snapped shut and tight on my right ankle.

I put on my shirt, and checked the hidden pockets in my sleeves. One already hid a vial of Margherita's fix-it-all. Another held a potion intended to help me crack the safe. I picked up the vial of red liquid, and slid it into the third hidden pocket. Then I touched my silvery chain, and let it slide up my wrist. It looped several times and latched into a loose bracelet.

"Angustus," I murmured, and the bracelet tightened, flawlessly fitting my wrist.

I went up to the mirror, and put my Bluetooth earphone in my left ear. Then I carefully combed my hair until it covered it completely. I grabbed a can of "Extra Super Hold Professional Hair Spray" from my night table, and sprayed the hair covering the earphone with it thoroughly. I moved my head around a bit, verifying that the earphone remained well hidden under the stiff hair.

Amateur burglars often forgot to pee before a job, and found themselves trying to crack a safe while cross-legged. I was anything but an amateur. I quickly went to the bathroom and sat on the toilet, realizing a fraction of a second later that it was still wet from my shower. I did what I had to, dried myself up a bit, and fixed my clothing again, making sure in the bedroom mirror that all was well.

I checked the time again, muttered the obligatory "Fuck," and dashed outside, grabbing my purse on the way and shouting apologies at Magnus, who howled at the door, mortally offended that I wasn't taking him with me.

TWENTY-THREE

I reached the mansion only five minutes early, which was, to my taste, cutting it a bit close. I immediately noticed that the gate now held three guards, not two. Jonathan Roth waited in the entrance and tried to hurry me inside, but the guards checked my ID meticulously, and verified my name was on the list. There would be no mistakes tonight. As Jonathan briskly led me to the dining hall, muttering angrily that I could have been a bit earlier, I noticed there were two patrolmen with dogs walking alongside the outer wall. They didn't want *anyone* crashing this party. We went past a hostess standing by a table with dozens of seat placement cards, around through the back door, and into the kitchen.

"Each table needs to have a bread basket and a bottle of wine before the guests show up," Jonathan told me. "Each bread basket should contain a dozen buns. After that's done, we begin setting the salads. Hurry, the rest of the staff are already working at it."

I joined the waiters in the dining hall. Sally, a nice waitress I had befriended the day before, whispered that Jonathan had already changed his shirt once. Apparently, this was his first big banquet, and his armpits were drenching his suit. Though he was a thoroughly annoying individual, I couldn't help feeling sorry for him.

Going to the farthest table, I took out my phone and logged into our voice chat.

"I'm here," I murmured. "Baroness Fleurette? How are you doing?"

"Wonderful, darling," Sinead's voice rang with a rich Dutch accent. The engine of the car hummed in the background. "I am on my way in our lovely car, driven by my *ravishing* butler, Bente Visser."

"Hardly ravishing," Kane's voice interjected.

"You're just upset because I made you leave that ghastly coat of yours behind," Sinead said, her baroness accent becoming even more pronounced.

I stifled a smile. "And your personal assistant?"

"I'm here," Isabel's voice was soft. "Looks like we'll get there at eight sharp."

"No rush," I murmured. "Reception is until eight-thirty. You can be ten minutes fashionably late. Harutaka?" He was supposed to be in the nearby mansion, monitoring us.

"Right here," he said. "Watching you through the security camera. A waiter behind you is checking out your ass."

"Well, if she's wearing her black pants, her ass looks delicious in them," the baroness said.

"Yes, thank you for keeping this chat professional," I muttered. "Okay, I'm going to set some tables. Baroness, remember, once you're here, you need to order a—"

"Bloody Mary, yes darling. You've only told me eleven times."

I placed twelve buns in the bread basket, and moved to another table. In the background, Jonathan was yelling at a waiter that there were no bathroom breaks until nine o'clock. I tuned his nasally voice out, feeling irritated.

Something nagged at me, but I wasn't sure what. Had I forgotten something? I made sure that I had the potions and the lockpicking kit. Setting a bread basket on another table, I began going through the plan. The baroness and her entourage would get here in their car. They would go to the front gate, give the invitation to the guard. The guard would verify that the baroness is on the guest list, then usher her in. She would sit at her table, and order a Bloody Mary. I would serve her the drink after adding the potion to it and—

She would sit at her table.

"Harutaka," I said quietly, my lips hardly moving. "Did you add the baroness to the seating arrangements?"

A few seconds went by. I counted twelve buns. Put them in a bread basket.

"No," Harutaka finally admitted. "I didn't think of that. I'll do it now."

"It's too late now," I said, feeling the blood leaving my face. "The seat placement cards are already outside, waiting for the guests."

"You'll have to switch them," Sinead said urgently, the Dutch accent gone from her voice.

I glanced at Jonathan, who watched the action around him, his eyes intense. "Yeah. Leaving might be tricky, but I'll have to try."

My mind whirled, trying to find a good excuse to leave the dining hall.

"Sinead, don't show up until I tell you to," I finally said. "I'll fix this."

Jonathan's garment bag hung on one of the chairs. I went over to it, carrying a bread basket. Once at the table, I set the basket down, glanced around to verify no one was looking, and quickly grabbed the garment bag. Marching quickly to the corner, I slid it under a table, dragging the tablecloth slightly so it hid the bag.

Then I went back to work, eyeing Jonathan and repeatedly checking the time. We began setting the salads. Six dishes to each table, each portion fit for a king. I checked the time. Almost eight. There were two large matching stains on Jonathan's armpits, but he was distracted by the salads and didn't pay attention.

I went over to him. "Um, Jonathan? The tomato salad with the leaves—"

He rolled his eyes. "The insalata Caprese?"

I glanced at his armpits for a fraction of a second. "That's the one. Should it be placed by the salad with the lettuce and bread bits—"

"Good god, were you born in a barn? Those bread bits are croutons, and the salad is called Perigourdine."

I eyed his armpits again, then quickly glanced away. "Right, Perigourdine. So should it be to its right or—"

"Like I said before, the order of the salads is, in a clockwise direction, the insalata Caprese, the Rojak, the Taramasalata, then the Perigourdine…" He slowed down, seeing my eyes as they dipped to his armpits again. "The, uh… Cappon magro and finally the Karedok. Clockwise. Do you know what clockwise means?"

"Sure, thanks!" I said brightly and strode away. From the corner of my eye, I saw him check his armpits, then hurry to the chair where his bag had been. He looked around frantically, checked under the table, then circled around several other tables.

I had expected him to go look for it somewhere else—in the bathroom or in his car—giving me time to sneak away, but he seemed to be circling the same tables over and over, his eyes widening in panic.

I sighed and approached him. "Is everything okay?"

"My bag! It was right here! Did you see it?"

"Did you check the kitchen?" I asked. "Or maybe the bathroom?"

"I would *never* leave my bag in the kitchen. And I wasn't even *in* the bathroom today." His voice croaked and a sad little squeak emitted from his nose.

"Hang on, is that the big gray bag?"

"Yes!"

"The one you had on your shoulder when you met me at the gate?"

"Yes… I mean… What?"

"You had a big gray bag on your shoulder. Remember?"

His eyes were unfocused as he tried to recall it. "I must have left it there," he said miserably.

"Yeah."

He glanced around him. "It's eight o'clock," he whispered. "The guests…"

"Do you want me to go grab it for you real quick?" I asked.

He gave me a sharp, grateful nod.

I ran outside and down the gravel path to the entrance. The first guests were already milling in, grand-looking men and women, some fussed over by personal servants, all dressed in fancy clothing and glittering jewelry. I approached the table with the seat placement cards. They were situated in rows on the table in front of the hostess, each folded into a neat looking V. A small stack of empty cards stood in the corner of the table, probably for last minute changes.

The hostess faced an elderly man, his arm intertwined in the arm of a woman about my age with an enormous cleavage.

"Name?" she asked.

I walked by the table and tripped, colliding with the young woman and knocking down some of the cards on the table. The woman shouted in outrage, while I stood up, apologizing profusely, helping the hostess rearrange the cards. I carefully palmed one of the empty cards, as well as a filled one, and the pen from the table. Then I slunk into the shadows. Hidden in the darkness, I took a look at the card in my hand. It said "Mr. Boris Vasiliev, Table Eighteen."

Copying the flourished handwriting as well as I could, I wrote "Baroness Fleurette van Dijk, Table Eighteen" on the empty card, and folded it into a carefully shaped V. I shoved Boris Vasiliev's card into my pocket. Then I returned to the table, where the hostess had just handed the placement card to the old man.

I approached the young woman, sidling by the table. "I just wanted to say I'm sorry again." My fingers flicked the V-shaped card onto the table. "I hope you're all right."

The woman shot me an icy look and nodded. I gave her an embarrassed smile, and then glanced at the hostess. She peered at me as if I was a snail inside her shoe. I'd made good impressions all around.

Walking back, I murmured, "Okay, Baroness, you're good to go."

"Wonderful, darling," Sinead's Dutch-inflected voice answered. "You heard her, Bente, you can start the car."

"Harutaka," I said. "Find the seating arrangement file and change Mr. Boris Vasiliev's name to the baroness. He was at table eighteen." That way, when poor Boris got here and began shouting for his seat, they wouldn't find out about the switch even if they checked with the computer.

"On it," Harutaka said.

I slunk back into the dining hall, where the first guests were already being seated. Unseen, I removed Jonathan's garment bag from under the table where I'd hidden it, and then sauntered over to him carrying it over my shoulder.

"There you go," I said. "It was right where you left it, by the front gate."

"Thanks," he muttered. "I'll just be a moment."

He rushed to the kitchen to change his shirt, and I took a long breath. The night was just getting started.

TWENTY-FOUR

I served the first few guests who sat down in the dining hall, while listening intently to my earphone. Sinead—or rather, Baroness Fleurette van Dijk—had just passed through the gate with no problem. The forgery of the invitation was flawless, and when they checked her name on the computer, it was there, just where Harutaka had put it.

"The couple at table fifty-seven both want martinis," I told the bartender.

"Sure," he said, smiling at me. "What are you doing later?"

"Going home to my boyfriend." I smiled thinly.

"Hello," the baroness' voice buzzed in my ear.

"Good evening," I heard the hostess reply. "Name?"

"Baroness Fleurette van Dijk."

"Here you are, madam, table eighteen. I hope you have a lovely evening. Your personal servants can wait in the servants' quarters, right over there."

The servants' quarters were in a separate structure, disconnected from the mansion. We had known this beforehand, and were prepared.

"Go on, darlings, I'll be fine," the baroness said. "Oh, Bente, would you please take my bag with you? I swear, the thing weighs a ton."

"Yes, ma'am," Kane's voice answered.

There was a moment of silence in the chat. I served the martinis to the elderly couple who had ordered them, smiling politely.

"Okay," Kane whispered. "Isabel and I are entering the servants' quarters, and Sinead is on her way to you. This place is unguarded."

"It doesn't need guards," Harutaka said. "Every inch of the quarters is visible on the security feeds. I promise you there's someone watching carefully to make sure none of the servants decides to take a walk."

I tensed as a man entered the dining hall and glared around him with piercing eyes. Maximillian Fuchs, the security chief. The vampire.

"Maximillian just entered the dining hall," I murmured.

"If you say so," Harutaka said. He couldn't see him in the security footage, of course.

"And here's the baroness," I added.

A lot of heads turned when Baroness Fleurette van Dijk entered the room. Dressed in a gorgeous scarlet dress with a glimmering translucent gray shawl on top, hands clad in feminine silk gloves, Sinead looked like a woman who could launch a thousand ships. She had the careless air of an aristocrat who was used to being the most sought-after person in the room. She glided with catlike grace to table eighteen and sat down, smiling at the other people at the table and introducing herself.

The vampire didn't even glance at her twice. He didn't care about beauty, or youth, or charm. She meant nothing to him. We would have to change that.

I began making my way toward Sinead the baroness when, ahead of me, I saw Jonathan hurrying toward her. I clenched my jaw, realizing he would reach her long before I would. Dammit! I needed to be the one serving her.

I flicked my wrist and my bracelet detached, the chain slinking into my palm. Almost imperceptibly, still walking toward Sinead, I tossed the chain forward. It coiled in the air, flying low, and entangled itself around Jonathan's feet. He yelped and tripped, slamming to the ground. Everyone turned their eyes to him as I crouched by him, the chain slinking up my sleeve, now hidden.

"Are you okay?" I asked.

"Something… tripped me!" he winced.

"Everyone is looking at you."

"Oh, god." His nose squeaked.

"Don't worry about it, just go to the kitchen for a bit. We've got you covered, chief." I winked at him, with the expression of a soldier covering for her beloved commander.

He nodded and I helped him to his feet. He limped away, and I sidled over to the baroness, who gazed at the events with an expression of mock horror.

"Is the poor man okay?" she asked me, her Dutch accent bordering on outrageous.

"Yes, ma'am. I'm sorry. His shoelaces were untied."

"I see." She sniffed. "All this chaos has made me thirsty. Tell me, do you people know how to make a Bloody Mary?"

"Yes ma'am."

"Good. Go light on the Worcestershire sauce, but don't skimp on the vodka." She flicked her hand at me imperiously.

"I'd like a glass of whiskey," the man sitting next to her said. "No rocks." He seemed distinctly pleased with himself for drinking straight whiskey.

"Vodka martini for me," the woman next to him added. She had a mouth that reminded me of an angry llama video I'd once seen. "With *four* olives please."

Because five olives would totally ruin her drink. Everyone thinks they're special. Then again, at this VIP banquet, everyone probably *was*.

"Coming right up." I smiled politely at them all and walked over to the bar. I gave the bartender the drink orders, and turned to watch the crowd.

Something was going on.

All heads were turned as a man entered the room. At first I couldn't see what was so interesting about him—just another man in an old-fashioned suit. He had a cigar between his lips, a plume of smoke drifting from his mouth. Then I realized the cigar was unlit. And the smoke kept coming.

This was Ddraig Goch, the dragon.

Though I had known that dragons could wear the shape of men when it suited them, I was still caught by surprise. Once I understood who he was, I noticed a hundred little details. His eyes, predatory and lizard-like, the irises huge and green. The subtle scales that ran down the back of his neck. His fingernails, much too long.

His smile. The smile of a god among ants. Of a predator surrounded by food.

He stopped every few steps to swap a few words with an acquaintance, to shake the hand of a duke, to nod politely at the French ambassador.

Did these people know who he was? Did they realize he could open his mouth and incinerate us all? I doubted it. If any of them noticed the unlit cigar, they probably assumed it was some sort of trick. Most of them just thought he was a very powerful businessman. A man who could change fortunes with his endless resources, topple governments, create kings.

And they were right. But he was more. Much more.

I glanced at Sinead, and our eyes met. Her eyes were full of excitement, and fear. This was the creature we were about to rob. It was complete insanity.

"There you go," the bartender said in a low voice, placing the drinks on the bar. "Man, to be that guy, huh? Must be great, knowing you're at the top of the food chain."

"Quite literally," I whispered to myself.

I twisted my right hand, and the vial hidden in my sleeve dropped into my palm. I popped the cap open with my thumb. Then I picked up the drinks, pouring the contents of the vial into Sinead's Bloody Mary. The crimson drops sank into the thick red drink, disappearing from sight.

I walked over to the table, placing the drinks in front of the guests. "One Bloody Mary. One vodka martini with *four* olives. And one whiskey, no rocks."

None of them thanked me, too busy with their hushed conversation. The man was telling the baroness and llama-face that he had heard Ddraig Goch had made his initial fortune by smuggling opium and blood diamonds to France. I rolled my eyes and moved away, approaching another table.

From the corner of my eye, I saw the Baroness chugging her Bloody Mary as if it was a contest. Good. The potion would take a few minutes to start working. The sooner she finished it, the better.

It was probably my finest work.

Vampires drink only blood. The very thought of consuming anything else is abhorrent to them. I couldn't spike the security director's drink with a truth serum.

So I spiked Sinead's blood instead.

The potion was aimed to do two things. First, it enhanced Sinead's blood's scent, hopefully making it a temptation Maximillian Fuchs couldn't ignore. Second, her blood now contained a mixture of truth serum and a soporific drug. It should make anyone drinking Sinead's blood woozy enough for her to pick his pocket for the keycard, and get the code to the vault door from him. If there was a Nobel prize for alchemical concoctions, this potion would be a potential candidate.

"Okay guys," I murmured under my breath. "The baroness just drank the potion. You should probably get out of the servants' quarters."

"Sure," Kane said. "Harutaka, can we leave?"

"Just one moment…" Harutaka said.

My heart pounded as I waited for Harutaka to do his magic. Kane and Isabel were being watched via the security cameras. Harutaka's job was to tinker with the feed, overriding it with older security footage, from before they were there, making them invisible to whomever monitored the feeds.

That was his main responsibility this evening—to make us digitally invisible.

"Okay," Harutaka said. "Just inserting a bit of static to mask the replacement... there we go. You two are invisible. Go forth and make trouble."

"We're out," Kane whispered.

Harutaka began murmuring instructions to Kane and Isabel, guiding them through the garden in a way that would avoid the patrols he followed via the untampered security feed. I tuned this out, focusing on my job. I glanced at Maximillian Fuchs. If he was sensing Sinead's blood scent, he didn't show any sign. I checked the time. Five minutes since she'd drunk the potion. It should have begun working by now. Was it not strong enough? Or was he much more in control than I had thought?

"Baroness, perhaps you should inspect that picture on the far wall," I murmured.

The painting I referred to was only six feet from the vampire. It should be enough.

The baroness smiled thinly as she listened to the man beside her talking. Then she placed her hands on the table, and said, "Excuse me for just a moment."

She got up, and made her way to the picture, her pace calm and certain. She sidled right past Maximillian Fuchs, and I focused on his eyes. A tiny frown. A fraction of head movement. And then he blinked, and looked away. *Damn it.*

"Baroness, can you get your heart rate up?" I asked.

"It's as high as can be, darling," she murmured. "I'm a bundle of nerves."

"The potion isn't strong enough. You'll have to get your chest closer to the vampire's nose."

"Closer? What do you want me to do, darling, shove my cleavage into his face?"

Maximillian began to pace the room, looking around, occasionally stopping to talk to someone. I clenched my jaw tightly. "Okay, go back to your seat, I have an idea."

I approached the bartender, trying to look much calmer than I felt. "I need a glass of red wine."

"For you, or one of the guests?" He winked at me.

"I definitely need one for me, but no, this one is for one of our esteemed guests."

"They have wine on the tables."

I cursed myself. Of course they did. "He's some kind of pretentious asshole. Said the acidity lingers too much."

The bartender rolled his eyes. "Oh god. Tell you what. I'll pour a glass of the cheapest wine we have here, and I bet you ten dollars he drinks it without noticing a damn thing."

"You're on." I smiled.

"Acidity my ass," he muttered, pouring the drink.

I picked up the glass and turned to look at the crowd. Maximillian was still making his rounds between the tables, and would reach Sinead's table in a few minutes. She was back in place, making conversation, and again, I couldn't see even a glimmer of nervousness in her.

I crossed the room, pacing myself so that I would reach the table just as Maximillian walked by it. I had to walk a bit slower than my usual pace, my heartbeats mismatched with my footsteps.

Thump-thump-thump, step, thump-thump, step, thump-thump-thump, step.

I was close enough to the vampire to see his predatory eyes, the whiteness of his hair, his ageless skin.

I tripped and my glass tipped, most of it spilling on the table, some splattering the baroness.

"Oh!" she said, and stood up in mock shock, her boobs thrust as closely to Maximillian Fuchs as she could possibly bring them.

He paused, and I saw the dazed look in his eyes as the enhanced blood scent hit him. Bingo.

"I'm so sorry, ma'am," I blubbered.

"It's quite all right." She flicked her fingers imperiously. Our eyes locked and I saw the twinkle in her eye, the rush we both felt.

Maximillian's attention snapped to me. "You clumsy oaf!" he hissed. The blood had brought out the predator in him. The animal. His eyes were brimming with bestial rage, and my heart dipped, suddenly thinking that instead of going for the bait, he would tear my throat wide open.

The baroness laid a hand on his wrist. "It's quite all right, sir." She smiled gently. "No harm done."

He blinked, his attention back to her. "I'm sorry for this incident, madam," he said. "Please allow me to escort you to a private room where you can clean up."

"Thank you, sir. I wish all men were as courteous as you."

He glanced at me, his eyes cold. "You're fired," he said. "Get out of here."

I did my best to look upset as I turned and left. In my ear, Harutaka whispered in excitement at our shared act. We had done it. Sinead was inside.

TWENTY-FIVE

J onathan accosted me as I tried to leave the kitchen.

"Where are you going?" He limped, and I felt an inkling of guilt, which dissipated once he added in an angry voice, "Get back in there. Now!"

"I was just fired," I grumbled, letting my voice quiver in indignation.

"What? By who? Only I can fire you!"

"That weird pale guy."

"Maximillian Fuchs?" He seemed to blanch.

"Yeah." I paused. "So he can't fire me? Would you mind talking to him? Because I could really use this job."

"Um…" Jonathan eyes frantically avoided mine. "I suppose if he fired you he had a good reason. I'm sorry, you have to leave."

I snorted and left the kitchen, slamming the door behind me.

Once I was out, Harutaka said, "Okay, Lou. Walk down to the gate. There's a guard looking at you right now. I'll tell you what to do."

I began striding toward the front gate. About midway, the path circled a fountain. There were yellow garden lights beaming around it, the water shimmering in the darkness. Just as I passed by it, all the lights around me suddenly died, plunging me into darkness.

"Okay," Harutaka's voice said, sharp in my ear. "Go east. Fast!"

I marched quickly down the garden, shrouded in Haru-taka's manufactured darkness.

"Good," Harutaka said. "Now cut north. You're not far from Kane and Isabel."

"What about Sinead?" I began walking back, the large structure's eastern corner in front of me.

"She's making her way through the mansion. I presume the vampire is with her, because she's talking to someone I can't see."

I reached the wall and began walking along it, picturing my location on the blueprints. I was near the place where we had agreed to meet, a small nook in which we could all stand without being seen by the patrolling guards.

"Freeze," Harutaka said. "Right there. One of the patrols is walking by. I don't think he can see you if you stand still."

Praying he was right, I didn't move a muscle. I heard the footsteps of the guard, saw the flashlight beam accompanying him near the outer wall. If he aimed it at me, he would see me easily. But he just pointed it ahead, to illuminate his way. After a tense minute, he was gone.

"Okay, go," Harutaka said. "Just a few more yards."

I almost ran those last steps, feeling giddy and nervous. Then a figure moved out of the shadows, and I stifled a scream.

"It's me," Isabel whispered. Behind her, I saw Kane, his back against the mansion wall. The location we had selected really was perfect. It could hardly be seen even if you searched for it. I looked up the wall, gauging the climb. It was completely smooth, with no handholds nearby, no windows or drainpipes to help. A very difficult climb for me. Probably impossible for Kane and Isabel. But this was the best location to do it unseen.

"Where's the rope and gloves?" I asked.

Kane moved forward, holding the baroness' handbag. He opened it, and took out three pairs of gloves. I slid mine on, flexing my fingers. Once we were inside, these would keep our fingerprints off everything.

Kane handed me a large coil of nylon rope. It had knots along its length, to make climbing easier.

I twisted my wrist and the silvery chain uncoiled from it, dropping to my gloved palm. I tied a small loop in the rope's end, and then touched the chain with it. It slithered and coiled around the loop.

"How does it know what you want it to do?" Kane asked, looking mesmerized.

"You tell me, you're the sorcerer."

"I've never heard of anything like it."

I took a step back, staring up, estimating the distance to the roof. Then I whirled the rope several times and let go. The chain, attached to the rope, flew upward. It arced over the roof, and landed beyond it, somewhere above. The rope jerked in my hand as the chain located something to latch itself to. Then it was still. I tugged. It held.

"One at a time," I said. "I'm last."

Isabel went first, grabbing the rope, and began climbing it nimbly.

"I was worried for you," Kane said. "It sounded like a bit of action took place there."

"Nothing I couldn't handle," I answered.

"I'm starting to think that's generally the case."

I looked away, trying to hide my embarrassed smile. "Harutaka, how are we doing?"

"Looking good," Harutaka said. "The baroness is in a large, comfortable-looking room on the third floor. She's sitting on a sofa, talking... I'm presuming she's talking to the vampire."

"Baroness? Are you okay?"

"She can't hear you," Harutaka interjected. "She muted the chat."

That made sense. The vampire's ears would be sharp enough to hear us through her earpiece.

"I'm up," Isabel said.

Kane grabbed the rope and began climbing, Sinead's bag on his shoulder. I half-expected him to struggle with it. He was much larger than Isabel, after all, and it would take a lot of strength to pull his body up the rope. But his movements were smooth and agile, and in a few seconds he was already ten feet up.

"I thought the vampire would lunge at her once they were out of sight," Harutaka said.

"I guess this one is gentlemanly," I answered.

"Aren't you worried he might... drink too much?"

"The tincture should make him woozy," I said, trying to keep the unease from my voice. "She should be able to pull back after a few seconds. He won't have a lot of time to drink."

"I'm on the roof." Kane sounded breathless. Strong or not, those cigarettes probably weren't helping his lungs.

I grabbed the rope and began scaling the wall. As a teenager I had practiced climbing daily, learning how to wedge my fingers into the smallest cracks, how to push myself up with only one limb, how to lunge for handholds. Climbing this knotted rope was a walk in the park. I shimmied up, enjoying the height and the rush.

Then a movement drew my eye. I glanced sideways. Through a small window, I gazed into a large, lavishly furnished room. There was a huge bed covered in silk bedsheets. An oak wardrobe, its surface carved with intricate designs. A large, comfortable sofa.

Maximillian Fuchs sat on the sofa, Sinead, the baroness, beside him.

She leaned toward him, murmuring something in his ear. He seemed hypnotized, the scent of her blood probably tantalizing him beyond belief. I doubted he understood a single word she said.

He whispered something, smiling. His fangs glittered in the light. The baroness cupped his cheek, gazing into his eyes. Then she lowered the front of her dress, uncovering the tops of her breasts. She tilted her head back and said one word. I read her lips. *Drink.*

He moved with lightning speed, one hand snaking around her, his face plunging to her chest, his fangs biting through her delicate skin. I let out a whimper of fear. Although I knew we had staged it, I suddenly felt insane for endangering my friend this way. Putting her in a room with a vampire, after spiking her blood to be more enticing—what was I thinking?

He drank in a frenzy, his body clenching with something that looked like pure passion. I counted the seconds. One… two… three… four…

It should be enough. I glanced at Sinead's face, expecting to see her expression alert as she prepared to pull him away.

She gazed at the ceiling, her eyes wide and blank, biting her lower lip in ecstasy. Something was wrong.

"What's going on?" Harutaka whispered in my ear. "She isn't pulling him away."

"He did something to her! She looks… drunk." I clenched my jaw. "Turn her voice chat on. We have to snap her out of it."

"I can't. Only she can turn it on."

"Damn it!" How many seconds had gone by? Ten? Fifteen? How much was he drinking from her? He'd kill her.

I hesitated, then thumped at the window.

Neither of them seemed to care. He sucked more and more. Was she becoming pale? I thumped the window again, harder. Nothing. She wrapped her hands around his head, pulling him *toward* her, instead of pushing him away. What the hell was happening? Horrified, I watched the vampire about to drain my friend dry. My heart beat wildly, my breathing shallow, a bitter taste in my mouth.

The fear pulsed in me, in my hands, and before I could stop it, my right hand burst into flames, burning the glove off instantly. I quickly let go of the rope, clutching it only with my left hand and my legs. An orange glowing spot materialized where the flame had touched it, a wisp of smoke rising from it. But it held.

My left hand became infernally hot as well. Pulling back my burning fist, I hit the window as hard as I could. I heard the glass crack slightly.

Sinead's eyes sharpened. She glanced at the window, saw my face, my blazing hand, then gaped downward, at the head of Maximillian Fuchs.

She yanked him back and pushed herself away. I let out a small breath of relief. The vampire seemed dazed, confused. My potion had done its job.

Sinead fumbled at her ear, and suddenly I could hear her heavy breathing in my earphone. She had unmuted the chat.

"I'm fine," she mumbled, sounding far from fine.

Her voice calmed me down enough to quench the flames on my hand. I could only hope none of the guards below had seen this momentary flicker of fire. I glanced at the vampire. "He isn't," I said. "He drank much more than he should have. He'll fall asleep in a few seconds. Get the combination from him, now!"

She nodded at me through the window, then turned her eyes to Maximillian.

"Maximillian," she said. "I have a question for you."

"Wha…?" His voice was heavy, sleepy.

"There's a combination to the vault's door, Maximillian. I want to know what it is."

"I shouldn't have drunk so much," he mumbled. "But you tasted so good. I need more." He fumbled toward her.

She gently held him back. "Soon, darling," she said. "But first I just need to know this one small thing. And then you can drink your fill. What's the combination to the vault door?"

"The combination?" His eyes were closing.

"That's right, darling. Just give me the combination."

"It's four digits."

"Okay. What are they?"

"It's… hang on. The room is spinning."

"You're very tired, Maximillian. Just give me the combination, and you can sleep."

"It's… six… three…"

He tumbled to the floor, his arms spread to the side, a trickle of Sinead's blood on his lip. He was unconscious, and he had given us only half the combination.

TWENTY-SIX

—◆—

Through the glass pane, my eyes met Sinead's. For a second, it seemed as if she were about to cry. Then her jaw clenched firmly, and she studied the unconscious vampire at her feet.

"Do you think we'll be able to wake him?" she asked, her voice soft in my earphone.

"Not likely. That was a powerful soporific, and he ingested a lot more than I had intended. Can you stand up?"

"Sure." She rose to her feet and then gasped, and wobbled.

"Sit down before you faint," I hissed at her. "You lost a lot of blood."

She sat back on the sofa. There were twin puncture marks on the top of her breast, and a trickle of blood ran down from it to her dress. She was definitely pale, and her eyes fluttered. She looked like she was about to faint, and my heart plunged. But then she stilled herself, palms on the sofa, and began breathing deeply, shutting her eyes.

"Take your time," I said.

"Said the girl hanging ten yards above the ground, waiting for me to move," she mumbled.

"I'm very comfortable here, don't worry about it." But now that she mentioned it, I suddenly noticed how tired my muscles were. I shifted my grip on the rope, transferring some of the weight to my legs. I would have to climb up to the roof soon.

"Okay." She opened her eyes. Very slowly, she stood up, stilling herself against the bedpost. She approached the unconscious Maximillian, and crouched by his side. Her movements were slow, and her fingers trembled. She began going through his clothing, finally retrieving a keycard from his right pants pocket.

"Okay, got it," she said.

"Good." Harutaka's voice buzzed in our ears. "Sinead, the door to the greenhouse is not far from where you are. There is no one on your floor, you're good."

"See you in a bit." I smiled at her encouragingly. Then I began climbing again. My muscles were trembling, but it was still an easy climb. In the background, I heard Harutaka guiding Sinead through the house, and her answers. Her voice sounded a bit more firm, or at least that's what I wanted to believe.

I reached the ledge of the roof in three seconds. Kane crouched above me and offered me his hand. I took it, and he hauled me up. For a moment we stood facing each other, him holding my right hand, his breath heavy and warm. Then I pulled away.

"Thanks. I need another glove."

He wordlessly produced a pair of gloves from the bag, and I took the one for my right hand. I'd anticipated this sort of accident as well, though this was the only spare we had.

I looked for the edge of the rope. It was attached to a small pipe on the roof's surface, my chain coiled tight around it. I grabbed the rope, and touched my chain gently. It quickly slid up my hand, and twisted back into a bracelet. I retied the rope to the pipe, this time without my chain. Then I began pulling it up.

"What will we do about the password?" Kane asked me.

"Plan B," I said shortly.

Isabel cleared her throat. "I told you, I don't know if it can be done."

"You can do it." Coiling the rope calmed my frayed nerves. I began feeling a bit better. The password was a small setback, nothing more. "Did you find the greenhouse door?"

"It's over there," Isabel said, pointing in the darkness.

I followed her finger with my eyes, saw the large glass dome of the dragon's greenhouse about twenty yards away. I finished coiling the rope and put it on the roof's surface. "Let's go."

I led the way, Kane and Isabel walking silently in tow. We reached the door and I peered inside through the glass. It was hard to see anything in the dark, but I spotted a murky figure making her way to us slowly. It was Sinead. She reached the door, and searched around her. Finally, she pressed a button on the wall, and the door clicked, opening slightly.

The way into the mansion was unlocked.

TWENTY-SEVEN

The greenhouse was humid and warm. The relief of being away from the cold night air evaporated almost instantly, replaced by a sense of stuffiness and discomfort. The others shuffled past me as I hugged Sinead gently.

"How are you holding up?" I asked in a low voice.

"A bit dizzy," she answered. "I'll be good once I rest a bit."

"You were amazing in there."

"Yeah, I was great, how I almost let him kill me." She seemed pale, shaken. "I couldn't stop him, Lou. For a few seconds, all I wanted was for him to keep drinking. I can't explain it."

"Vampires are rumored to have ways of making their victims docile. I guess the rumors are true." I squeezed her hand. "You did good."

She smiled weakly.

I looked around me. It was hard to see the plants in the dark, but I glimpsed strange shapes. Huge twisted cones, long toothy leaves, gnarled branches looking like claws. Some of the plants seemed almost to move in the darkness, leaning toward us, as if noticing the intruders. The atmosphere was oppressive, hostile.

"Okay." I glanced at my three companions. "Sinead will rest here. The rest of us go on to the vault door in the basement. Once we open the vault door—"

"*If* we open the door," Isabel said.

"We will. Once we do, Isabel will join Sinead. Both of you will go down the rope, assume the roles of the baroness and her personal assistant, and drive away. Kane and I will crack the safe, grab the scales and the box, and teleport to safety."

"My PowerPoint presentation explained it all much more succinctly." Sinead grumbled.

"We can all watch it again once we're out of here," I muttered. "Harutaka, how are we doing with the security guards in the manor?"

"There are still two in the dining hall, with the guests," he said. "One in the security room, watching the monitors, and a fourth patrolling the floors. But he seems to be spending a lot of the night in the security room with his friend. They've procured a bottle of wine from the banquet."

"Where's the dragon?"

"Still in the dining hall, talking to the attorney general."

"Has anyone noticed that the mansion's security chief is missing?"

"No… but if that patrol guard finds him unconscious on the floor, there might be questions."

"We'll take care of it," I said. I pictured the blueprints in my mind, and thought of the room where I had seen the vampire bite Sinead. I could find the way there easily. "The floor is empty, right?"

"So far."

"Let us know if that changes." I turned to Sinead and held out my hand. "Can I have the card please?"

"I almost forgot." She laughed shakily, and retrieved Maximillian's magnetic card from her pocket. She handed it to me. "Be careful."

"See you in an hour." I tucked the card into my own pocket.

I crossed the greenhouse, Kane and Isabel behind me. I did my best to keep my distance from the creepier-looking plants, imagining one of them suddenly snapping at me. At the far end of the greenhouse, I found the stairs leading to the third floor. Eight stairs. With each one, the familiar sense of exhilaration and excitement that came with breaking into someone's home intensified. It was difficult to acknowledge to myself that I had missed this feeling, the rush of knowing that getting caught here would mean prison or death, the giddy feeling of traipsing through someone else's home without his awareness or consent, his valuables a mere touch away.

And what valuables they were.

Dragons live for centuries. And they dedicate their entire lifetime to collecting *things*. But they weren't like typical hoarders, with rooms full of stacked newspapers, or balls of twine. No. They hoarded things of beauty and value. Every room we walked into was decorated with works of art, with cases displaying intricate pieces of jewelry. One room had a collection of Ming vases and other ceramics. Another had two curved swords crossing each other, hanging on the wall, their scabbards lined with jewels. Paintings hung on almost every wall, the colors vibrant, the details staggering.

The decorations weren't necessarily in good taste. One room had two paintings I guessed belonged to the Renaissance period, hanging next to a huge postmodern painting of a yellow square and a red dot. The room's carpet was Persian, and in the middle stood an enormous jade statue of an elephant. Dragons were known for their ferocity and attraction to treasures, not for their interior design capabilities. Ddraig Goch probably couldn't care less if a marble statue of a Greek goddess didn't match the Japanese swords that lined the walls in the room. In fact, maybe he liked it that way. Maybe it was just another way to demonstrate how he viewed us. After all, I didn't bother to decorate my bedroom in a way that matched the expectations of the occasional cockroach that visited it.

"Look at all these things," Kane said, staring wide-eyed at a jeweled crown in a display case.

"Don't touch anything," I reminded him. "He'll know."

He flashed me an irritated look, and I shrugged.

We finally reached the room of Maximillian Fuchs. He still lay on the floor, unconscious. The drug he had consumed should keep him sleeping for a few more hours at the very least.

I approached his inert body, motioning Kane to join me. He grabbed the vampire's feet, while I slid a hand under his neck.

His head instantly twisted to the side, the mouth gaping open, reaching for my forearm. I hissed in fear and pulled my hand back, letting his head drop to the floor. His mouth snapped several times, making sharp clicking sounds. His eyes were still shut, the body inert. Kane dropped the vampire's feet again, and we shared shocked glances.

"Jesus," I muttered.

"What is it?" Harutaka whispered in my ear.

He couldn't see the vampire, I remembered. "Looks like this thing's reflexes are still sharp, even when he's unconscious," I said. "We should probably stay away from his teeth."

We ended up pulling him up to the bed by his feet. It was clumsy work, and his head banged against the bedside twice.

He could blame only himself for the headache he would have when he woke up.

Once Maximillian Fuchs was comfortably sleeping in his bed (feet on his pillow, shoes still on) we turned to the stairs. I knew the layout of the mansion by heart and didn't hesitate as I strode across the hallway toward the stairs that would take us to the first floor. At one point, Isabel touched my shoulder and pointed upward. From the ceiling's corner, a tiny lens watched us. It made me think of Harutaka, looking at us on his monitor, verifying that any security feed nearby us was overridden with a loop of twenty-minutes-old footage, turning us digitally invisible. Without him, all the guards in the complex would have surrounded us by now.

We reached the stairs in less than a minute. They went down two floors, and would take us straight to the lobby on the first floor. We began to descend them in a hurry, when Harutaka's voice buzzed in the chat.

"Guys, the patrol just left the security room and is coming your way. Hide, now."

I had just reached the second floor, and dashed toward the closest door. I opened it to find a small bathroom. I slid inside and was shutting the door when it was pushed open violently, smacking me in the forehead.

Kane slid inside and swung the door closed. It made an audible click as it shut, and my heart sank.

"I think he heard that," Harutaka whispered.

We stood in the narrow space, our bodies inches from each other. I felt Kane's heavy breathing on my skin and realized I was clutching his left hand. Was I doing it to quiet him, or to calm myself? I wasn't sure, but I didn't let go. Very carefully, I turned my head and peered through the tiny crack in the door. I could spot slow, careful movement. The guard, as he crept toward us.

I couldn't really see his face; the crack was too narrow. Was he curious? Suspicious? Wary? Impossible to tell. But he was definitely coming our way. He had heard the door shut, and was investigating.

"He has his gun raised," Harutaka whispered.

Would I be able to disarm him with my chain before he shot? No chance. And even if I miraculously managed to, he could shout for help.

Very carefully, I lifted my left leg, leaning it against the opposite wall. Kane stared at me in confusion, his body wedged between my thighs, my leg touching his waist. I put a finger to my lips, and then gently leaned forward, my head brushing against his chin, and eased the Glock from my ankle holster.

Understanding blossomed on his face, mingled with worry. Needless to say, using a gun right now would alert everyone to our presence. I wasn't thrilled about it either. I peered through the crack and saw the guard almost at the door. My hands became hot, the fire threatening to burst free again.

The lights outside the bathroom suddenly flickered strangely. The guard paused. Another flicker. The light was turning on and off sporadically in a different room, somewhere behind the guard. I could glimpse movement as he turned around, saw his hand holding the submachine gun, fingers tensing at the grip.

The light kept flickering. On. Off. On. Off.

The guard moved away from the door, toward the light.

"I don't know how long I can distract him like this," Harutaka whispered in my ear. "Better get out now."

I signaled Kane, and he gently opened the door. He slid out the doorway, and I followed close behind. The guard was only ten feet away, creeping in the direction of the flickering light. It *looked* like someone was playing with the light switch. Which, in a sense, was exactly what was going on. Except the person toggling the light was almost a mile away, sitting by a computer.

Isabel materialized by my side. She had been hiding in the shadows, not far from the stairway. We crept downstairs, reached the lobby, and half ran to the hallway that led to the northern part of the mansion.

"That was fucking close," Kane whispered.

We found the stairway to the basement without any trouble. At the bottom waited a solid metal door, runes etched above it, a metal keypad by its side. It was the door to the vault.

TWENTY-EIGHT

I watched the door for a long moment, mentally cataloging the security measures I knew would be there. The keycard slot was to its right, and easy enough to deal with. Below the slot was a 10-digit pad for the combination. Several runes were inscribed above the door, intended to kill any intruder who opened the door. "Okay. The door is locked with a combination lock and a keycard. I have the keycard that Sinead took from Maximillian, but we have only half the combination. Isabel will figure the other half."

"How?" Kane asked.

"Lou thinks I can read it in the tea leaves," Isabel said.

Kane looked incredulous. "Can you?"

She hesitated. "Maybe. I have to be close to it. And I've never done something like this before."

"We have three tries," I pointed out. "And we just need two digits."

"It doesn't work like that, Lou. The psychic signs—"

I raised one finger. "Less talky-talky, more drinky-drinky."

Isabel rolled her eyes and unslung her backpack. She retrieved from it a metal cup, a thermos, and a bag of tea leaves.

"I don't believe this," Kane muttered.

"If you can counter the runes protecting the door while you're complaining, that would be great," I said. "Harutaka? Anything we should know about?"

"The patrol is on the third floor." Harutaka's voice was tense and excited. "The guard in the security room looks drunk. And they just rolled the desserts into the banquet."

"They're good desserts, too," I said, recalling the menu. My stomach rumbled.

Kane approached the door and examined the runes above the door. He traced his finger over them slowly, deep in thought. Isabel had put some tea leaves in the cup and added hot water. While she waited for the leaves to settle, she drew her tarot pack from her bag, and began to shuffle the cards.

"You think the cards will help?" I asked.

"I don't know, but I'll take any help I can get."

"Okay," Kane said. "This spell is a bit tricky and, uh… I need blood from a maid with a pure heart. Which one of you has a purer heart?"

"Isabel," I said, just as she said, "I do."

"Well, no arguments there, apparently." Kane grinned. He withdrew his pin. "Give me your palm."

She held out her hand and he took it gently. I glanced away, annoyed at myself for being annoyed. I checked my Glock. "Harutaka, what about Sinead?"

"I'm here," Sinead's voice interrupted. "Still in the greenhouse. I'll be happy to get out of this place."

"How are you feeling?"

"Like someone drank two pints of my blood."

"You're a champ," I muttered distractedly, looking back at Kane and Isabel. She sipped from her cup while frowning at her cards. Kane dabbed at the runes with Isabel's blood.

"Kane," Harutaka said. "That rune is the Eihwaz. You need more blood on it."

"I knew that," Kane grumbled.

Isabel upended the cup on the floor and studied the messy tea leaves.

"That one looks a bit like a three," I said.

"Lou, be quiet." She stared at the cup in concentration. "Maybe... seven. I need more tea." She began to prepare another cup.

I wanted to *do* something. To pick a lock, to creep through a room, to climb a wall. Waiting like this felt useless, and wrong.

Time went by. My stomach rumbled again. Kane chanted and the runes pulsed in an orange light. Isabel upended another cup, and studied the tea leaves for a long time.

"Guys?" Harutaka said. "I don't want to rush you, but the banquet is ending. People are starting to leave."

"Already?" I felt a wave of anxiety. "Don't these people know how to party?"

"These people definitely do *not* know how to party," Harutaka answered. "Once they leave, Ddraig Goch will probably go to sleep."

I swallowed, saying nothing. Ddraig Goch's bed was inside the vault, just beyond the door.

"There's so much here." Isabel's voice was faraway, her eyes half glazed as if in a trance. "Darkness, and misery. It's hard to see the numbers within this cloud of torment."

"The first two numbers are six and three," I said, quoting Maximillian's words.

"I know that, Lou. Try... six, three, seven, one."

I keyed in the four digits. A red LED blinked.

"Nope."

Isabel began to put more leaves into the cup.

"Isabel, there's no time."

"I need another reading. It's too vague. And the darkness is too strong. Where does it all come from?"

"The dragon, probably," I muttered. "Torment and misery sounds like what will happen to us once he catches us here."

The runes above the door flashed with a bright light, and then dimmed.

"Done," Kane said.

Isabel sipped her tea patiently, as we both stared at her.

"Can you… gulp faster?" Kane asked.

"It's very hot," Isabel said. "And if you rush the drink, you get a rushed future."

Kane looked at the door. "Maybe we can try six, three, one, seven?" he suggested. "She might've gotten the digits right, and the order wrong."

I folded my arms. "We have only two tries left."

Isabel stared into the three piles of tea slush with concentration. "Try six, three, seven, five."

I keyed in the combination, and the red LED blinked again.

"The dragon is leaving the dining hall," Harutaka warned. "I think you should pull out."

"Not yet," I answered, feeling as if my heart was about to burst. "Isabel? Please?"

"Six three five five," she said, uncertainty in her voice.

"Are you sure?"

"Try it."

I keyed in the combination.

A green LED blinked. I let out a shaky sigh and swiped the magnetic card. The door clicked open.

I gaped at Kane and Isabel in disbelief. "We did it. We're in the vault."

TWENTY-NINE

"Isabel."

She gazed at the tea leaves' slush piles, her forehead creased.

"Isabel!"

She glanced up. "What?"

"You need to go," I said. "Join Sinead and go to the car. We'll meet you in the offices of HHT."

"Yes… yes, of course."

She took one last look at the leaves, and rose to her feet.

"The patrol is back in the security room," Harutaka said. "Your way up is clear, Isabel."

"Do you have eyes on the dragon?" I asked.

"He's watching his guests leaving from the balcony upstairs. Hurry, Lou."

I pushed open the door. It was heavy and thick, hard to move, a metal door built to withstand crowbars and even explosives. When the crack was wide enough, I slid through it. Kane followed in my wake.

I stopped two steps into the vault, my jaw going slack.

All the valuables upstairs had been only a fraction of the dragon's possessions. And the rest were here. Piles of glittering coins, jewels, works of art, ancient weapons—all were scattered in the vast hall. It looked like one of Scrooge McDuck's vaults—enough treasures to swim in. Here, the dragon gave up on the pretense of order altogether. The treasures were littered around as if someone had taken fistfuls of them and just tossed them inside the vault, letting them land where they would.

But as my eyes ran across the room, I began seeing a strange pattern. The piles of treasure were lower in the center, their tops flat. In the corners they grew high, toppling on each other. This created a sort of crater in the center of the vault. And as my perception adjusted, I saw what this really was. It was a bed. The treasure was the bedsheets, crumpled and tossed to the corner, like I would do on a summer night. This was where the dragon slept. And once I understood that, another fact sunk in.

The dragon was huge.

I had been thinking of Ddraig Goch as the man I had seen in the banquet. Scary-looking, powerful, dangerous—sure. But a man. The thing that slept here was not a man. It was an enormous beast, its body spanning ten yards, maybe even more.

"How much treasure does one dragon need?" Kane asked in a hushed voice, and his words echoed in the vast vault.

"All the treasure," I said.

I tore my eyes from the glittering piles, and stared across the vault. There was a steel door, about two feet high, set into the wall. It was the dragon's safe. I touched Kane's arm, pointing. "There it is. Let's open it before the dragon returns."

As I crossed the room, I retrieved a small vial from the hidden pocket in my sleeve. I uncorked it and drank the contents, grimacing. It tasted like I imagined dirty socks would taste, if anyone was inclined to try.

I then reduced the volume of my earphone to the bare minimum. The concoction I'd just consumed would make my hearing sharp and sensitive. Harutaka's voice in my ear would sound like a roar once it kicked in.

Kane was already by the safe, muttering arcane whispers. The safe door was covered in runes. I wouldn't be able to touch it until he countered them. He rummaged in his pocket and retrieved a yellow parchment, placing it against the safe door.

The parchment's surface had a strange, swirly pattern on it, and as Kane spoke it began to shift and move in a mesmerizing spiral. After a while, the pattern began crawling off the page, intertwining itself between the runes on the safe, like an inky snake. Each rune it coiled around seemed to dim somehow, as if broken.

Kane's voice rose, almost to a shout. But no—I was just hearing it louder. My ears were a stethoscope now, the sound of the world enhanced. My earphone constantly emitted a faint annoying static crackle that I hadn't noticed before. From far beyond the room, I heard people speaking—the guests, bidding goodbye to each other. In the vault, there were thumping noises. Our hearts, beating almost in unison.

The chanting had stopped. The ink pattern had crawled through each and every one of the runes now, rendering them inert. Kane moved aside.

"You're up," he said, and the words pierced my skull like blades. I winced, and placed a finger on my lips, my eyes pleading for silence. He nodded in understanding.

I crouched by the safe, and gave the dial a few quick turns to reset it. Then I put my right ear to the safe door and began to turn the wheel slowly. The sounds of the rest of the world were distracting—Kane's breathing, the rustle of his coat as he moved, a lady with a sharp voice summoning her driver somewhere above me. I put my left hand on my left ear, blocking everything as much as I could, and kept turning the dial.

To crack a safe, one must find the contact area—a point between two numbers where there's a small click. I turned the dial slowly, one number at a time, and suddenly there it was, as loud as someone kicking a metal bucket. *Clank.* The contact area was between thirty-four and thirty-five. I turned the dial again, just to be sure. There it was. I was right.

Kane cleared his throat, a rumble, like a volcano. I glanced back at him, furious. He raised his palms apologetically.

Now I had to count the wheels. I parked the wheel opposite to the contact area and began turning the dial. Every time it went past the contact area I heard it again. *Clank—clank—clank.* I counted the clicks, praying for a small number. Three would be a dream come true. Four would be great. Five would mean we'd be here for at least half an hour. Six or more would be… terrible.

The dial went through the contact area without clicking. That was it. Four clicks. I breathed in relief. That meant it was a combination of four numbers.

Now it was time to find the four numbers. I began turning the dial again listening for the clicks, my mind noting the results. It was slow process, and I had to be sure I had it right. If I made a mistake here, we would waste a very long time. Finally, I had them all. Four numbers.

Five, twenty-five, forty-two, eighty-three.

"The dragon is moving," Harutaka said. Even at the low volume I tensed in pain as his voice tore through my ear canal.

"Just a few more minutes," I whispered. "Kane, get the circle."

I had the numbers, but I didn't know their order. It could be twenty-five, eighty-three, forty-two, five. Or it could be eighty-three, five, twenty-five, forty-two. Or any other combination. Four numbers gave me twenty-four possible combinations, and I would have to try them all. If it was a five-numbers safe, there would be one hundred and twenty combinations. Six numbers would mean seven hundred twenty combinations, and trying them would take all night.

Behind me, I heard loud scratching. Kane, drawing the teleportation circle on the floor.

I began trying the combinations one by one. Kane chanted, his voice loud and pounding, and I gritted my teeth. I was sure he was chanting as quietly as he could. By the eighth combination I was a bundle of nerves. What if I'd gotten it wrong? I wouldn't have time to start over. Thank god there were only four numbers.

Were there only four numbers? I began to doubt myself. Wasn't there a fifth click? That would change everything. That would...

Another click, much louder. It was my twelfth attempt. The safe was open. I backed away from it, amazed that it had worked. That it had *all* worked.

I pulled the safe door open and peered in. There were two items inside: a small, worn-looking leather pouch, and a black box, the size of my palm, its surface smooth. The box had a tiny lock, with an intricate key inserted in it. Kane and I just stared, frozen.

Once we touched either of them, the dragon would know.

"Is the circle ready?" I asked in a whisper.

"Yeah." He did his best to lower his voice.

"We move on the count of three. One…" I tensed, could hear Kane hold his breath. "Two…" Our heartbeats were racing, a cacophony of beating drums. "Three!"

I snatched the box. Kane took the pouch.

I could almost feel the heaviness of the gaze suddenly upon me. Somewhere above, Ddraig Goch paused, realizing there were intruders in his vault. That they were touching his most valuable possessions.

Almost instantly, the vault door clanged shut. I heard the mechanical clunking as it locked, shutting us inside. Trapped. The dragon must have moved it with his mind.

Something roared above us. I cried in pain, falling to my knees, hands on my ears, trying to mute the sounds. It was impossible. There was nothing beyond that roar. I couldn't think, couldn't talk, couldn't move.

And then the roar slowly dissipated.

Harutaka said something, but it was hard to hear him over the throb of my skull. "Dragon… moving… tore a gate… get out!"

I looked at Kane. He already stood in the circle. The pouch was in his left hand, and one huge, blue, gleaming scale lay atop his right palm. His lips were moving as he muttered incantations, tapping into the power in the dragon scale.

Another roar shook the mansion, and suddenly the world ruptured. A black, pulsing void appeared in the air just a few yards away from us, growing larger. A tear in space. The dragon was ripping apart dimensions to get to us.

The circle of charcoal began to glow with a blue light. It grew brighter as Kane kept chanting.

"Get into that circle!" Harutaka roared into my ear.

I stumbled to the circle, but it seemed small, almost too small. I stared at Kane standing in it, wondering if I was about to be abandoned here, stuck, as the dragon appeared. Was Kane going to leave me behind? Memories hit me full blast as I gazed at him, my head pounding and dizzy. Of a job years ago. Of the man I'd loved, who ran away without me. Of the handcuffs latching onto my wrists…

And then Kane shifted, moving aside slightly. He grabbed my arm and pulled me into the circle, hugging me close to him.

I could smell the scent of clove and pine. Kane's scent. Above me, his voice rose to a crescendo that vibrated through me.

Would the spell work? It *had* to work. In a minute, we would be safe and sound, in the conference room of HHT.

Beyond Kane's body, the void widened, and in it, the silhouette of the dragon's head began to materialize. Its jaw opened, emitting an ear-shattering roar. Harutaka yelled something, but it was impossible to hear, and Kane's voice shouted strange ancient words above the din as his arms pulled me to him, one around my waist, the other on the back of my neck, pressing my head to his chest.

A sharp glimmer, like lightning, and then, suddenly, darkness. We were out of the vault.

My shuddering breath of relief caught in my throat. We weren't in a conference room at all. We were surrounded by looming, dark shapes.

The shapes of plants.

THIRTY

For a few seconds I just stood frozen, petrified. Kane still held me tightly, protectively. His heartbeat was much louder now, with my ear to his chest. A fast, deep drumming sound.

Then I pulled away. "Where are we?"

"I don't know," Kane said. "Something went wrong. The dragon sensed the spell, he tried to pull us down. I took us as far as I could, but—"

"I have eyes on you!" Harutaka shouted, and I winced in pain. "You're in the damn greenhouse on the top of the mansion!"

A sudden loud, sharp noise screamed around us, the wail of a siren going off.

"Sinead, we need you to pick us up," I said, praying she was still on the chat.

"Turning the car around!" Her voice crackled above the sound of the car engine screaming. "I'll be there in ten minutes."

"Make it five, or we're dead."

"Get the hell out of there, guys," Harutaka said.

The night was flooded with lights as spotlights were suddenly lit. Enormous beams of light moved, searching. Somewhere in the distance, I heard men shouting. Below us, the dragon roared again. The cacophony in my ears was hard to bear.

We ran out of the greenhouse, the cold night wind momentarily taking my breath away. It was difficult to spot the roof's edge in the dark, and I had to crouch as I ran, my hands before me, my eyes straining to see. I reached the edge of the roof and spotted our rope, dangling down the wall, where Sinead and Isabel had left it after climbing down.

"Not there," Harutaka said. "That way is full of guards. And you'll never get out the front gate."

I looked around us. The roof spread in every direction, a mess of pipes, wires, and antennas. "Which way, then?"

"You have to go to the rear of the house. If you climb the wall there, you'll drop not far from Newton Street. Go to the western wall. There's a drainpipe alongside the wall. Only one guard is currently there."

I knelt by the rope. It was taut and quivering violently. Someone was climbing it. Leaning over the edge, I could spot the burly shape of a man, pulling himself up clumsily. I tried to untie the rope, but the weight of the man climbing it made it impossible. I unfurled my hand, and it burst into flames. I gripped the rope and it caught fire immediately, breaking, snapping and peeling my skin as it slid across my palm. It flew over the edge of the roof, its tip still burning. I heard shouting from the men below, and a loud crashing noise as whoever had climbed the rope fell to the ground.

"I have eyes on four men running up your way inside the mansion. They'll be on the roof in a few seconds," Harutaka said. "Get to the drainpipe, now!"

I ran, Kane by my side, jumping over a small chimney, and again over a discarded bucket, then whipping my head down to avoid a stretched wire.

"I'm about to kill the lights in the entire mansion," Harutaka said. "It'll buy you a few seconds until they figure out what's going on. But after that, they'll reset the system, and I'll be kicked out."

"Don't do it yet," I said, my voice shuddery as I leaped over a small platform. "I want your eyes. Sinead, what about the car?"

"I'm almost at Newton Street, but it's a long street," Sinead said. "Where should I go?"

"Stop fifty yards after the turn to Doublet Hill Road," Harutaka answered. "I'll guide Lou and Kane there."

"On it," Sinead answered.

We reached the edge of the roof, and I peered over. A long stretch of dark lawn stood between the mansion and the western wall; I estimated it to be about twenty or thirty yards. Behind the walls, I saw the shadowy outlines of the trees that surrounded the mansion. Newton Street was just beyond the trees, but I couldn't see it in the dark. Looking down, I spotted the drainpipe Harutaka had mentioned, running along the wall.

"The guards are in the greenhouse. I'm killing the lights," Harutaka said. "Lou, your hand!"

Damn! It was still burning. If Harutaka killed the lights now, I would be the only thing visible on the roof. Silhouettes of men moved urgently inside the greenhouse. I clenched my fist, breathing deeply, thinking of Tammi's chiming laughter. The fire died.

"Do it!" I barked.

Almost instantly, we were drowned in darkness. I heard multiple shouts as men scrambled to figure out what was going on.

I grabbed Kane's arm. "The pipe is here," I said in a low voice. "Go."

"You first."

"Don't go gallant on me, you idiot. If you fall, I don't want you taking me with you."

He hesitated, then crouched, following my guidance. He grabbed the drainpipe and began sliding down.

I heard the greenhouse door opening, the guards pouring onto the roof, shouting blindly, searching for us. I counted seconds, giving Kane time to reach the ground. One... two... three.

Then I vaulted over the wall and slid down.

It turned out I had overestimated Kane's ability to go down quickly. I hit his body as he was climbing down, about one floor aboveground. He tumbled down with a shout, and I jumped after him, landing on the soft grass.

"Are you okay?" I asked in a low voice.

"I think so," he groaned.

"Sinead, how are we doing with the getaway car?"

"On my way!" she shouted, the engine of the car roaring in the background. "Just one minute!"

"I doubt we have that long," Harutaka said. "A guard is on his way to the server room. He'll reset the system."

I helped Kane stand up. "Come on."

We ran to the wall, Kane limping.

"They just reset the system," Harutaka informed us. "I don't have eyes on you anymore. The lights will probably turn on in about... twenty seconds. And the security cameras."

A car screeched somewhere beyond the wall.

"Give me a lift," I said to Kane.

He hesitated for a moment, then interlaced his fingers to create a human ladder. I put my leg in it, and he gave me a boost up. I scrambled, my fingers feeling the edge of the wall, then pulled myself up. I vaulted over the iron poles at the top, landing on the other side, in the midst of bushes and trees. I could spot the dark shape of the road through the thick foliage.

I bolted to it, stumbling over a gnarled root, crashing into a tree trunk, careening to the road. The car was about dozen yards away, its lights bright. I waved at it, and its tires screeched as it drove over to me. Sinead and Isabel leaped out of the car.

"Rope!" I shouted.

Sinead popped the trunk, took out a coil of rope, threw it over to me. I ran back through the trees, breathing heavily. Heaving, I slung the rope over the wall, and it tightened as Kane gripped it and began climbing.

Lights flooded the mansion again. Sinead and Isabel were by my side, helping me pull the rope. Kane's face appeared over the wall, and he struggled to climb up. From behind, I heard people shouting.

He leaped over the wall, and his shirt snagged one of the iron spikes. There was a loud tearing sound, and he collapsed to the ground. Isabel and I grabbed him, hauling him to the car. Sinead held the door as Isabel and Kane crawled inside, then she slammed it behind them.

I opened the front passenger door just as Sinead slid behind the steering wheel.

"Buckle up!" she barked at me, and slammed her foot on the gas pedal.

With a lurch, our car hurtled into the night.

THIRTY-ONE

F or a while, none of us said anything. My heart hammered, my hearing still too sharp for comfort. The roads of Boston were mostly empty, traffic low this time of night. Twice, police cars with screaming sirens shot past us, probably on their way to the mansion of Ddraig Goch. Had the dragon found his unconscious security chief yet? Had they located the remnants of the burnt rope, tied on the roof? Had they checked the security feed from the evening, looking for us, only to find it had been deleted in its entirety?

I kept going over the evening in my mind. Did we leave anything behind that would lead them to us? No fingerprints, no security feed, no names. Despite the evening's mishaps, we'd handled ourselves well.

We had broken into a dragon's vault, stolen the contents of his safe, and gotten away with it.

I let out a small giggle, the sudden feeling of euphoria blooming in me. Then the giggle morphed into a rolling wave of laughter. Sinead joined me, and we both laughed helplessly, tears clouding my eyes. Just as I was about to calm down, I glanced into the rearview mirror and saw Kane's face as he gaped at us, aghast, which made me collapse into a new fit of laughter.

"Stop," Sinead begged amid bursts of laughter. "I'm going to pee myself."

"I also have to pee," Isabel said. "I drank a whole thermos of tea."

This made us start laughing all over again.

Sinead slowed down as we approached a gas station.

"What are you doing?" Kane asked, incredulous.

"We all need to pee," I said. "And some celebratory ice cream couldn't hurt."

"We have a dragon, a vampire, and the police looking for us," he pointed out. "And we have the dragon scales in the car, which are very incriminating—"

"We. Need. To. Pee," I explained again. "We'll only be a second."

If he argued, the sound of it was muffled as we slammed the car doors. Sinead and Isabel went to the bathroom while I

273

stayed outside, breathing in the smell of gasoline while watching the car, just to make sure Kane didn't decide he was better off running with the loot. When they came back, Sinead went inside the all-night store to get us some ice cream while I went to the bathroom. The tiny space stank, but I found a reasonably clean stall and peed for what felt like a blissful eternity.

When I came out, Sinead and Isabel were already back in the car. I quickly got in, smiling at Sinead.

"What did you get?" I asked.

"One container of chocolate chip cookie dough, and one peanut butter and fudge."

"I love you, Sinead."

"I love you too, sweetie." She started the car, and steered it back into the sparse night traffic. I turned on the radio, and Katy Perry's "Chained to the Rhythm" filled the silence. I raised the volume a notch and leaned back, shutting my eyes.

Something rumbled, followed by a patch of static, the radio hissing loudly. I tensed, could almost feel the predatory eyes from above.

"What was that?" Sinead asked.

Katy Perry was singing again, and I wanted to say it was a small earthquake, or distant thunder, but I knew better.

"The dragon," I said. "It's hunting for us."

Another rumble, a roar. Did I imagine it, or did the light outside dim as the dragon's body blocked the moonlight?

"Can it sense us?" Sinead asked. "Can it feel its scales?"

"I think we're about to find out," Kane said.

I could almost feel the oppressive weight of the dragon's searching gaze. I imagined him above us, watching the tiny car, so easy to incinerate with one breath. Or he could swoop down, pluck us up, fly with the car in its clutches back to his lair, where he would take us apart, limb by limb. Fear thrummed through my chest, and wisps of smoke floated from my palms. I tried to breathe deeply, to calm down, clenching my fists as if that would stop the fires from erupting.

What did the regular citizens of Boston make of it? Did they think it was some sort of plane, flying low above the city? Were people pointing at the sky, at a dark shape far above them, thinking it was some sort of bird? Did some of them suddenly realize there were monsters in the night, that the world was a much darker place than they had originally thought?

And then came another roar, much farther off. The dragon was flying away. He could not sense us, could not find us. I let a victorious smile materialize again. *We've done it.*

Harutaka reached the meeting room of the Hippopotamus Hunting Trips office a few minutes before us. When I walked inside, a huge smile broke across his face. It mirrored my own smile, and I approached him, thinking of shaking his hand, or maybe slapping him on the shoulder. Then Sinead whisked past me and caught Harutaka in a long, squeezing hug.

"You wonderful, magical man," she said, grinning at him. "You were amazing."

He gave her an embarrassed smile, and then glanced at the shopping bag in her hands. "Is this it?" he asked, his voice full of awe.

"Yes, Harutaka," she whispered. "The dragon's safe had so much more than you'd ever believe." She lay the bag on the table, and opened it to display the contents. "Not one, but *two* ice cream containers. One is peanut butter *and* fudge."

Harutaka blinked, and I let out a snort of laughter. Kane strode forward, shaking his head in amusement, and drew the leather pouch from his coat pocket. "I have the dragon scales right here."

He opened the pouch and poured its contents on the table. We all strained forward, looking at the small pile in awe.

"They're beautiful," I said softly.

On the smooth wooden table lay five scales. They seemed to be mostly blue, though they caught the light strangely, the color at the edges seeming to move and change constantly. Green, yellow, orange, red. Tear-shaped, each the approximate size of my palm. They glimmered hauntingly, emanating their own ghostly light.

Harutaka picked one up between thumb and forefinger, and raised it to the light. The scale's light reflected in his eyes, giving them an eerie color.

"What about the box?" Isabel suddenly asked. "Do you have it?"

"Yeah," I said, and pulled it from my pocket. I hesitated for a moment, then lay it on the table. I turned the key in the lock, and lifted the lid gently. Inside was a white crystal sitting atop a black velvet material. A thin golden chain was latched to it, a necklace, the crystal its pendant. I slid a finger under the necklace and lifted it, plucking the crystal pendant from its velvety home. A strange orange glow seemed to pulse inside the crystal, but I couldn't decide if it was really inside it, or simply a reflection of the ceiling light.

"Is this the Yliaster crystal?" Kane asked. "Is there a soul inside?" His voice was intense, almost eager.

"I don't know," I admitted. "As far as I know, the Yliaster crystal is a myth. I've never even seen a picture or drawing of one."

The crystal mesmerized me. I watched it, slowly convincing myself that the light really was within. A warm, pulsing, orange light. I had an urge to clasp the crystal, to touch it to my chest.

Instead I lowered it back to the box, closing the lid and locking it shut. This was Breadknife's part of the loot.

"It's ice cream time," Sinead declared. She opened both containers and retrieved a dozen plastic spoons from the shopping bag, which she scattered on the table. I picked up one, and dug into the peanut butter and fudge container. The world is flawed and full of pain, and the only perfect thing in it is peanut butter and fudge ice cream. I put it in my mouth and closed my eyes, inhaling through my nose, becoming one with the euphoria in my mouth.

After a few minutes of eating, Sinead left the room, and returned with a bottle of Jack Daniels and a stack of plastic cups. She poured half a cup for each of us and toasted to Ddraig Goch.

Ice cream and whiskey blend well.

It's a special kind of feeling, to come out victorious with a good team. It brings you closer, cements a special kind of connection that's hard to explain to outsiders. That night, as we sat and drank and ate ice cream, a pile of treasure on the table, my heart filled to the brim. Too often in my life I felt as if I were alone, but now I was part of a unique, wonderful group, and I had to blink away the tears of gratitude that materialized in my eyes.

At some point, when the ice cream was gone, Sinead put on music and, to my amazement, Harutaka jumped atop the table and began to dance. It was a clumsy sort of dancing, full of twisting limbs and ridiculous hops. Sinead, not one to be beaten at partying, joined him on the table and tried to teach him some basic salsa moves, to no apparent success. I just watched them, smiling, feeling content and calm and full of warmth.

Then a chilly breeze brushed my cheek. I glanced aside and saw Kane standing by the window, a cigarette in his hand. He had cranked the window slightly open, letting in the cold night air. He gazed outside, his body still. He took a drag on his cigarette, its tip glowing against the dark cityscape, and breathed a plume of smoke out the window.

"Scrumptious, isn't it?" Sinead whispered in my ear. She was kneeling on the table, her lips by my ear.

"What?"

"His ass. You were staring at it for the past minute."

"I was not!" Blood rushed to my face.

"Uh-huh." She stood back up, and shook her head despairingly at Harutaka's latest attempt at the basic salsa steps.

I got up and sidled over to Kane. My heart beat fast, and I told myself it was because of the sugar rush from the ice cream.

His eyes had a sad glint in them, as if his mind was somewhere far away. I thought of his tales about his sister, playing her viola. He had the same look now as he'd had then, when he'd told me about her.

"Would you mind giving me a drag of that?" I motioned to his cigarette.

He handed me the cigarette, our fingers brushing. "You said you didn't smoke."

"I don't." I put the cigarette between my lips, tasting the tobacco, knowing his lips had touched the same cigarette. I took a quick drag and returned it to him, keeping the smoke in my mouth, imagining that I tasted Kane and not just tobacco and smoke. "But I used to. And occasionally I get an urge." The smoke made my voice heavy, raspy.

"I hope this won't be the cigarette to make you fall off the wagon." He smiled at me. "These things can kill you."

"What do you think?" I gestured at the Boston cityscape. "Beats every other city, doesn't it?"

"Does it?" He took one last drag of the cigarette and dropped it in his almost empty plastic cup. "I prefer New York."

"Were you born in New York?"

"Born and raised."

"And your sister? Is she still there?"

He tensed. "Yes."

"What happened to her?"

"She's… in a coma."

"Oh, I'm sorry. How did it happen?"

His jaw tensed. "That's not something I want to talk about."

"With me?"

"With anyone."

I touched his arm gently. "If you ever change your mind—"

"Thanks, I won't."

We stared outside in silence. The city was a myriad of lights—radiating from windows and streetlights, the moon glowing from above. The plethora of lights reflected in the river below, a blurry second city, its skyscrapers pointed downward, the rippling shape of the moon below it.

"My parents died when I was eight," I said. "In a fire."

"I'm sorry."

"You probably think it's ironic. A girl whose hands regularly burst into flames lost her parents in a fire."

"I didn't think that, Lou."

"I was in school. And a teacher… I don't even know her name… she came into my classroom and escorted me out. She took me to the principal's office. It's probably hard to believe, knowing me now, but I was a good girl back then. I'd never been in the principal's office before. The principal sat with the woman from social services… I didn't know it back then, of course. She was a stranger, but the way she looked at me— as if she knew more about me than I knew myself… It chilled my blood. And they told me. That our house burned down, and my parents died."

Kane offered me his cigarette pack. I shook my head. He seemed about to take one for himself, but then changed his mind, sliding it back into his pocket.

"We had no living relatives, and my parents had no will. Not a lot of money, either. Many years later, I found out they had left me something"—a book, with alchemical recipes. The *Tenebris Scientiam*—"but back then I thought I had nothing left. You'd think I'd focus on the fact that I'd lost my parents, that they were gone forever, but I distinctly remember that there was a dress I had gotten for Christmas a few months before. And I kept asking about that dress. I was really upset about losing that dress. My mother loved it when I wore that dress."

I blinked a tear away, the memory as fresh and searing hot in my mind as the day it had happened.

"They put me in foster care. The first couple were fine, I guess, but I was still in shock, didn't talk to anyone. After a while, they moved me around and I ended up in the second house, where my foster father slapped me the first night for not answering a question he asked."

Kane's eyes sparked in anger, and I saw his reflex to lash out at the past, to find that man and make him pay, to shelter that scared, nine-year-old girl.

"After that... well. It wasn't the worst place I ended up in." I suddenly didn't feel like talking anymore.

"That sounds rough." Now it was his turn to touch my arm, his grip strengthening me.

"I guess it was." I cleared my throat, trying to banish the past. This was a night for celebrating, after all. I wiped my eyes. "So... what will you do now with your precious dragon scale?"

"I'll take it back to New York," he said. "I know someone who might be interested in it."

"Oh." I tried to ignore the wave of disappointment. "You're not staying here?"

"I don't think so. I have unfinished business in New York."

"Right."

"It was a pleasure to work with you, Lou Vitalis."

I was about to tell him I felt the same when he suddenly bent forward, tilting his head, his lips meeting mine. A small peck and he drew back, looking at me, gauging my reaction. I licked my lips, breathing heavily, and then leaned toward him, pulling him closer. Our lips met again, and my tongue darted, feeling for his.

He tasted of tobacco, and smoke, and man.

THIRTY-TWO

A paw scratched at my cheek, accompanied by the high-pitched whine of a canine with a full bladder. He had already tried several of his favorite methods—the nose licking, the incessant ear-barking, the back-and-forth bed-tromping. He was clearly getting desperate. And somewhere in my alcohol-marinated brain, I knew if I didn't wake up soon, I would have a puddle of pee in my bedroom.

I groaned, and pushed myself to a more-or-less sitting position. The events of last night were muddled in my brain. There had been more drinking after the kiss, and then some more kissing, and possible thigh-stroking, though that part could have been a dream. Then, disappointingly, Kane had turned out to be a gentleman and helped me into a cab.

I was pretty sure the thigh-stroking wasn't a dream.

I recalled stumbling home and struggling with my boots. The task of removing them before going to sleep seemed difficult and annoying. I seemed to have given up halfway, the left boot discarded on the floor, the right still on my foot. Pathetic.

"Mommy is disgusting," I told Magnus.

He barked excitedly, and wagged his tail, probably already thinking of all the fire hydrants he would defile this morning.

I dragged myself to the bathroom and brushed my teeth, Magnus barking at me from below, trying to explain that I was confused, the front door was the other way. Then I returned to the bedroom, and put on my left boot. I'd remove them both and confront my socks after Magnus had his walk.

I grabbed the leash and tried to tie Magnus, but he began spinning like a deranged dreidel, excited beyond belief at the prospect of a morning walk, and leashing him became impossible in my hungover state.

"Please stand still," I muttered with zero authority.

He stood still. A miracle. I clipped the leash on him and was about to leave, but then hesitated.

To Magnus' chagrin, I went to my lab. There, on the counter, stood the black box and the dragon scale. Last night I couldn't get the safe open to put them inside. Now I berated myself in anger. What if someone had broken in? I grabbed them both, went to the safe, and unlocked it, then put them in and shut it. Breadknife would come later, and I would give him the box and clarify that this was it. My debt was paid, and we were finally *done*.

Somewhere in my mind, the voice of a jaded, clear-headed Lou whispered that we weren't done, not so long as he could threaten to expose my identity to my daughter and her adoptive parents. But I ignored that voice. Breadknife would leave me alone. He had promised.

Endless questions about the job popped into my mind. Who was Breadknife's client, and what did he want with the crystal? Could it be the real Yliaster crystal? Did it hold a soul? Was that what he was after?

I reopened the safe, and took out the box. Yesterday it had seemed as if something was inside the crystal. But we had been giddy with excitement, feeling magic in the air. I wanted to look at the crystal in the morning light.

I turned the key in the lock. Opened the lid.

My heart sank.

The box was empty.

I pried the velvet out, thinking that maybe the crystal was somehow wedged underneath, but it wasn't. Underneath, all I could see was the dark surface of the box. I looked around the lab's floor, searching inanely, knowing I was ridiculous. The box was locked. There was no possible way it could have fallen out.

Only one explanation was possible, and it made me sick to consider. Someone had taken it last night. And the list of suspects was awfully short.

A sudden angry knock rapped on the shop's door. I jumped in fright, my mind whirring. It was too early for a customer, and the knock was too violent to be a welcome face. This was Breadknife and his goons, coming for the crystal they knew was here. What would he do when I told him it was missing? Burn the shop? Torture me to find out its location? Tell my daughter about me?

All three, perhaps?

My recently purchased backpack was in the corner of the room. I grabbed it and quickly threw the box inside. I grabbed some of the potions in reach, not knowing if I would be able to return here anytime soon.

Then I opened the lab door. Magnus stood outside, his head tilted quizzically. Miraculously, he wasn't barking at the door. I grabbed his leash, and walked him to the bedroom. Silently, I unlocked the window and pried it open. It squeaked noisily and I winced. It was raining outside, and I hoped the steady pattering of raindrops would mask the shrill sound.

Another knock on the door, and Breadknife's voice hollered, "Lou, open up!"

I took Magnus in my hands, and he tried to twist away.

"Stand still, boy," I whispered. "We're going for a walk."

Going for a walk were words he definitely understood. He wagged his tail once and stopped twisting. I eased him out the window, and then crawled out as well. The bedroom window led to a small alley, around the corner from the front door.

Not daring to even try and get a glimpse of Breadknife and his goons, I ran silently in the other direction. Magnus trotted after me, pausing to pee and yelping when I pulled him onward before he was able to finish his business.

Three blocks away, I took out my phone and called Sinead.

"Wha?" she answered.

"Are you home?" I asked. "I need to see you, now."

"I'm still at HHT. I slept on the table. I feel awful."

"I'm on my way." I hung up and began running again, with Magnus in tow.

THIRTY-THREE

Auntie Rosa is scared.

The words blossomed in my mind as I hurried down the streets of Boston, backpack on my shoulder, dragging Magnus after me. The rain pattered on my head, my shoulder, my face.

When I was six, my aunt was hospitalized. When I went with my mother to see her, she seemed strange. As if she were sleeping, but awake. She could hear us, occasionally nodded or glanced our way as Mom talked, but other than that, there was nothing. My aunt had always been a loud woman, quick to laugh. This dormant, dead-eyed thing frightened me, and I asked my mom what was wrong with her.

She had been medicated, my mom explained, to calm her down.

"Why?" I asked. As a child, *why* is the strongest word in your vocabulary. It can open doors, torrents of explanations, of ideas, of facts. It's a word that keeps things going. A perpetual motion machine.

"Because she had a nervous breakdown," my mom said after a long pause.

"What does that mean?"

"Auntie Rosa is scared, Lou."

And that was the gist of it. Auntie Rosa was so frightened, she had to be medicated. She preferred to be this unresponsive, sleepy thing.

"Scared of what?"

"Of everything."

It seemed so strange at the time, to think Rosa found the world such a scary place that she had to be sedated.

A few years later, the concept was not so alien. My second foster father had taught me that the world could be a scary place indeed.

And for a while, it was. Then, slowly, I began to take control of my life. I built something around me. I had a job, a store, some friends, a dog. A daughter I could catch a glimpse of every day.

Walking like a zombie, the sound of morning traffic loud in my ears, my head throbbing, I began to feel the fear crawling back. My phone rang, and I glanced at the display: *ABC.* Anthony Breadknife Cisternino. I didn't answer the phone. I had left the window open after my escape. They would break into the shop, and see that the dog was gone, that the window was open. Would they realize I'd fled?

Of course they would. This was Breadknife.

Auntie Rosa is scared, Lou.

I was good at keeping fear at bay. Fear, used correctly, is a drive, propelling you forward. If you fear something, you do what you can to stay away from it, or to fight it. But what if you fear more than one thing?

Scared of what?

Of everything.

It was probably the lack of sleep. The hangover. The after-effects of the potion I'd drunk the night before. But terror was taking root.

I had angered a dragon, and he had a vampire working for him. A criminal warlord was searching for me. He knew where I lived, where I worked, who my friends were, who my *daughter* was.

And speaking of friends, one of them had betrayed me. Had taken the crystal from the box. How could I trust *anyone*?

My phone rang again. Breadknife.

Auntie Rosa is scared.

Suddenly, the faces of the passersby in the street seemed hostile, suspicious. Breadknife had dozens, maybe hundreds of informants. Ddraig Goch could have realized the waitress the night before had disappeared just before the burglary. Maybe there were records, an image of my face somewhere. A police car went by, and reflexively, I hid my face, sudden tears of fear in my eyes.

My palms were hot, smoke rising from them. I tried to think of Tammi, of my parents, of anything, but my mind was a jumble, I couldn't concentrate. A flame flickered on my skin, then sizzled and died, the rain putting it out. I tried to breathe, looked around me. Did anyone notice? It didn't seem that way. But what if someone had? What if he was calling the police right now, telling them he'd seen a girl with smoke rising from her hands?

I let the rain drench my palms and crouched by a puddle, submerging my hands in it. The water grew warm with the heat. I got up, walked away, ignoring the stares of a couple standing under a shared umbrella.

I was walking to meet Sinead, but what if Sinead was the one who had stolen the crystal?

Sinead would never do that. I trusted her with my life.

But someone had, hadn't they? Could I really, honestly trust anyone?

When everything scares you, when nowhere is safe, the fear doesn't propel you forward. Instead, you try to draw into your shell, like a snail, waiting for the danger to pass. For the dragon and vampire and criminal warlord to lose interest and walk away.

My phone rang a third time. It was a number I didn't know, but I could guess who it was. Breadknife, using a phone belonging to one of his goons, trying to trick me into answering him.

My heart beat wildly in my chest, my breathing was short and quick, my vision narrowed to a small circle. Where was I going? What was I doing here? A tall building stood in front of me. I hazily recalled I needed to be here. On the thirteenth floor.

I stumbled into the elevator, picking up Magnus in my hands, trembling as the elevator rose. My phone blipped—a new text message. It's unhealthy to use the phone in an elevator because of cancer. But I took a look anyway.

A message from Breadknife. *You don't want to run from me, Lou.*

I lost a bit of time, my thoughts becoming a fractured thing. There was a glass door, on which there were letters. I tried to read them, but they swam in front of me, not making sense. The longest was Hippopotamus, which couldn't be right.

And then the glass door opened and Sinead was holding me in her arms and talking, asking me what was wrong while Magnus jumped around us, yipping. I tried to summarize the morning adventures, but I couldn't breathe, couldn't talk, tears were streaming down my cheeks, and flames flickered around my fingers.

Scared of what?

Of everything.

"How are you feeling?"

I sipped from the mug of ginger tea. I let it swirl around my tongue, considering my response, wondering if I would break into tears again if I spoke.

"Better," I finally said.

We were in Sinead's office. I vaguely remembered refusing to enter the meeting room. I wanted a small place. A shell I could retreat to. She had hugged me while I cried, shaking, trying to speak, to explain.

"Who the hell is Auntie Rosa?" Sinead now asked.

Clearly I hadn't done a very good job of explaining. "It doesn't matter. What matters is that someone took the crystal. And Breadknife wants it now."

"Why didn't you tell him what had happened?"

"What do you think he'd have done if I'd told him I lost the crystal?"

She didn't answer. We both knew how ruthless and cold Breadknife could be. How dangerous when angry. And though he wasn't particularly sadistic, the people who worked for him often were.

"So now what?"

"I need to get the crystal back, and get it to him," I said. "That's all he really cares about."

"And who took the crystal?"

"Kane did."

It was funny how I knew it without really thinking. The knowledge had been hiding in my brain the entire time. Waiting for someone to ask the question.

"He was *really* interested in the Yliaster crystal," I said. "He asked about it several times. And there's something he wasn't telling me. About his sister. She's in a coma, and he might think he could use the crystal to heal her."

"Did he have an opportunity?"

I thought about last night. Two drunken visits to the bathroom came to mind, as well as five minutes when I had nodded off on one of the chairs. "Yeah, several."

She shook her head. "I find it hard to believe. He seems like… a good guy."

"Who, then?"

She didn't answer.

"If he thought it would save his sister, he would take it, even if he was a good guy," I said. "Besides, both of us know that supposedly good guys turn out bad." I was exhausted from my earlier meltdown. I wished I could curl on the floor and go to sleep. But I couldn't.

"What are you going to do?" Sinead asked.

I stood up, placing the empty mug on the desk. My body felt shaky, and the feeling of dread still clung to my gut, but hiding here would only make things worse. "I'm going to get the crystal back."

THIRTY-FOUR

It's weird how sometimes holding a gun can inspire confidence. I'd been dreading this moment since I'd left the offices of HHT on my way to Kane's office. But, in front of his door, I pulled my gun from my backpack, and felt resolve harden my nerves. I tried the doorknob.

The door was locked.

Compared to a dragon's safe, this lock was child's play, and I had it open in less than three minutes. Kane's office, though empty, smelled like Kane. It brought back memories of the night before, of his lips on mine, his hand tracing my back, sliding downward.

I crushed those memories in anger, reminded myself how Kane had looked when I'd opened the box.

Is this the Yliaster crystal? Is there a soul inside?

I searched the office, checking the scattered papers on his desk, opening and closing drawers, looking for a clue to his whereabouts. Had he left already? Gone to New York? He could have gone last night, after the party, dragon scale and crystal in his pocket.

I could talk to Isabel. She could probably locate him. I'd seen her find a man using nothing more than his hat, a pendulum, and a map.

She'd need something that belonged to Kane. I glanced at the ashtray on the table, overflowing with stubs. Would that be enough? Probably not. She'd ask for something more personal.

I began tossing the office again. The desk drawers seemed to contain nothing more than random stationery, a week-old newspaper, and a receipt for two bottles of scotch. The papers on the desk were a mess. Some of them were related to our burglary—a photo of Ddraig Goch's mansion, a diagram of the runes that protected the vault's safe, several sketches of the circle Kane had used to teleport us. There was other stuff that meant nothing to me—a police report about a man who died of an overdose in New York; a hospital bill dated last month for someone named Georgia Baker; a note in his own handwriting that said *She has no clue*, the word "no" underlined three times. Was this note about me? I got the sense that it was, a fragment of Kane's thoughts. What did it refer to? To the fact that he had planned to steal the crystal all along?

I went through the drawers a third time, pulling each one out, looking behind them.

The second drawer had a small nylon bag taped to the back. I tore the tape, removing the bag, holding it up to the light. I recognized it almost instantly. It used to contain children's dreams. I had sold it to Ronald. I remembered seeing Kane there that night. What had he been doing there? It was nearly empty now. Had Kane used it?

I was staring at the bag, trying to think, when I heard footsteps. I drew my gun quietly and aimed it straight at the door, leaning against the desk, waiting.

A key scraped at the lock, but the door was unlocked and opened as soon as the key twisted. Kane gaped at it, confused, and for a moment didn't even see me. Then his eyes rose and met my gun barrel.

"Step in, close the door. Slowly," I said.

"Lou, what—"

"Do it. Now. Don't talk."

His eyes narrowed, morphing to a dark black. His stare did not waver. This was a man who had faced guns before. He closed the door behind him.

I kicked the chair over to him. It tumbled to the floor, clattering. "Sit down."

He picked up the chair and sat on it. Then his hand went to his pocket.

"Don't!"

"I was just going for my cigarettes," he said. His voice was chilly.

"You can do without, for once. Those things can kill you, remember?"

"Okay. What's going on?"

"Where is the crystal?"

"The crystal?"

He seemed genuinely taken aback. But I'd seen liars who could convince you of anything. Hell, my best friend was one. It didn't matter. If there's a person no one can lie to for long, it's an alchemist.

I shoved my hand into my pocket, and retrieved a copper vial. It was the truth serum I had brewed before we knew that Maximillian Fuchs was a vampire. I tossed it over to him.

"Drink that."

"No offense, but I don't think so."

"Do it, or I'll shoot you."

"You won't."

"You don't know me, Kane Underwood. You don't know what I'm capable of. The potion is a truth serum, nothing more. Drink it."

He hesitated, then uncorked the vial, and drank it all in one swig.

"Now what?"

"Now we wait." The truth serum was fast. It would start working in less than a minute.

"Lou, you've made a mistake. I didn't take the crystal. When did it go missing? Last night?"

I said nothing, just looking at him.

"Have you considered that Harutaka might have taken it? A man obsessed by chaos? A man who broke into the library of the Shades, for a reason none of us know?"

I concentrated on my breathing, keeping it steady. Waiting. I wanted to be convinced. Maybe it *was* Harutaka. That would mean that Kane, the mysterious, sexy man who made my chest feel warm when our eyes met, whose touch made me shiver in excitement, had not betrayed me. I *wanted* it to be true.

But I also remembered Kane's eyes when he'd seen the crystal. And the way he refused to talk about his sister. Besides, Harutaka hadn't known about the crystal beforehand—I'd never told him about it. Kane had known about it—I'd stupidly told him in a moment of weakness.

Kane's pupils were sharpening, and his entire posture became relaxed, tired. The truth serum was working.

"Kane, did you take the crystal from the box last night?"

A long pause. "No."

It was possible that the serum hadn't completely affected him yet. I waited for another minute. His eyes glazed over, becoming distant.

"Kane, did you take the crystal that we stole from the vault?"

"No. You did."

"Someone took it out of the box last night. Was it you?"

"No."

I bit my lip. Was I wrong? Was it really Harutaka?

"You have the distilled dreams I made. Why do you have them?"

"Because I needed to stop the supply."

My phone blipped with the sound of a new message, and I ignored it. "What supply?"

"The supply of the drug to New York."

I blinked. He made no sense. "What drug?"

"Ice dream."

The frustrating thing about the truth serum was that people weren't really engaged in the conversation. They just reacted to questions. It was up to me to make sense of Kane's answers. I decided to change tack.

"Do you know where the crystal is?"

"No."

"Can you guess where it is?"

"I thought you had it."

"Why were you so interested in the crystal?"

A pause. I waited. His fists clenched.

"Kane, answer me. Why were you so interested in the Yli-aster crystal? You kept asking about it."

I saw something in his eye. A glint of consciousness. He was still trying to take control of the conversation. He spoke slowly, as if each word was a huge strain. "Lou. I did not… take the crystal. This is what… you wanted… to know. My… interest… is my own."

"This is about your sister. You were interested in the crystal to help your sister?"

A point-blank question he couldn't ignore, couldn't talk around. "Yes." He clenched his jaw tightly, as if trying to prevent words from emerging.

But as strong as he was, I was a superior alchemist. And my serum was in his veins. A little voice in my mind begged me to let it go. Kane hadn't betrayed me, and he was entitled to his own secrets. Questioning him about his sister under the influence of the drug wasn't right.

But I was curious. And I told myself that perhaps his secret would help me track the crystal somehow.

"What happened to your sister? Why is she in a coma?"

For a moment all his body strained, and then he slumped, defeated. "Her soul is gone. I sold it."

I stared at him, aghast.

"She was dying of cancer. I summoned a demon, to cut a deal with him. It was quite a good deal. My soul for my sister's life. When he gave me the contract, I read it carefully, and signed. I was bloated with self-importance, thought I was too clever to be tricked by a demon. Assumed my soul was a huge prize for him."

"Okay, stop," I said. I had pried into the man's hidden past, uncovering his shame and hurt. For nothing more than curiosity.

He smiled at me, a joyless, angry smile. "Didn't you want the truth? Then listen to all of it. After we signed, he healed her body. And then he left, leaving her asleep. She never woke up. Her body is a husk. Her soul is gone, stolen. I had signed it off. That's the real prize. My soul was worthless, the soul of a jaded, angry man. Her soul was pure. And in my stupidity and cockiness, I had given it away."

His face was deflated, suddenly tired and sad. "Are you done with your questions? I didn't steal your crystal, Lou Vitalis."

I nodded, hating myself. I retrieved a fix-it-all from my pocket and approached him with it. "Drink this," I said, my voice hoarse. "It's an antidote to the truth serum."

He took it from my hand, taking care to avoid touching me. He uncorked it and drank the contents, his eyes never leaving mine.

We both stood, looking at each other. Slowly, his eyes swam into focus, the truth serum's effect fading.

"Get the hell out, Vitalis," he said. "Leave me alone."

Perhaps I should have apologized, but forcing him like that suddenly felt too intrusive for a simple apology. Instead I walked to the door. I took out my phone on the way out, more as a way to avoid Kane's eyes than anything else. One new message from Breadknife. An image. I opened it, stared at it, trying to understand what was in front of my eyes.

Then I stumbled, the strength seeping out of my muscles. I grabbed the door handle, trying to steady myself, the phone tumbling from my fingers, facing up. Smoke began curling from my palms, a flicker of a flame.

"What is it, Vitalis?" Kane's cold voice asked behind me. "Need help opening the door?"

"Breadknife." My voice was hollow, empty of the turmoil in my gut. "He kidnapped my daughter."

THIRTY-FIVE

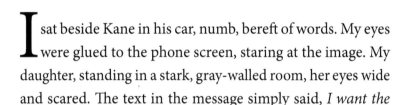

I sat beside Kane in his car, numb, bereft of words. My eyes were glued to the phone screen, staring at the image. My daughter, standing in a stark, gray-walled room, her eyes wide and scared. The text in the message simply said, *I want the box. You have 24 hours.*

I tried to convince myself that it was a clever image editing trick. He had taken a photo of Tammi in the street and changed it. Perhaps he had used a filter called *kidnapped*, or maybe he had one of his computer kids change it with Photoshop. Wasn't there a strange difference in the image lighting, as if my daughter and the background didn't match? Didn't her face appear unnatural, as if the image had been manipulated?

But I knew the truth. Her face seemed unnatural because I'd never seen her scared before. The background didn't match because I couldn't imagine my daughter in such a place, held by this monstrous man.

"Here it is," Kane said, his tone grave.

I had asked him to take me to my daughter's address, hoping to see her already back from school. I had intended to knock on the door, throw caution to the wind, just to make sure everything was all right. But there was no need. There were two police cars parked in front of the house. In the window, I caught sight of Jane, Tammi's adoptive mother, staring outside, her face streaked with tears. Her gaze was desperate, as if she hoped Tammi would suddenly materialize in the street, unharmed.

"Drive on," I said, my voice hoarse.

"Don't you want to talk to the police?"

I shook my head. "ABC has informants in the police. If he finds out… if he even smells a whiff of cops…" I couldn't finish the sentence. Couldn't utter the possibility that my daughter would be harmed.

"Where to, then?"

"Park around the next corner. Please."

I thought he would argue, would try to figure out what my plan was, but he didn't. He followed my instructions, turned right at the next intersection, pulled up out of the cops' view.

I opened my contact list. He was always on top, his nickname dictating his position in any alphabetized list. I hit the contact *ABC*.

Three rings, and he answered. His voice lacked any pretense of warmth, of pleasantry.

"Lou Vitalis. We had a deal."

"I didn't break it. I was about to deliver the box to you."

"And instead you disappeared. Fled through the window when we knocked on your door. That was unwise, Vitalis. I don't like betrayal. You have something precious of mine. And I have something precious of yours."

"Don't hurt her." I meant it to sound threatening. A Liam Neeson moment, where I let him know that if he hurt my daughter I would find him and kill him. Instead, my words were broken, scared. I was pleading.

"You shouldn't be worried about it at all. We can meet right now if you want. You'll give me the box with the crystal, and I'll give you your daughter, still unharmed."

Still unharmed. I shut my eyes.

"I don't have the crystal on me."

"You sold it to someone else. That's why you fled when we came for it."

Once, when I still worked for him, Breadknife had found out that one of the boys had snitched. Nelson, only fourteen, had been persuaded by the police to give them a bit of information, enough to start building a case against Breadknife. However, they didn't know that one of them was on Breadknife's payroll. Nelson's betrayal was exposed. ABC summoned all of us to let us know. His voice had a strange property to it, as if it was the only thing standing between us and an erupting volcano. It trembled and shook in a manner I found terrifying. And Nelson disappeared, of course, rumors of the manner of his death fueling many nights of hushed whispers.

Breadknife's voice now had the same tremor.

"I didn't sell it to anyone," I blurted. "It..." What would he do if he found out it was stolen from me? Would he even believe me? What would happen to my daughter? No. He couldn't know that. I had to buy some time. "It's in a safe place. I was afraid the dragon would find me, so I hid it."

"Hid it where?" The rage was still there, slightly more in control.

"I'll get it to you," I said. "I need more time."

"You have until tomorrow morning, Vitalis." The line went dead.

I breathed hard, my fingers trembling.

"We need to find Harutaka. Get the crystal back from him."

"We don't know where he is," Kane pointed out. "I haven't seen him since last night. We have no way to contact him."

Just like he intended. "Isabel will be able to find him," I said, desperately believing that was true. "She lives nearby."

As I guided Kane through the streets of Roxbury, I tried to map out my course of action. If Isabel could find Harutaka, I would go to him, armed with everything I had, get the crystal back and deliver it to Breadknife. If he received his precious crystal, he would let my daughter go.

But what if Isabel couldn't find him? Harutaka was clever, and knew of Isabel's powers. Perhaps he could find a way to hide.

Then I would ask her to locate my daughter instead. We could go to Jane, ask her for Tammi's belongings. Surely Isabel would be able to find her. And then I would free her. Somehow.

I had a feeling that something was wrong as the car got close to Isabel's shop. The door was hanging slightly open, a crack of darkness. Even as Kane pulled up to the curb, I was already pushing the passenger door open and leaping out, barging into Isabel's shop.

"Isabel? Isabel!" My shouts hung in the air, unanswered. My eyes slowly got used to the shop's dark gloom, and my feeling of dread grew. The floor was littered with shards of glass, papers, books, and bits of cloth. Isabel's wooden furniture had been toppled and smashed. Almost nothing in the shop remained whole.

In the corner, a small limp form was curled, inert. I rushed to it, a sob in my throat as I saw it was Isabel. Her face was bloody and bruised, her hair tangled, her clothing torn. She lay in a fetal position, as if she had been trying to protect herself from the beating. Her right hand was outstretched, two of the fingers twisted at unnatural angles. I was relieved to see her chest rising and falling—she was breathing. But when I whispered in her ear, tried to shake her gently, I got no response.

This was ABC's doing, I knew, and a molten kernel of pure rage blossomed inside me. He should pay for what he'd done to my friend.

"Is she alive?" Kane was by my side, horror and worry in his voice.

"Barely," I answered. "ABC got to her. He probably tried to get her to tell him where I was. Maybe he asked her to find me for him."

"I'm calling an ambulance," Kane said.

I nodded distractedly, caressing Isabel's hair, not daring to move her. "Call Sinead too. Tell her to get here."

Kane spoke urgently on the phone behind me. I tuned him out, focusing on Isabel, whispering in her ear, apologizing, begging her to wake up, promising vengeance. She was lying amid her tarot cards, which had been scattered on the floor.

One drew my eye, the image on it disturbing. It was the card of the Lovers, but it looked wrong. Different.

I picked it up and stared at it. The nude man and woman stood across from each other, as before. But above them stood a strange creature, its body a mass of darkness. The couple's expressions were masks of pain and fear. Their bodies were etched with scars and wounds.

I picked up another card, the High Priestess. The woman in it was fighting off a dark creature as it slashed her with its claws, her cheek torn and bleeding.

The Empress was dead, several shadowy creatures looming around her body. The Fool cried as a creature tormented him with a barbed blade. The Emperor sat in mute horror as creatures committed atrocities around him.

"Sinead is on her way," Kane said behind me. "So is the ambulance. What is that?"

"It's the future," I answered. "It's the future Isabel saw."

THIRTY-SIX

W e sat in Isabel's torn up shop. The ambulance had gotten there first, Sinead a few minutes after, just in time to see Isabel carried out on a stretcher.

I gazed at the floor. There were specks of blood everywhere, a reminder of what Isabel had gone through in here mere hours before. Sinead was picking things up, trying to busy herself by restoring a shred of order to the chaos around us. Kane smoked a cigarette.

"Are you sure it was ABC who did this?" he asked.

I bit my lip. "Who else could it have been?"

"Harutaka. Trying to make sure we didn't find him like we planned to."

"Then why beat her up and ruin the shop? Why not kill her instead? Whoever did this wanted something from her. It was Breadknife. And he wanted me."

"He called me several times after you left," Sinead said. "I didn't answer. I haven't been home yet."

"He realized I was gone," I said. "That I was hiding from him. He went for Isabel and Sinead, because he knows they're close to me. He couldn't find Sinead, but he found Isabel, beat her up, bashed up her store. And then he… went for my daughter."

"He *what*?" Sinead snapped.

I showed her the message he had sent me on the phone. Her eyes widened with horror.

"There's something about this crystal," I said. "I've never seen him that obsessed about anything."

"What does he want to do with it?" Sinead asked.

"I don't know. But I have to get it to him. He has Tammi. He'll hurt her if I don't hand it over."

"Is there a way we can find Harutaka without Isabel?" Kane asked.

"I can't think of a way…" I tried to think of a solution. "Can you create some sort of… forgery? I don't know, something that looks like the crystal? An illusion?"

Kane nodded slowly. "Yes, but I'd need the original to do it."

I groaned. "That doesn't help us, then. We still need to find the crystal."

"I can ask around," Sinead suggested. "Maybe someone knows where Harutaka is. And hopefully Isabel will wake up and help us find him."

"If they hadn't hurt her…" My words faded as I gazed at the cards scattered on the floor.

"Lou? What is it?" Kane asked.

"What did Isabel ask the cards?" I pointed at the twisted images strewn on the floor. "She wanted to know something. Something specific. What was it?"

"Couldn't she have just… asked about the future?"

I shook my head. "Isabel always looks for specific answers. She doesn't believe in a generic pointless reading."

I suddenly recalled what she'd said last night when we were breaking into the vault. *Darkness, and misery.* She couldn't see the numbers because of the suffering.

She had seen something in the tea leaves. Something terrible. Thinking back, she had been distracted for the rest of the night. Hardly speaking, her mind somewhere else. When we had celebrated our success, she had remained silent. Whatever she had seen had worried her.

But she did ask about the box. Asked where it was. The truth suddenly hit me. Harutaka hadn't taken the crystal after all.

"Isabel saw the future when she read the tea leaves last night," I said. "She saw something that scared her. She saw…"

I gestured at the cards. "This. Or something like it. Maybe it wasn't entirely clear. But she saw something very bad approaching. And it had to do with the crystal."

"*She* took the crystal," Kane said.

"She was worried that whatever Breadknife was about to do with it would result in this. So she took it, probably just to buy time, and then came home, and began reading the cards to see what he wanted to do with the crystal. And *this* is what she saw. Somehow, if Breadknife gets hold of the crystal, it will unleash... whatever this is."

"But if she took the crystal, and Breadknife was here, he might have found it," Sinead pointed out. "So he would have it already."

I shook my head. "He came here before he kidnapped my daughter, I'm sure of it. That means he still thinks *I* have the crystal. Isabel must have hidden it somewhere."

Kane looked around the broken store. "Well, they would have found it, if it was here."

"It's not here," I said. "It's in her family's mausoleum."

THIRTY-SEVEN

The sun was setting, its rays filtering through the brown and red leaves of the trees in Forest Hill Cemetery. Kane and I walked down Canterbury Lane, glancing around us, waiting for a safe moment to hop over the cemetery's fence. It was past visiting hours and the cemetery was closed. I would have waited until night settled, but I wasn't sure I could find my way to Isabel's family's mausoleum in the darkness. In fact, I wasn't convinced I could find my way there during the day, either.

Sinead was in the hospital, waiting by Isabel's side. The doctors said she wasn't in immediate danger, but were keeping her sedated. Our hopes that she would be able to guide us to the crystal were evaporating. We would have to trust my hunch that it was in the mausoleum, and my ability to find the place by following my hazy memories from our childhood.

I shivered, but not from the cold. I didn't want to be here. I didn't want to touch those memories, that dark time of my life. Did other people have that part in their past? A cluster of memories that felt like a stormy sea that would wash over you and drown you if you waded close to it?

Most kids who lived on the streets surely did.

I pushed my apprehension away and glanced at Kane. He gazed at the cemetery, avoiding my eyes. I followed his stare to the cracked gray tombstones protruding from the thick layer of brown leaves. The graves were scattered in a seemingly random manner, some bunched close together, some standing alone. I turned my eyes back to him.

"Thanks for coming with me," I said. "For helping me after..." I couldn't end my sentence.

He nodded curtly. "Let's find this thing and get your daughter back."

I didn't correct him, didn't say I wasn't getting her *back*, I was simply trying to save her life.

"Where is the mausoleum, exactly?" he asked.

"I don't remember... yet."

"Better figure it out."

"Yeah." Would I? How long had I left those memories untouched, to rot and crumble and dissipate? Were they even still there, hidden in my skull?

I glanced to both sides. No traffic. No dog walkers. It was time. "Come on."

I went to the waist-high fence. With practiced ease, I climbed it and hopped—

—to the other side, Isabel already waiting for us impatiently in the cemetery grounds, her hands in her pockets, her hair a tangle of dreadlocks. There was a light drizzle, just enough to make it a bad night to sleep outside. Usually, we'd go to a shelter, but Sinead had found a stray kitten, which she was looking after. The shelters wouldn't let us in with a pet. And then Isabel, staring into the distance, had said she knew of a safe place.

"Lou, can you help me with her?" Sinead said, holding out the small bundle. I took it from her gingerly. The bundle meowed piteously. Sinead had wrapped the kitten in a blanket from her pack. The rest of her pack was slung on her back, along with her guitar. She always carried more than the rest of us. She would joke that while Isabel and I were homeless, she was a snail, her home on her back.

She climbed over the fence and jumped, landing in the wet grass, the leaves crunching under her feet.

"Okay, you can hand her back."

I did, hesitating just for a moment. We kept telling Sinead the cat was nothing but trouble, but now, holding her, I realized there was something special about her. She was so helpless, so small, so light in my hands. She wasn't something one could simply abandon.

"Okay." I hunched my shoulders against the rain. "Where to, O wise one?"

"Through here." Isabel began to cross the long stretch of grass. Sinead and I walked side by side, following her, passing near a tall gravestone shaped like a—

—cone, an intricate engraving of a cross on top. I was lowering my head, as if trying to protect my face from a rain that did not exist. I looked around me, trying to remember the exact path, but it was impossible. Like trying to remember a dream that was already fleeting away. I walked over the leaf-covered ground, smelling the unmistakable scent of the cemetery, a smell of wet earth and of foliage. The stench of the city was somehow left outside the fence, among the living.

"We used to come here some nights," I said. "It was safer than sleeping in the streets; we weren't hassled by cops or threatened by drug addicts."

"You were homeless?" Kane's voice was flat, but there was an edge of curiosity there. He was still angry, but he wanted to know more. And I wanted to talk. I'd forced Kane to reveal his past. Telling him about myself would, perhaps, be the first step in making amends.

"Yeah. Sinead, Isabel, and me. Before we joined Bread-knife's gang." Focusing on the memories wasn't only helping me find the way. It was keeping the fear at bay. I let them flood my mind—images, smells, and sounds from long ago.

"And you slept here? In the cemetery?"

"The dead didn't bother us." *Not usually.* "We could sleep deeply here. When you sleep on the street, you never really sleep well. You're always tense, listening to faint sounds, trying to figure out if someone is coming for your stuff, or for your body. But here, there was no one. It was peaceful."

"Peaceful," Kane repeated.

I let out a small smile, remembering. "Sinead had a small kitten. So tiny. Sinead called her Trouble, because we kept telling her she was only trouble."

"Wasn't it cold? Living in the street, in Boston?"

"You wouldn't believe how cold it could get."

I brushed my fingers against one of the—

—gravestones, looking at the name. Anne Rose. Her remains were here, somewhere below. Along with countless others.

"Did you ever hear the story about the lady in black?" Sinead asked me.

I looked at her. She wore the purple parka she had received one morning from an old lady who felt sorry for her. Underneath, she had her orange T-shirt on. Sinead had three shirts. The orange T-shirt with the torn collar, the off-white T-shirt with the ketchup stain, and the green T-shirt with the faded print of an alien smoking a joint. Lately she avoided the green one. She had been wearing it when a drunk had lunged at her and groped her, and she said she could still smell him on it.

"What lady?"

"The lady in black. So this Confederate soldier was being held prisoner at Fort… what's it called? The one on the island."

"Fort Warren," Isabel said. She walked ahead of us, and we could hardly see her in the settling darkness of the night. Just a silhouette of a kid, walking purposefully, occasionally stopping to focus on something that neither I nor Sinead could ever see or hear.

"Right! Fort Warren. This Confederate soldier had a wife. Her name was Mrs. Lanier."

"Didn't she have a first name?"

"I don't know. Shut up and listen. Mrs. Lanier found out her husband was being held in Fort Warren, so she crossed the water one stormy night on a flimsy boat with nothing but a small pistol and a pickaxe. When she reached the fort, she whistled a Southern song her husband knew well."

Sinead whistled a soft tune. Hearing it in the dark grave-yard, surrounded by the dead, made me shiver.

"Her husband repeated the whistled notes." Sinead whis-tled again, repeating the same—

—tune. I was whistling to myself, the same tune from that night, when we had first entered the cemetery.

"That way," I said with certainty, leading Kane to a small path. "Sinead used to scare the hell out of me with ghost stories when we walked here. Whenever we entered the graveyard, she always had a new ghost story to tell. I was only fourteen, and those stories sounded so real…" I smiled, shaking my head.

"My sister and I used to tell ghost stories to each other some nights," Kane said. "She would fall asleep straight away afterward, but I'd stay awake for hours, too scared to sleep."

"Did you hear the one about the lady in black?"

"I don't remember." His voice suddenly became slightly colder. Perhaps he realized he had forgotten to hate me for a few seconds.

"This woman entered Fort Warren with a pickaxe and a—"

—————◆—————

—pistol. That's all she had," Sinead said. "She managed to wiggle through one of the cell windows, and with the help of the Confederate prisoners, she began tunneling with her pickaxe."

Fog was starting to gather on the ground, wisps of it curling around the gravestones. I hefted the pack on my shoulder and stuck my hands in my pockets. All my attention was focused on Sinead and her story.

"But Mrs. Lanier got caught, and when the guard went for her, she raised her pistol and fired. Unfortunately, the pistol was old, and in bad shape after her long travels in terrible conditions. It exploded in her hands, and a shard lodged in the brain of the man standing next to her, killing him instantly. That man... was her husband."

You knew the scary part of the story was coming when the person telling it lowered their voice to a hoarse whisper. I wanted her to stop. I wanted her to carry on.

"She was hanged for her crimes, in the black robes of a traitor, and with the knowledge that she had killed her own husband."

Sinead's voice took a strange tremble, almost as if she had scared herself by telling the story.

"Not long after the hanging, people began reporting strange experiences they had in the Boston graveyards. They could occasionally hear a quiet sobbing, accompanied by a steady clunking. Almost as if someone was endlessly trying to dig a tunnel with a pickaxe nearby. And then people began sighting a strange figure. Dressed all in black, hovering above the ground. And she was whistling an eerie Southern tune."

She whistled the tune again. Somewhere, in the fog, I could almost imagine the tap-tap-tapping of a pickaxe. I shivered, telling myself it was because of my wet clothing and hair.

"Shhh," Isabel suddenly hissed at us. She stood alert, her eyes unfocused, listening to things we couldn't hear.

"What is it?" I asked.

Isabel was the main reason we had managed to survive on the streets. Every so often she would stop to listen, or to stare at a pattern in a pile of street garbage, or at a strangely shaped puddle. And then she'd say something like, "We can't go to the shelters tonight. It would end badly." Or "There's a restaurant with a blue sign somewhere close, and there's lots of food in the garbage bin behind it." Or "There's a predator nearby. We need to move west, to keep away."

We always followed her advice. She had an uncanny ability to see things we couldn't, to catch glimpses of the future, see the truth in random patterns. She said this ability ran in her family.

"We need to move to the—"

—left." I pointed, and strode past a large weeping willow.

"It's getting dark," Kane said.

"We're nearly there," I muttered. "There should be a statue of a woman." I looked around.

"There's one." Kane gestured.

"That's it!"

It was gray and intricately carved. A woman with curly hair, one hand raised up high, fingers splayed. She wore some sort of cloth shirt, its folds and curves all sculpted to make it almost seem as if its touch would be soft, silky, instead of hard and cold.

I approached it, circled around it, and peered at the—

—road, where a single light shone. A security guard, probably. He walked down the path, shining the beam of his light around him, coughing every two or three seconds. The light cast in all directions, and I was worried that at any moment he would point it at us.

But he didn't. We stood still behind the statue of the standing woman, and he stalked past, his cough puncturing the silence.

Now that I was motionless, I realized how hungry I was. We hadn't eaten since that morning. We had some food—Sinead had managed to earn thirteen dollars playing her guitar, and I'd scammed ten more from passersby. We'd bought a few pastries and some cheese. But just as we were about to eat, Isabel had become tense and said we should keep moving. So the pastries and cheese all went into Sinead's huge backpack, and we walked on. Thinking about them now, my stomach rumbled. It was a low, growling sound, loud enough to wake the dead, not to mention the security guard only ten yards away. I clutched at my abdomen, pressing it, hoping to muffle the sound, my heart pounding hard. Would he hear it? Would he chase us?

But he kept walking. By my side, Isabel and Sinead were stifling giggles as my stomach kept growling and humming like some sort of cartoonish motorcycle. Finally, its rumble stopped, the security guard none the wiser. He kept coughing, getting farther away. After a few minutes we could hardly even hear his coughing, and we all relaxed.

"God, Lou." Sinead snorted with laughter. "What do you have in there? A lawnmower?"

"Shut up."

"You should do street shows! We'll hold a mic to your belly." She raised her hand in a theatrical gesture, the other pointing to my stomach as if holding an invisible microphone. "Come closer, ladies and gents, come listen to the rumbling-belly woman. Not too close, kids! She's so hungry, she might eat you up!"

"I'm Lou's ravenous tummy!" Isabel boomed. "Brrrr-rm-brrrrrm."

"It has more pitch," Sinead corrected her. "It's like… brr-raaw-merrrrow-wowowow."

"Flee, mortals, Lou's belly is coming! Rrrrrooooom-broooaaaaw."

"Is it an earthquake? A volcano? No! It's Lou's tum-tum! Wrrrrrr-rrrraw-brawawaw."

They were walking side by side, making outrageous groaning and roaring sounds, intermittently collapsing into helpless laughter.

I rolled my eyes, fighting to keep a grin off my face. "Idiots."

We were walking into a deeply forested area. The tombstones around us seemed older, some broken, mold and moss covering their surface.

"Come on." Isabel sounded excited. "It's not much farther. Over here."

She led us deeper into the foliage, where trees clustered around a small hill, only a few feet high. Isabel climbed it, practically running, and disappeared beyond it.

I climbed after her, Sinead following me, breathing hard. She was getting tired, carrying the cat around, with the enormous pack on her back. I was about to call Isabel—tell her to stop for a bit, because Sinead needed a rest—when I saw it.

A small stone structure, its walls covered with moss and ivy, with thin, twisting cracks decorating its surface. There was one doorway, as uninviting as any doorway I'd ever seen—a metal grid, brown with rust, a huge lock in its frame. Isabel stood next to it, her hand on the wall, looking at it as if she had finally come home.

It was her family's mausoleum.

I was already reaching for my pocket, where I kept a few bits of twisted metal I used as lockpicks, when she raised an iron key. She slid the key into the lock and pulled open the gate.

She walked inside, but Sinead and I paused at the threshold. Sinead's ghost story was still fresh in my mind, and I found myself terrified of the dark space beyond the gate—a space meant for the dead.

"Come on," Isabel said, and a small flame appeared. She held her lighter in one hand and a single candle in the other. "It's dry here."

Dryness sounded wonderful. We entered the crypt and closed the creaking, rusted gate behind us.

THIRTY-EIGHT

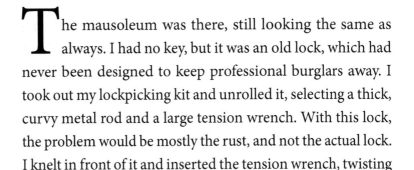

The mausoleum was there, still looking the same as always. I had no key, but it was an old lock, which had never been designed to keep professional burglars away. I took out my lockpicking kit and unrolled it, selecting a thick, curvy metal rod and a large tension wrench. With this lock, the problem would be mostly the rust, and not the actual lock. I knelt in front of it and inserted the tension wrench, twisting it, then started feeling for the pins with the rod.

"We used to come here whenever it rained and we couldn't go to a shelter," I said, nudging the first pin. "After the first night, we always tried to come with some sticks and newspapers."

"Why?" Kane crouched next to me, watching my fingers as I picked the lock.

"For a fire. It was good at keeping the rain out, but it could get hella cold in there. I guess there's no real insulation in the floor. The dead don't mind the cold."

"Didn't you find it… creepy?"

"It might sound weird, but Isabel said her ancestors didn't mind. And it's not like she meant that they didn't mind because they were dead. She literally meant she knew they didn't mind. I had some weird dreams in there once or twice. Voices whispering in my ear, or the sensation of something touching my cheek. But maybe it was just my imagination. I was only fourteen."

"Why do you think she hid the crystal here?"

"Even after we grew up, Isabel kept coming here. She would talk to her ancestors, ask for advice, tell them about her life… that sort of thing."

"I can't imagine it was much of a dialog."

"Who knows, with Isabel. But I don't think that was the point. She felt like she belonged here. We all tried fighting our loneliness in our own way, I guess. Sinead and I tried to find relationships that would fill the hole. And Isabel had her ancestors."

"Did any of you find a relationship that satisfied your loneliness?"

I hesitated. "No. Mostly random flings. Sinead had a good thing for a while, with a really smart guy. And I…" I thought of a young man with a rakish smile, one of his front teeth slightly broken. And his nose and chin identical to Tammi's. "Well, I had one very intense relationship. And it ended with me having a daughter."

He said nothing.

I felt the first pin catch, and began playing with the second. It tended to stick because of the rust, and I had to keep poking it to set it loose. It was exhausting work.

"I didn't know. That I was pregnant, I mean. I was working for Breadknife at the time, and he began pushing me harder and harder. I was breaking into homes almost every night. It was a never-ending cycle—scout the place in the morning, break into it at night. I was constantly on edge, afraid I was about to be caught. And some of the homes Breadknife chose... it seemed almost cruel. A man who'd recently lost his wife. A single mother with several kids. An old woman living alone. But I couldn't refuse the jobs. You don't say no to Breadknife."

The tension pin nearly slipped in my grip, and I muttered a curse, forcing myself to work more carefully, ignoring the pain in my tired muscles.

"And then I got caught. I broke into a couple's house while they were out on a date, but they came back home early. Saw movement in their house through the window and called the police. The lookout hadn't noticed them; I guess he wasn't paying attention. And when we suddenly heard the police sirens... he drove off. Leaving me behind."

The memory floated back unbidden. The shocking moment of disappointment and betrayal. I'd thought he was so perfect. Quick to laugh, passionate, clever. I'd fallen in love with him when we were working together on a job, the excitement and adrenaline fueling our lust. That's why you should never listen to your heart when pulling a job. Never.

"I was arrested, and got one year in prison. It probably would have been more, but it was a first offense—or so the judge thought. And I was an orphan, failed by the foster system. Inside, I found out I was nine weeks pregnant."

The second pin caught, and I leaned back, keeping the tension on the lock while flexing my shoulders. Then I leaned back in, started working the third pin.

"What did you do?"

"I decided to keep the baby. Part of it was because I wanted a child. I had these fantasies about being a mother. And part of it..." I paused. "It's really shitty. Part of it was that I thought it was a way out. For some reason, I assumed Breadknife wouldn't keep me around if I was a mother. I tried to *use* my daughter as a one-way ticket out of my life. I even hoped they'd release me early. But they didn't. And once she was born, I realized how selfish I'd been—using this child for leverage. Risking her exposure to people like Breadknife and his goons. I didn't want my baby to grow up in a prison. And her father... I didn't want him to know about her. So I gave her up for adoption. It was stupid. She wouldn't have remembered the short time in the prison's nursery ward anyway. I could have kept her. I just had a few months left. We would have been together now."

"It's not stupid," Kane said quietly.

"Anyway, once I was out, I asked Isabel to find her for me. I still had the cloth they'd wrapped her in when she was born. Isabel said it was immersed with her essence, or whatever. She found her in less than an hour. I rented a place nearby, started working on my alchemy."

"How did you get into alchemy?"

"My mother was an alchemist."

The third pin caught, and the tension wrench turned, the lock clicking. I pulled the metal grate open, relieved that my success had interrupted our chat. If it hadn't, he would have asked more about my mother and my knowledge of alchemy. And I wouldn't have answered anything about that. He couldn't know about the book. That was the one secret I had to keep.

"Hang on, I have a flashlight app," Kane muttered, rummaging in his pocket for his phone.

"No need," I said. I lifted my right hand and focused on it. Flames burst from my palm, licking my fingers, illuminating the mausoleum's walls with their flickering orange light.

I stepped into the cold room, the memories flooding me. A small black smudge marred the floor where we used to light our campfires. We always made sure to clean the ashes the following day, but the black mark remained. The walls were lined with the family's tombs, their names engraved in the ancient stone. An alcove across the room contained a line of urns. Isabel told me that when the space in the mausoleum began to run out, the family had begun cremating their dead. My eyes immediately went to the right-hand wall, and I knelt by the bottom tomb, looking at the engraved letters illuminated by the orange firelight, even though I knew what they said by heart.

Eleanor King, 1864-1886.

"This was my spot," I said. "Where I'd sleep. I used to watch this engraving, imagining that Eleanor was lying on her side facing me. She was Isabel's great-great-aunt. She died in childbirth."

"Do we need to start opening these tombs to find the crystal?" Kane asked. He sounded uncomfortable, almost like the concept of a girl regularly sleeping next to an entombed skeleton bothered him.

"No." I stood up. "We had a cache. The right urn over there is empty. We used to hide some stuff we needed there."

Kane picked up the urn I pointed at. He removed the lid, and carefully upturned it on the floor, shaking it to empty the contents.

An assortment of items fell out. Two ten-year-old cigarette packs, a lighter, a small knife, a pack of cards. And in the midst of it all lay the crystal. Now, in the dark cemetery, there was no mistaking the light that pulsed in it. I let the flames on my hand dissipate, and the mausoleum was cast into a gloom, illuminated only by that strange, warm, pulsing light.

I picked up the crystal by the chain and looked at it closely. What did Breadknife want with it? Did he really intend to unleash the horrors we had seen in Isabel's cards? In any case, it was obvious we couldn't give it to him.

"Okay," I said. "It's time for you to create the fake crystal. And make it look *real*."

THIRTY-NINE

The street corner was unusually dark, since two of its streetlights weren't working. The third emitted a sharp electrical hum, perhaps the streetlight equivalent of a dying man's breath. Across the street was a nearly empty parking lot and a closed McDonald's, the yellow *M* looking faded and old. The traffic lights in the corner had changed endlessly since I'd shown up here—green, yellow, red.

I checked my phone again, rereading Breadknife's message for what must have been the twentieth time. *Corner of Warren and Dale. Half past midnight. No one but you. Come only with the box.*

It was now twelve forty-three and I was getting anxious, even though I knew it was part of Breadknife's strategy. He wanted me stressed and full of doubt. He knew me well enough to guess I might try something, that this evening was the equivalent of a very violent chess game between us, with everything on the line.

A battered gray Lexus slowed down as it got closer, and I tensed. The driver was obscured in the darkness, and for one moment I almost believed it was Breadknife himself. That he would step out of the car, shoot me, and take the box.

But when the car stopped, the brakes squeaking, I saw it was only Steve O'Sullivan, Breadknife's flat-headed, obedient soldier. Of course; Breadknife would never risk an ambush. He'd sent one of his minions to fetch me.

Steve stepped out of the car, leaving the engine running, and approached me. His face was blank, an expression of a man with one goal in mind—following his boss' orders. He looked at me, at the small pouch in my hand.

"Is it in there?"

"It is." I tensed. Would he try and take it from me now? Leave without freeing my daughter? "Where's the girl?"

"You'll see her soon enough. Open it."

I opened the pouch, cursing myself for telling Kane to stay far away. I needed backup right now. If Steve took the box, I would have to stop him from leaving myself.

But he never even touched it. He examined the pouch, verifying it was empty aside from the box, feeling the fabric for any hidden pockets. Then he patted me down to make sure I carried nothing else. He did a shoddy job, and I suspected that deep inside, Steve O'Sullivan was wary of becoming too intimate with a female body. He found nothing, which demonstrated his carelessness. I had two items on me that he should have confiscated. He did take my phone, and removed the battery. Then he swiped me with some sort of electrical device, which hummed and buzzed as it brushed my body. He was looking for a wire. There was none.

"Get in the car," he said, holding the rear passenger door open.

I did, hugging the pouch close to me. The car stank of sweat, accompanied by a moldy smell that hinted of a forgotten snack left to rot, probably under one of the seats. Steve got into the driver's seat and started the engine.

The ride was long, and Steve drove in a roundabout way, circling Boston, taking side roads with little traffic, trying to spot anyone who was following him. I was relieved that I had expressly forbidden Sinead and Kane to do that. I'd known Breadknife would suspect a tail.

I also knew something else, and the knowledge made me tremble in fear. Breadknife suspected a decoy. That was the only reason for not simply shooting me on the spot and taking the box. Breadknife knew I might use a forged crystal, and not the real one. And if that was the case, he wanted me alive to find out where the real crystal was.

How good was Kane's forgery? The incantation had taken more than an hour, slowly morphing a piece of wood into an identical-looking crystal. I couldn't spot any difference. Even the strange light in the crystal looked the same. But there was no ignoring the fact that the crystal that currently sat in the box was a stick, disguised with glamour. If Bread-knife checked hard enough, he would spot the forgery. And then this night would probably end very badly, for both my daughter and for me.

Finally, the car stopped by an abandoned warehouse in Hyde Park. Its gray walls were marred by unimaginative graffiti and dirt. The door had been white once, but was now covered in brown rust, its color cracked and peeling. Steve got out of the car, and waited for me to get out as well. He did not hurry me, did not seem to care if I got out of the car or not. He simply waited.

Following the script, I got out of the car. I walked behind him to the door, which he unlocked with a key from his pocket. Then he motioned me inside.

To say my chest thudded would be an understatement. It boomed. It shook. It seemed as if my entire body was one pulsing, panicky heart as I stepped into the dark warehouse.

The warehouse seemed to be half-full of long forgotten building supplies. Discarded timber logs, some long iron scaffolding, rusty cans of oil paint. Three men waited inside. One was a huge man I didn't know, though something about him was familiar. He leaned against a small door at the far end of the empty space. The other two men stood by the table—Breadknife and his cruel right-hand goon, Matteo "Ear" Ricci.

Steve closed the door behind me and locked it. Then he crossed the room to stand by Breadknife and Matteo. I was surrounded and outnumbered. All the men in the room had guns strapped to their waist, except for the large man in the corner.

That rang a bell in my mind. I *had* seen him before. He was one of the four assholes who had robbed me, the night before Breadknife had showed up in my store asking for his money. He was Hardy! And he was one of Breadknife's goons.

Breadknife had orchestrated that robbery, probably knowing in advance that I was returning with a lot of cash in my bag. Enough to make his monthly payment. But he had *wanted* me to miss my payment. To know I was indebted to him. To make sure I would break into the dragon's vault for him.

His smile widened when he saw the realization on my face. He had wanted me to know. That's why he'd told this goon to be here tonight. Another chess move. He wanted me to feel outmaneuvered, weak, foolish. And it worked.

341

"Where's my daughter?" I asked, trying to keep my voice natural.

"She's over there," he motioned to the door that Hardy leaned against. "I didn't want to wake her up. She was exhausted, poor thing, constantly crying for her mommy. The wrong mommy, of course."

"Did you tell her?" My tone was cold.

He shrugged. "I didn't exchange one word with her, Lou. Why would I bother?"

I raised the pouch. "I have your damn crystal here."

Breadknife nodded at Matteo. The man strutted over to me, a cruel glint in his eye, gun in hand.

"Frisk her," Breadknife said. "Take everything. Lou is a cunning woman. She could turn a pin into a deadly weapon."

"You really overestimate me," I said.

"Take any jewelry, too. She owns a bracelet that can do some quite deadly tricks."

Matteo began running his hands over me. He didn't suffer from Steve's aversion to touching me. In fact, he relished it, groping my body thoroughly. I kept my face neutral, knowing that showing any disgust or outrage at his prodding would only delight him.

"What's this?" he asked, feeling a slight bump in my sleeve. His fingers investigated, finding the secret pocket, and he retrieved a small vial of purple liquid.

I let a small flicker of despair show on my face, then quickly masked it. "Open it and find out."

He laughed, and kept searching me, the vial in his palm.

The truth was, the vial contained water and a drop of artificial food coloring. Breadknife would never have believed I didn't have a plan of some sort when I walked inside, so I hid the vial as a red herring. Make him think that the vial was part of my foiled plan to outsmart him.

Breadknife's strategy was to fill me with doubt. My strategy was to fill him with false confidence.

He located a cigarette packet in my back pocket and retrieved it, smirking. "Marlboro Light, huh? This brings back memories." Matteo used to take those from me whenever he found them, when I was a teen, delighting in smoking them in front of me while I trembled in anger.

Finding nothing else, he returned with the cigarettes, the vial, and the pouch to the table, laying them down one after the other.

Breadknife picked up the pouch, and took out the box. He looked at it for a long moment with wide eyes, and then his gaze flicked to me. "Why didn't you hand it over as soon as you had it? Why take us through this elaborate... mess?"

"There were some complications," I said evenly. "Why didn't you wait a few hours before kidnapping a five-year-old girl?"

"When I smell a stench in the air, I act. You know that, Lou." He sighed, shaking his head sadly. "Now, let's see. If I open this box, will I find the crystal inside? Or will my finger be pricked by one of your poisonous traps?"

I rolled my eyes. "You're paranoid, Mr. Cisternino."

"Am I?" He glanced at Hardy, who picked at the dirt in one of his fingernails. "If something happens to me when I open the box, walk into that room, and kill the girl."

The man nodded. Breadknife raised an eyebrow, looking at me expectantly. I said nothing.

He twisted the key once in the lock, and pried the lid open. He picked up the chain holding the crystal and gazed at it. Despite myself, I tensed. Would he notice a flaw I couldn't see? Could he see through the glamour?

And then he discarded it with disinterest on the table. My heart plunged. He knew. He had seen through it somehow. Now he would torture me. Or my daughter. Do whatever he could to get the real crystal.

But he didn't. Instead, he focused on the black box. Caressing its lid with a trembling finger. Touching the key in the lock. I had no idea what he was thinking.

"What does your client want with the crystal?" I asked. "Is it really the Yliaster crystal?"

"The crystal?" He frowned. "I don't know."

I blinked. He didn't know? What was he...

And then it dawned on me. I was dizzy with horror, the knowledge of what I'd done terrifying. "It was never about the crystal," I said. "It was the box you were interested in."

"It's amazing how something so small can contain such a huge change," he whispered, half to himself, still looking at the box.

"But there was nothing in it! Nothing except the crystal."

"That's what the first woman who ever received it thought as well—at first. She opened it, only to find it empty. But then she found out you could twist the key in the lock over and over. And if you twist it eleven times… the true contents of the box are exposed." He put it on the table, shutting the lid.

Eleven times. My mind whirled. What was in that box? Whatever it was, it would lead to what Isabel had seen in the cards.

He twisted the key, and it clicked. One. No, along with the first twist from before, Breadknife had twisted the key twice already.

He twisted it again. Three.

"Can you guess her name? The woman who first received the box?" His voice quavered.

I thought hard. A box that contained horrors, kept in a secure vault. And then I recalled his words when he had first told me about it. *The box was lost when Troy fell.* Troy. Ancient Greece. What box could it be? But I already knew.

345

"Was her name... Pandora?" I asked.

The key turned again in the lock, the click echoing much louder than it should have in the empty warehouse. Four.

"You were always a smart girl, Lou. That's right. This is Pandora's box. The gods placed all the horrors of the world inside it, and when Pandora, overcome by curiosity, opened it, those horrors were unleashed on humanity. Oh, and supposedly the box also contained hope or something. I don't know, sounds ludicrous to me."

Click. Five.

"But the truth is that before all the horrors got out, Pandora managed to shut the lid and lock the box. Only *some* of the things in the box got out. But many remained."

"Who is your client? Why does he want it opened?"

"My client is a *she*, not a *he*."

Click. Six.

"And she wants it open because she was one of the things unleashed back then. And I guess she misses her family."

Click. Seven.

Nervous, Matteo picked up the Marlboro pack from the table and knocked out a cigarette. He put it in his mouth and lit it, looking at his boss, who paused between each key twist as if drawing out the moment of triumph.

I was desperate. "Mr. Cisternino, if you open that box, it will destroy the entire world. Isabel saw it in the cards."

"Not the entire world. Some of it. I would remain. And would receive a more than adequate compensation for my actions."

Click. Eight.

"Steve, Matteo... you can't be fine with this? Your boss is insane. He wants to kill us all!"

Steve's face remained impassive. Matteo's eyes were anxious, but he said nothing, taking another puff on the cigarette.

Breadknife glanced at me. "Loyalty, Vitalis, is an amazing quality. You could learn something from these men. If you had any time to do so."

Click. Nine.

Shadows began gathering around the warehouse, the lights dimming. Each twist of the key sounded louder than the last, and by now they were like loud drums, vibrating long after the key had turned. I took a step toward the table. Steve raised a gun and pointed it squarely at me, his eyes blank, free of emotion. He scared me even more than Matteo. I could understand Matteo; I've seen others like him over the years. But Steve's motivations were something I couldn't fathom.

Click. Ten.

The shadows lurking around us seemed to be taking on forms. Strange, predatory creatures, all waiting for the box to open, for hell to be unleashed upon the world. Breadknife's fingers hovered over the key, as if even he was suddenly hesitant to turn it one final time.

"Mr. Cisternino… Anthony. Please think about this."

"I have, Lou," he whispered. "I've thought about it long and hard."

Steve's attention was on me, while the rest of the men were looking at the box. No one looked at Matteo.

He was, unbeknownst to him, smoking one of my nightmare cigarettes. I'd transferred the contents to a Marlboro light, hoping that he wouldn't be able to resist the allure of stealing my smokes again, especially if they were his favorite brand. Now, as the shadows loomed above us, his body transformed. It became thin, bony and pale, with numerous leering mouths pocking his skin. His hair grew longer, turned white and wispy. The kids who had dreamed this particular nightmare had been quite imaginative.

I glanced at him, letting my mouth drop, my eyes widen in fear. Steve, attention focused solely on me, glanced sideways to see what I was staring at. And he saw a nightmarish, deformed witch, standing over his boss, close enough to touch.

He swiveled his gun and began shooting, the explosions sharp and painful in my ears. The bullets tore through Matteo's bony form as if he were made of paper, and he howled, a tormented, screechy wail.

I lunged forward, flames erupting from my fingers, burning high up to my elbows and casting a hellish light. I grabbed for Steve's gun hand, and he screamed as I gripped him, the fire sizzling on his skin. He pushed me away and I tumbled back, falling to the floor. But he was too late.

The fire had caught his sleeve, and spread up his shirt. He let out a tortured screech, and began running around, waving his arm, trying to extinguish it but only fanning the flames. I used the distraction and lunged for the table, going for the crystal.

A gun barrel smashed into my face, and I stumbled backward, my vision blurry and tinged with red. Breadknife held his gun pointed at me.

"Good try," he said vehemently, his words echoed by Steve's wails as he ran around the room, his whole body a blazing inferno. On the floor, Matteo lay dead, the numerous mouths on his body slack.

"What were you going to do with this?" he asked, raising the crystal from the table. "Smash it and let loose the soul inside? Or did you have an even cleverer plan?"

There was a sudden detonation, and both of us flinched. Steve, his body blazing, had knocked into one of the oil cans, and it cracked. The years-old vapors that had accumulated inside caught fire instantly, and it exploded. Then, exposed to the heat and the flames, other cans exploded as well. Timbers were now catching fire at an alarming rate.

I lunged for Breadknife's gun, but I was dizzy, my movement sluggish, and he simply stepped back, the gun still pointed at me, the other holding the crystal.

He draped the crystal's chain around his neck. "You were the best, Lou. I hope the things in the box will find you as useful as I did."

"I wasn't going for the crystal, Breadknife," I said. "Angustus!"

The chain around Breadknife's throat suddenly constricted, biting into his skin. His eyes went wide, and he began clawing at it with one hand.

"Angustus," I said again, making the chain constrict even more. His face became purple as his throat made rasping sounds. He raised his gun, but his aim wavered, and he shot wide, the gun dropping from his hand. He clawed at the constricting chain with both hands.

A movement flickered in the corner of my eye. It was Hardy, running toward me. I lunged at the table, grabbing the vial with the purple water. I swiveled to face the huge man, who was only five yards away. I lifted the vial high above my head, and shouted "Stop!"

He did, nearly tumbling down.

"If you touch me, I'll shatter this," I warned him. "And then we'll both be dead."

He blinked.

"Your boss is gone," I said, speaking steadily over the roar of the fire around me. Smoke filled the warehouse. "This place is about to burn to the ground. You have nothing left to do here."

For a long moment we glared at each other. Then without saying a word, he whirled and ran for the exit.

I breathed in relief, and waited for him to unlock the door and leave. Only then did I put the colored water on the table and pick up the box. Gingerly, I removed the key from the lock, placing it in my pocket.

Breadknife was motionless by my feet. His eyes were vacant, his mouth ajar in a wordless scream. I touched the tight chain on his throat, and it became lax, then slithered up my wrist, and linked into a bracelet. I grabbed the pouch from the table, and tossed the still-closed box inside. I had no idea what would happen if I left it behind to burn. Perhaps the things inside it would be free. Better to take it with me.

I stepped over Breadknife's body and ran to the door at the other end of the warehouse. I prayed that, for once, no lock would stand in my way.

None did. The door opened to a small room, which must at some point have been an office. Now, the only remnants of its original function were severed phone cables protruding from the walls, and abandoned electrical outlets. A sleeping bag was unrolled on the floor, and on it lay Tammi, asleep.

She was tucked in a fetal position, a stray curl on top of her cheek. I crouched by her side, brushing the curl away. Her skin was soft and warm. She breathed deeply, her lips in a pout, moving slightly as she dreamed.

The air became hazy and suffocating. I coughed into my sleeve, and then picked Tammi up, resting her head on my shoulder. To my amazement, she remained asleep.

She weighed almost nothing, and I easily carried her out of the room. The fire had spread to the far corners of the warehouse. The glass windows had cracked, then broken, and the flames roared as additional oxygen began fueling them.

The doorway out was engulfed in smoke. Flames licked at it, hungry for the air outside. I thought of my parents' death and shuddered.

But then, the longer I waited, the worse the fire would become. Holding tight to my daughter, I ran across the room, the heat becoming more and more unbearable. My breathing, heavy from the effort, became a coughing fit as I inhaled a lungful of smoke. Tammi began moving in my arms, slowly waking up to an inferno.

And then we were plunging through the flames and I hugged her tight as she screamed, half blind with my eyes blurring from tears, running, running.

It took a while for me to realize we were out, that the air was cool and fresh around us. That we stood in a dark street, and not in a warehouse, orange with flames.

Tammi cried and squirmed. I quickly put her down, checking her for flames, for burns.

"What is it, sweetie? Are you in pain? Where are you hurt?"

"I want my mommy," she sobbed.

She was whole and unhurt. Endless conflicting emotions drowned my heart as I hugged her, whispering, "Okay, sweetie. I'll take you to your mommy. Calm down now. Stop crying. You'll see mommy very soon."

FORTY

———◆———

I had no phone; it was now melting inside the burning ware-house. No car either—nor, to be frank, the knowledge of how to drive one. No money for a cab. Besides, the streets around us were empty and dark.

I could wait with Tammi for the inevitable firefighters and police to show up. But that would mean I'd have to answer questions. One of the policemen who were routinely paid by Bread-knife might have lingering loyalty to their barbecued boss, and I had no intention of risking Tammi or myself that way.

So I walked. At first, I told Tammi we would walk hand in hand. I wrapped my palm gently around hers, marveling at how small and soft it was. Then we began walking, but I quickly realized that walking with a five-year-old, even my daughter who was the best and brightest and most wonder-ful girl in the world, was… difficult.

Her steps were so small. She constantly stumbled, or paused for no clear reason. She was tired. She wanted her mommy. After what felt like a lifetime of walking, cajoling her to walk slightly faster and be a brave little girl, I looked back and saw that we'd barely crossed a hundred yards.

So I took her in my arms again and marched, already hearing the sirens of the first responders getting closer. I ducked with her into an alley as I spotted the flashing blue light of a squad car, and then moved on, keeping off the main streets to remain hidden.

She dozed off, her head bobbing on my shoulder, her hair tickling my nose. Though she didn't weigh much, carrying her around wasn't easy; her feet kept bumping my body, and my arms were starting to ache.

Nevertheless, I wanted this walk to stretch forever. My daughter in my arms, for the first time since she was born.

Finally, we reached an open bar. I stepped inside, looking around me warily. There were several men sitting around, drinking beers and playing pool, and one tired-looking pros-titute smoking by the bar. Not the most wholesome place to bring a five-year-old to.

"Can I use your phone?" I asked the bartender.

He was fat, and a faded tattoo of what looked like a snake decorated his neck. He took one long look at me, and said, "Are you okay? Do you need help?"

I glanced at the mirror behind him and saw that my face was sooty, my hair a mess. A large ugly bruise was developing where Breadknife had pistol-whipped me. "I'm fine. I just need your phone, thanks."

He handed me his own mobile phone, and I called Sinead, whose number I knew by heart. I gave her the address of the bar, refusing to go into any details other than "We're both fine."

While I waited, sitting on a bar stool with Tammi cradled in my lap, the bartender made me some tea. The prostitute stubbed out her cigarette, apologizing for the smoke. She gazed at my daughter and murmured that we were so much alike, a forlorn smile on her face. When I gazed around me, all I saw were kind eyes.

And then the bar door opened and Sinead and Kane walked inside. Sinead rushed to my side, hugging me carefully to avoid waking Tammi up. I followed them out, thanking the bartender profoundly for all his help.

Kane held the rear passenger door for me, and I carefully lay Tammi in the backseat. She shuffled slightly and murmured, "Mommy."

"We're getting you to your mommy now, sweetie," I whispered in her ear.

I stood up, gazing at my daughter asleep in the back of the car. Then I took three steps to the side and threw up.

Sinead was by my side in an instant, fulfilling the loyal role of hair holder as I retched and vomited again. The world spun. I shook violently.

"You're okay, Lou," Sinead whispered in my ear. "You're okay."

"I'm… not okay." My teeth were chattering. "I *killed* them, Sinead. I killed three of them. And I ran with Tammi through a fucking fire. She could have been hurt. I killed those men, Tammi. Matteo and Steve and ABC."

"You were protecting yourself. And Tammi. They deserved to die."

Tears were running down my cheeks. My body shivered violently. "But *I* was the one who killed them."

Something had changed in me when I'd killed those men. Something profound. I went from being someone who'd never taken a life, to someone who had. This was something I could never undo.

I would have done it all over again, and it was the right thing. The men I had killed really did deserve to die. Still, Steve O'Sullivan was my age, and we had joined Breadknife's gang almost together. His main crime was blind loyalty. And Breadknife used to be Anthony, and he had saved me from homelessness, and taught me things. We used to have a connection. And Matteo "Ear" Ricci...

Well, he was just an overall shitty person, and the world was infinitely better without him. But still, *I* had been the one who had taken his life.

But something else had changed in me. I had beaten four strong men, left three of them dead and burned, and come out almost without a scratch. And a small part of me, a part that used to be afraid, was now gone. I was dangerous. Predator, not prey. And if people messed with me—or even worse, with my daughter—they would pay the price.

"I'm okay now," I said, my voice steady. I wiped my eyes with the back of my hand. "Let's get Tammi back to... back home."

Kane parked the car a few houses down the road. There were no police cars at the home of Tammi's adoptive parents. But the light inside was on, although it was past three in the morning. I spotted a shadow of movement there. They were waiting. Waiting for news, waiting for a call, waiting for their daughter to come home.

"You'll have to take her," I told Sinead. She sat in the front passenger seat. I was in the back, Tammi's head in my lap, my hand on her hair, a gentle touch. I tried to etch that memory in my mind, that sensation of my daughter sleeping in my lap. It wouldn't happen again.

"What? No way. You should do it, she's your… you saved her."

We both refrained from saying anything that could be repeated later. It was impossible to guess how much Tammi heard, how much she'd remember. It was best if she didn't have details to tell her parents, and the cops.

"Her mother will recognize me." They saw me every day, walking my dog.

"Tammi didn't seem to recognize you."

"Because she was scared and exhausted and confused. But her mother will, I'm sure."

"I can glamour you," Kane said.

"What does that mean, exactly?" I asked suspiciously.

"They'll perceive you differently. It's like a very good disguise. And when they try to recall your face later, they won't be able to. It'll only last ten minutes or so, but that should be enough."

"Okay." The truth was, I wanted to stretch my time with her, just for a few more seconds.

I got out of the car, standing on the sidewalk. We were far enough not to be seen from the house in the darkness. Kane opened his own door, sliding out. He walked over to me, stopping only inches away. He gazed at me, his eyes intent and focused, and then he began chanting.

As always, his words were alien, strange-sounding, some of the syllables completely foreign to the English language. Each word had its own tone—some rising, some falling—and I instinctively knew that the tone was important, that it was an integral part of the spell. Mystical energy began to prickle my skin, mixing with the tingling I felt from his close proximity. His fingers began to brush my face, like a lover's caress, their tips shining with a pale blue light. He touched my cheeks, my forehead, and my eyelids. Then one finger slid down my nose, brushing my lips, and I found myself parting them slightly, wishing for it to linger there. But it kept going to my chin and throat, and by that point I was completely taken by the touch, wanting it to dip even lower. My breathing became husky, thick, my mind a turmoil of sensations and heat.

And then he stepped back, and stopped chanting.

"Why did you stop?" I whispered.

"It's done," he said, and pointed to the car's side mirror.

I glanced at it, and saw... someone else. I couldn't say who it was, or what she was like. As soon as I looked away, I couldn't recall any of her features. Her hair was... brown? Or maybe blonde? Her eyes were definitely rounder than mine... but then I thought they were actually narrower, almond-shaped. Her mouth...

It was impossible to keep that face in mind.

"You have ten minutes, perhaps just a bit more," he said. "Be quick about it."

I opened the back door and touched Tammi's cheek gently. "Tammi? Sweetie? We're home. Let's get you to your mom."

She sat up, blinking woozily, and got out of the car. I picked her up and strode down the street, to her home.

Even before I reached the house's front yard, I heard someone inside cry, "Oh my God! Frank, it's Tammi!"

The door flew open and Jane ran outside in her nightgown, her face swollen and stained with tears. I put Tammi down, and she rushed to Jane's arms. "Mommy!" She was sobbing, as was Jane. I blinked a tear away, lowering my head.

For a long moment Jane just crouched, hugging Tammi. Her husband, Frank, ran out of the house. He had been sleeping. I hated him for being able to sleep when my daughter, who was in his care, had been kidnapped. I hated Jane for loving my daughter so much that she had stayed awake, constantly looking out the window, waiting for her. I hated them both for everything they had that I didn't.

"Thank you," Jane said to me. "How… Where…"

"The detectives will explain tomorrow, ma'am." My voice was flat and pleasant. "But she's safe, and unharmed, and the men who took her will never trouble anyone again."

She wasn't even listening. Maybe it was Kane's spell, morphing my words to ambiguous platitudes, or maybe it was just because now that she had Tammi in her arms, she didn't really care.

"Thank you for bringing my daughter back."

I wanted to say, "She's not your daughter." Or, "In return, I want to spend time with her every day." Or, "She just came to say goodbye, she's going to live with me now."

"You're welcome, ma'am. Have a good night." I turned around.

"What's your name?" Frank called after me.

"Smith," I called back. "Officer Smith."

Sinead would have been displeased with my unimaginative response. But it was all I was capable of.

FORTY-ONE

Isabel's eyes filled with tears the moment I stepped into her small room in the hospital.

"I'm sorry," she said, her usual soft, low voice replaced by a trembling squeak. "I'm so sorry."

She looked so out of place, her usual colorful clothing replaced by a hospital gown, her golden skin pale and bruised, her braids disheveled and scattered, some unbound. Only her pink flamingo lips were freshly done. I knew that Sinead stayed by her almost constantly, applying the lipstick again and again whenever she felt it had faded.

It had taken me a day to find the resolve to come and visit her, and a sliver of anger shot through me when I first saw her. Then it faded, replaced by sadness.

"It's fine. I'm fine. *Tammi's* fine." If I put a bit of emphasis on my daughter's name, that couldn't be helped. I'm not a fucking saint. I wanted Isabel to remember the cost of her actions.

But it was clear that she did, and a second later I felt shitty for my vindictiveness. Sinead, who sat on a chair by Isabel's bed, gave me a furious glare.

I sat down on the other side of the bed. One of Isabel's braids was falling apart, the rubber band that held it torn. I gently removed it, and tied the ends together. Then I unwound the entire braid, carefully separated the three sections of hair, and began to braid them together again patiently. "Why didn't you just tell me? I think if you had said, 'Hey, Lou, bringing the box to Breadknife will usher in Armageddon,' I would have probably listened."

"I didn't *know* that. All I could see was darkness. And the darkness originated with the box that you took. I didn't know what would cause the darkness to erupt. And almost all the paths I saw to the future were dark. *Even* telling you."

I thought about it. What would I have done if Isabel had told me? She hadn't known that the danger was the box itself. Assuming she could have convinced me that bringing the stolen box to Breadknife would end in disaster, I would have probably done just what I did—forged the crystal and handed the forgery to him when he came for it. He'd have left and opened the box once he was back home, unleashing the monstrosities inside. She was right. Telling me about it wouldn't have prevented the box from being opened.

I held the braid tightly and looped the rubber band around the end a couple of times.

"Lou, I would never—"

"It's okay, Isabel. I understand. Don't worry about it."

And I did. She had done what she had to do; there was no other way. And saving the world was a pretty good incentive, too.

But I also knew that when I saw her next, a small part of me would remember that her actions had put my daughter in danger. That she had betrayed my trust. What she'd done had resulted in a tiny fracture between us, and I could only hope this fracture would eventually heal.

I cycled slowly down the dark street, my mind heavy with worry. The damage Breadknife's goons had done to my shop had been extensive. Though the safe was still as I'd left it, most of my alchemy tools had been shattered, the ingredient jars smashed, the store's shelves bashed and knocked down. The front door's lock had been destroyed. I'd managed to save most of my ingredients, but it would take a lot of time and money to restore the shop to a reasonable state. Time in which I should be working. Money that I lacked.

It would be nice if I could sell the dragon scale. But doing that right now was tantamount to suicide. It was more than probable that most of the potential "buyers" for the scale would be bounty hunters, hired by the dragon to find the thieves who had taken his scales. It could take years to sell it safely.

Sinead had dismantled HHT's offices, leaving a bunch of confused and angry hippo hunter wannabes. She claimed she had managed to stay a few thousand dollars ahead, and had shared some of it with me, saying that it was a "participation bonus." So I could fix the door and pay this month's rent. But the future was a desperate and worrisome thing.

It became even more worrisome when I stopped a few yards from the shop's door. A man leaned on the door, his arms folded.

Or rather, a vampire.

Maximillian Fuchs looked at me with gleaming eyes. A smile stretched across his face, hinting of long fangs beneath.

My legs tensed as I prepared to cycle away, the chain on my wrist already unwinding, feeling my need. My palms began to smoke, the heat making the rubber on the bicycle handles grow soft.

"You know you can't outrun me—definitely not on that ridiculous thing," he said, his voice crisp and cold. "And I hope you don't think you can burn me to a crisp, the way you did to your old boss."

I had to buy time, come up with a plan. "How did you find me?"

"I'm very, *very* good at what I do."

"So am I."

"Yes, you are!" His smile brightened. "I must congratulate you. The security footage for the entire week before the burglary had been erased from our servers; I have no idea how. You left no fingerprints behind, no useful witnesses."

"Then how…"

"Never underestimate a vampire, Lou Vitalis. You left behind your scent."

I wanted to punch myself. Of course!

"It was all over the safe. And then I remembered that clumsy waitress, her scent quite similar. Tracing her back to you wasn't easy… you cover your tracks well. But someone *did* help you get the job. And he was more than happy to give me your name. I barely had to rip off three of his fingernails. I didn't even get to his teeth."

Sinead's man. Wasn't he from the Secret Service? I guess that wasn't enough to deter a vampire. "He didn't know that I was about to steal anything. He just helped a friend."

"I know *everything*. Like I said, I'm good at what I do. Don't worry. He'll recover. Well, he'll recover *physically*. I don't know about mental scars. Mortals are quite fragile."

"So what now?" I asked, letting the chain on my wrist snake into my palm. I would throw it at his feet, immobilize him, then burn him. Vampires burned, I was sure of it. "Are you going to take me to Ddraig Goch?"

"That's a good question." He narrowed his eyes. "I could do that. You would tell me where the box and the crystal are. And, of course, those six precious dragon scales. And then I'd take you to the dragon."

"What if I don't talk?" I could throw the chain around his neck. Would it cut through his neck if I tightened it enough?

He rolled his eyes. "Everyone talks. They think they won't, because they don't understand how real pain feels. But when they find out, they talk. There could be another solution, though."

I didn't take the bait, didn't ask what the solution was. Instead I watched him calmly, my thumb running against one of the chain links.

He seemed irked that I failed to play my part. His smile lost some of its smugness. "You are quite a capable woman, Lou Vitalis. I wouldn't have thought stealing from a dragon was possible. Already, to Ddraig Goch's chagrin, your deeds are becoming a legend."

"Yeah, I'm awesome-possum. The best thing since sliced bread."

"Indeed, and—"

"Totally bitchin'. The bee's knees." I searched my mind for something else. "The cat's pajamas."

"Are you done?"

"Yes."

"And it occurs to me—"

"Oh! Peachy-keen. Sorry, it was on the tip of my tongue."

"*It occurs to me* that we could work together."

I nodded. "Would working together include me not being tortured and later incinerated by an irate dragon?"

"I think we can agree on those terms."

"Then I'm your girl." I smiled a wide, insincere smile. "Won't your boss be angry you didn't find the person in charge of that spectacular, legendary, peachy-keen job on his vault?"

"Let me worry about my boss. You can worry about keeping me happy."

"And how do I do that, exactly?"

"Baroness Fleurette van Dijk had an interesting… scent. I assume she was working with you?"

"I don't know what you're talking about."

"I'm thinking you do. Rumor has it that you're quite the alchemist. Did you make her blood smell and taste that way?"

"Maybe."

"I need more of what you gave her." His eyes had a sudden, hungry look. "Not whatever made me sleepy and stupid. But what made her blood so… peachy-keen."

"You almost killed her out of excitement," I said sharply. "If I make you some of that vampire Viagra, won't it end with a bunch of dead people?"

"Why is that any of your concern?" He frowned. When he saw my jaw clenching, he added, "Oh, relax. I never would have killed her. Do I look like some teenage vampire who can't control his impulses? I just want something that will improve my meals. Is that too much to ask? Should I remind you that the alternative is that you die, your friend the baroness dies, those servants of hers die... a lot of death for refusing me some food seasoning."

"Fine." I raised my hands. "I make you some seasoning, and you leave me the fuck alone."

"No." He laughed, a steely edge in his voice. "You make me some seasoning, and our budding relationship blossoms. And when I need something else, I'll come visit." He pushed himself from the door and turned to leave.

"I need some money for ingredients," I said hurriedly.

He groaned, and turned around. "Mortals," he muttered, as he took a checkbook from his pocket. "How much? Will ten thousand dollars be sufficient?"

"That," I said, my voice becoming slightly high, "would be a good start."

FORTY-TWO

The drill vibrated in my hand, and I leaned into it, pouring my frustrations into the materializing hole in the wall. Pieces of plaster and wall dust were scattered all around me, on my clothes, and in my hair.

I'd finished cleaning up my store, and was now installing the new shelves. There was a complex process. I'd measure the shelf, and mark the places I needed to drill. Then I would pray to the gods of drilling that my drill would not hit a water pipe or an electricity line. I would drill the holes, four for each shelf. Then, when installing, I would realize that one of them was not properly aligned. I would create a new, fifth hole. I would install the shelf, and see that it was crooked, and that the extra hole was very much visible and ugly.

And I'd decide it was good enough and move on to the next shelf.

Magnus was nowhere to be seen. The drill's noise had scared him half to death, and I suspected he was hiding under the bed, head on his paws, waiting for the nightmare to be over.

I was working on the fifth hole of the third shelf when a knock on the door made me stop and turn around.

"Kane!"

He stood in the doorway, his hands in the pockets of his trench coat. He'd showered recently, his hair still glistening with that post-wetness sheen. I glanced at myself. I wore a black tank top—well, originally black, though now it was gray with wall dust. I was sweaty with the hard work of the morning, and since I often wiped my face with my grimy hands, I was probably thoroughly smudged with dirt. In the past week, I had twice tried to see him after showering, dressing nicely, and putting on makeup, only to find his office empty. And now, this was how he saw me. The female version of Bob the Builder.

"I… I thought you went back to New York," I said. "I came looking for you."

"I did go back." He nodded. "Went to see my sister, and take care of some business." He looked around at the shop. "Renovating?"

"Yeah. Breadknife and his goons did a number on this place." I put the drill on a nearby shelf, which wobbled slightly. "So you returned to Boston?"

"Yeah. I encountered some promising leads about my sister here, and I want to investigate them. Actually..." He seemed to hesitate. It was the first time I'd seen him struggle with what he wanted to say. "I was hoping for your help."

"My help in what?"

"Finding my sister's soul."

I stared at him, feeling confused.

"I've been looking for years. With no success. I don't know where it is, and even if I did, I have no idea how to get it back. And I saw what you can do. Those things you create—"

"I'm just following recipes," I said. "I'm a good cook, nothing more."

"No! That's not true! There's magic in what you do, true magic. I knew it from the moment I first saw those distilled children's dreams. You're special."

I frowned, a sudden idea popping into my mind. "Is that one of the reasons you wanted to do this job with me? To see if I could pull it off? To see what I could do?"

He looked away. "*Everything* I do is about one thing only," he said hoarsely. "Returning my sister."

I thought about it, desperately wanting to help, not knowing how. "I can ask around. I *will* ask around. And if there's a potion or a crystal that you need—"

"I need you to search." His eyes were desperate. "To use your powers for my sister."

"Kane… I'm sorry. It's just simple alchemy, nothing more. I have a few good recipes, and I've become very adept at following instructions. But I have no clue how to look for a soul. Maybe Isabel…"

The hope flickered away from his eyes. "You're right. I guess I'll talk to Isabel."

"If there's anything I can do to help, just tell me and I will. I promise."

He was silent for a moment. "Did you find out if the crystal… is it the Yliaster crystal?"

"Maybe. I don't know. All the research I did so far tells me it isn't. The Yliaster crystal is probably a myth." And even if it wasn't, I couldn't see how it would be able to help Kane's sister.

"A myth like Pandora's box?"

I smiled weakly. "Exactly."

The silence stretched between us, and I was suddenly scared that this was how he would think of me. Another failure to help his sister. I cleared my throat and went to my desk, opening one of the drawers. I retrieved a small bottle.

"I have something we can drink," I said. "It's really potent. It can reduce inhibitions, and calm down nerves." I located two smudged glasses on the table.

Magnus padded into the room, casting a baleful look at the discarded drill. He then approached Kane, sniffing his leg with interest.

"What is this magical potion called?" Kane asked, a sad smile on his lips. He scratched Magnus behind his ear distractedly.

"I call it the wondrous stupidifier. But I've heard people calling it scotch, so whatever. Call it what you like."

I poured a glass of the amber-colored whisky for each of us.

"A bit more wondrous stupidifier for me, please," Kane said.

I doubled his shot, and gave him the glass. He raised it and I raised my own glass, clinking it with his. I sipped, letting the burning taste linger on my tongue for a bit.

"You have a… bit of plaster in your hair," Kane said. He reached forward, and touched my hair. For a moment his face was close to mine, and I could feel his breath on my face, his grass-green eyes staring intently into mine. My palms were trembling. I didn't know if it was because of his proximity or because of the intense work I'd been doing, but I didn't care. I may have fallen for this guy during a job, but it was *real* this time, not some sort of juvenile crush that would end in disappointment. And he came *back*. He was here. My lips parted slightly, and I moved forward, shutting my eyes, hoping that he wouldn't back away, feeling expectant and anxious. His lips touched mine, and one arm wrapped around my waist, pulling me to him, and the kiss was warm, and passionate, the taste of whisky on both our tongues, and all I wanted to do was melt into him.

And then he pulled back.

"I can't," he said, his face twisted in sadness and pain.

I blinked. "What? Why the hell not?"

"I like you, Lou, I really do, but… my sister."

"I know. But that doesn't mean you stop living, right?"

"Her soul is *somewhere*." His voice was on edge, ragged. "And as long as I'm alive, I can't let anything distract me from trying to get her back. I can't let *anyone* distract me. You understand that, right?"

The right thing to do was to nod, to tell him I understand. Of course, any moment he spent not trying to save his sister's soul was a moment lost. Every minute he spent with me was a minute he could be spending researching arcane rituals to restore souls. Every hour he'd be in my bed was an hour he could be scouring the streets, looking for a cure. Every night we would cuddle together was a night he could be doing some sort of work to pay for the hospital bills that kept her body alive.

But I didn't nod. I gritted my teeth, and glanced away, feeling the tears in my throat. I wouldn't let him see them, no matter what.

"Lou, I—"

"It's fine, I get it. I really need to hang this shelf. And you should talk to Isabel. She's the expert on souls, right?"

He hovered behind me, and I hoped he would say that he'd had a change of heart—that of course he could let me into his life, that it didn't mean he'd stop searching for a cure. That it just meant he could let himself live while he did it.

But then I heard the door of my shop opening and shutting, as he left.

I could cry now, throw myself on the counter, trembling in a sobbing fit, woe is me, the love of my life will not love me back. Perhaps I could smash a jar in a fit of rage, or go take a shower, letting my tears mingle with the water and the soapsuds. Full of pathos. The jilted girl, her broken heart, et cetera.

But I didn't do that. Emotions should be shut in a vault, buried deeply, never to see the light of day. After all, I had to be true to my motto, *let it fester*.

Instead I poured myself another shot of wondrous stupidifier and swallowed it in one gulp, some of it dribbling down my chin, because life mocks those who try to act dramatically. Then I returned to my shelf, which was the most crooked one yet. But it was good enough.

After finishing with it, I walked over to the lab and approached the safe. I unlocked it, pulling the door open. The crystal sat inside it. Light pulsed weakly within its core, a shimmering golden glow.

I picked it up, carelessly gripping it in my hand. I should have known better. An alchemist never touches a magical crystal directly, unless she's sure it's safe.

The surface felt warm, pulsing, *alive*.

A single image flashed in my mind, of a club, the music pulsing in my chest, hundreds of people dancing in the smoky hall, the lights flickering from purple to red to blue.

I'd never been there before in my life. It was someone else's memory.

Another soul.

I nearly dropped it in shock. Instead, I grabbed the chain that held it, letting go of the crystal itself. I held it up to my eyes, saw it glow brighter than ever before.

The Yliaster crystal was not a myth. I was holding it. There was a soul inside.

And if it was there, maybe I could find a way to free it. And if I managed *that*, could I find a way to free Kane's sister's soul as well?

Of course I could. I thought back to Kane's hopeful look when he'd asked if I could help. He'd said I was special.

I was Lou fucking Vitalis. A vampire had called me legendary. I'd beaten Boston's most notorious criminal, killing him and his goons. I'd broken into a dragon's lair, stealing Pandora's box from him. I'd stopped the end of the world. I was totally bitchin', the bee's knees, peachy-keen.

I would find a lost soul, and get it back.

ABOUT THE
AUTHOR

Alex Rivers is the co-author of the Dark Fae FBI Series. In the past, he's been a journalist, a game developer, and the CEO of the company Loadingames. He is married to a woman who diligently forces him to live his dream, and is the father of an angel, a pixie, and a gremlin. He has two voracious hounds that wag their tail quite menacingly at anyone who comes near his home.

Alex has been imagining himself fighting demons and vampires since forever. Writing about it is even better, because he doesn't get bitten, or tormented in hell, or even just muddy. In fact, he does it in his slippers.

Alex also writes crime thrillers under the pen name Mike Omer.

You can contact Alex by sending him an email to

ALEX@STRANGEREALM.COM.

ACKNOWLEDGMENTS

This book could never have been written without my wife, who is as a sort of super brainstorming part-ner-editor-coacher-psychologist-hand holder. What other authors do without my wife is always a mystery to me.

The first draft was read by Christine Crawford, who pointed out a long list of mistakes, stumbles and downright lazy writing that I had to fix and rewrite. And so I did, to make a tighter, well written book.

My sister, Yael Omer, gave her own list of irritations with the book, especially with some lines that Kane should never have said, and a pointless first chapter that would never see the light of day, and made the book even better.

My editor Elayne took that final draft, and with her usual thoroughness and hilarious remarks, helped me to smooth it to near perfection.

Robin Marcus took that final draft and with her sharp eyes, removed any remaining kinks to make it shine.

Karri Klawiter designed the lovely cover of the book, and has been a joy to work with.

Colleen Sheehan did the formatting of this book, giving it the professional and clean look it deserved.

Thanks to all my friends at Author's Corner whose consistent advice, cheering and friendship has been invaluable, and still is.

24689902R00228

Printed in Poland
by Amazon Fulfillment
Poland Sp. z o.o., Wrocław